Eve Makis was born in Nottingham to Greek Cypriot parents, who emigrated to England in the 1960s. After graduating from Leicester University she studied journalism and moved to London to work as a reporter for Middlesex Country Press. In 1994 she left London for Cyprus, where she worked as a freelance writer, radio presenter and as a stringer for the London Evening Standard. She returned to England with her Cypriot husband in 2001. They now live in Nottingham with their five year old daughter and run a ceramic business importing clay sculptures from the family workshop in Cyprus.

EAT, DRINK AND BE MARRIED

Anna's head reels with plans to escape life behind the counter of the family chip shop on a run-down Nottingham council estate. Her mother, Tina, wants nothing but the best for Anna. She thinks that Anna should forget going to college, learn to cook and find herself a suitable husband. Mother and daughter are at loggerheads and neither will give way. Anna's grandmother, Yiayia Annoulla, is her ally, telling her stories about the family's turbulent past in Cyprus. Anna longs for the freedom enjoyed by her brother, Andy, but it is only when family fortunes begin to sour that she starts to take control of her own destiny . . .

EVE MAKIS

EAT, DRINK AND BE MARRIED

Complete and Unabridged

ULVERSCROFT
Leicester

First published in Great Britain in 2004 by
Transworld Publishers
London

First Large Print Edition
published 2005
by arrangement with
Transworld Publishers, a division of
The Random House Group Limited
London

British Library CIP Data

Makis, Eve
    Eat, drink and be married.—Large print ed.—
Ulverscroft large print series: general fiction
    1. Greeks—England—Nottingham—Fiction
    2. Nottingham (England)—Social life and customs
    —Fiction 3. Nottingham (England)—Race relations
    —Fiction 4. Large type books
    I. Title
    823.9′2 [F]

    ISBN 1–84395–924–0

Published by
F. A. Thorpe (Publishing)
Anstey, Leicestershire

Set by Words & Graphics Ltd.
Anstey, Leicestershire
Printed and bound in Great Britain by
T. J. International Ltd., Padstow, Cornwall

This book is printed on acid-free paper

For George and Fanoulla

Acknowledgements

Thank you to mama for answering the questions she grew tired of and for being a wonderful cook. Who will remain happily oblivious to the contents of this book unless it is translated into Greek. Papa has been equally invaluable as a source of information and inspiration. Thank you to Giorgos and Maria Makis, Theo Costa and Thea Androulla for sharing their stories. I am indebted to the following for their guidance and encouragement: Nick and Judith Nicholas, my sister Des, Nikos Makis, Chrysa Somakou, Harold Culpin, Judith Murdoch and Diana Beaumont. Special thanks to Antonia Marcou for reading, enthusing and believing. For their love and laughter I thank TM and Emily.

Greek Coffee
Yiayia's Method

Pour a demitasse of cold water into a small copper pan called an *imbriki* (any small saucepan will do). Sit the pan on a medium flame and add a fully heaped teaspoon of finely ground Greek coffee and sugar according to taste. Two teaspoons for a sweet coffee or *ylyki*. One teaspoon for a *metrio* (medium sweet) and no sugar for a *sketo*. Stir ingredients and allow to cook, lifting pan from heat when the coffee begins to rise. A well-made Greek coffee should have floating on its surface a cinnamon-coloured froth called *kaimaki*. Serve with a glass of cold water.

1

Beyond the dingy darkness of the precinct there is life, a life that lies tantalizingly on the fringes of my own. While I stand here, smelling of fish, the good-time people are somewhere out there, living it up, basking in bright lights, indulging in a temporary upper before the onset of Monday-morning blues. My week is topsy turvy: peaking on a Monday, dipping at the weekend. My Saturday night is a squirt of eau de Chip Oil, a blue gingham overall, waiting for the stroke of midnight when I turn from pumpkin into person.

I work weekends at Tony's Fish Bar. Tony's my dad. He was baptized Adonis Georgiou Papamichael, in a ceremony that gained him considerable notoriety. Baby Adonis yanked at the priest's facial hair as he was lowered into the font, pulled out a fistful of white beard and waved it triumphantly in the air. He smiled when they poured water over his head and lathered him in olive oil, earning himself a reputation for resilience and physical strength. These have served him well in life. Tony is the strong and silent type, believing words are cheap and should be used in moderation. His verbal reticence is complemented by his wife's love of talking.

Mum took the name of her grandfather Constantine. She has a noble lineage, a long line of predecessors named after Constantine the Great. Her name has, for the sake of convenience, waned in grandeur, shrunk from a statuesque Constantina to a stunted 'Tina' or 'Teen'. Tina is a self-professed open book. She is what she is, she says what she thinks, she talks without thinking, take it or leave it. She is not as hard as her uncompromising views might suggest. When the metaphorical chips are down she capitulates, gives up where Tony would fight like a bull to the death. Thankfully, these days, there is little cause for bull-headedness, allowing Tony to fade into the background and enjoy the status of henpecked husband. Tony and Tina are a formidable duo behind the counter, quick and nimble. 'The lid rolled and found the saucepan,' Tina says of their compatibility. 'Your papa is the lid,' she adds, 'he did all the chasing.'

Tina fills up the salt pots and sings one of her favourite songs, her voice competing with the din of the extractor fan and crackle of the chip pan. 'Nikoli, Nikoli, *capetanye nter-tili* . . . ' she sings in a high-pitched warble, a

4

song about a seafaring captain called Nikoli, who is asked to reveal all he knows about kissing. A kiss in Athens is cheap and quick to get, he replies, but in Crete and Mani it is paid for with a wedding crown. Tina has the voice of a tone-deaf Edith Piaf but sings with gusto regardless.

I wipe down the counter in time to her singing and join in the chorus, infected by Tina's joviality. My mother is not demoralized by her profession. She enjoys her work and takes great pride in providing a good service. The shop is a means to an end and the end she has in mind is a return to the Arcadian isle, where the sun always shines and bystander apathy has not yet taken hold. Where elderly parents are cared for by their children and the weather is kinder to aging bones. Where the smell of jasmine and honeysuckle float thickly in the air and mingle with the aroma of meat juices dripping on smouldering charcoal. It is a land of incongruous bedfellows. Of fasting and feasting and barbed-wire partitions separating a community that yearns to be one. Of topless Swedes wearing G-strings within sight of the armed troops who patrol the dividing line, an arbitrary schism across which deserted Cypriot towns and villages can be viewed. And there lies a depressing vision of

5

crumbling façades and warped wooden shutters, of old stone houses left to ruin — a physical manifestation of political intransigence. 'One day, I'm going back to my village,' Tina says with utter certainty, though peace talks have so far floundered miserably.

★ ★ ★

Three girls dressed for a date with pneumonia stand outside the shop, rubbing their naked arms, stamping their goose-pimpled legs. Fairfield women like to bare their sun-starved skin on Saturday night, irrespective of the weather, irrespective of their size. They brave the bite of freezing wind to flaunt their charms. On a mission to turn heads they leave nothing to the imagination. They warm their insides with chips and pungent foodstuffs and stand on the forecourt, shivering like plucked chickens, while Tina looks on, beseeching God to give them sense.

The need to expose naked flesh is a concept alien to me. I cover up, rain or shine. I am too tall and ungainly to prance about in skimpy tops and skirts above the knee. I have bits that rub together when I walk, that gently concertina when I sit down, that quiver when I run. I hover on the brink of acceptable largeness. A gentle calorific push would have me plummeting over the edge into territory rife with prejudice and intolerance. For Tina, my size is a source of great pride. 'My daughter, she's tall enough to be a model,' Tina says pointlessly, since I have no other modelling prerequisite. My size engenders false impressions. 'Big' suggests I am also 'strong' and emotionally self-sufficient. My size masks my sensitivity and my need to be enveloped like a child in arms stronger than my own.

I wasn't born big. I came out of my mother's womb weighing 5.5lb. I was the tiniest baby on the maternity ward and as expected my growth curve followed that of a 'small baby'. I was, for a time, below average for height, weight and head size, until friends and relatives began commenting on my smallness and Tina convinced herself the evil eye was stunting my growth. She enveloped me in a cloud of incense, hung a tiny blue stone around my neck and fed me at every opportunity. Her efforts had the desired effect. I grew and grew, in height and girth, like a recalcitrant marrow.

The girls on the forecourt gawp unashamedly through the shop window at Andy, watching him battering fish and dropping it into the frying pan. Girls are drawn to my brother with fanatical intensity. They loiter outside the shop, wearing next to nothing, hoping to catch his eye and hook their catch — patient fisherwomen casting for red mullet in a sea of whitebait. Andy is dark enough to be exotic and light enough to be acceptable. He bears a striking resemblance to Tony-the-youth, before time overzealously pulled out clumps of his wavy hair. Andy's face is angular, his cheekbones chiselled, thick lashes frame eyes like molten chocolate, flecked with mint-green specks. His sexual magnetism is boosted by an armoured phallus, parked within viewing distance of the shop: a metallic-silver Capri that draws the eye like an oil-basted bodybuilder in a room full of wimps, arousing envy, resentment, covetousness and admiration.

My brother has simultaneous girlfriends who inhabit the periphery of his life. I see them fleetingly, like birds flying across the horizon, flitting through the back door into or out of the potato room, climbing into the Capri at the end of the night, to be driven to a club or a quiet country lane. Andy doesn't talk about his love life and I don't ask. I believe it to be active and densely populated.

Tina views her son's promiscuity as a natural part of a young man's life before he settles down. The more girlfriends he has now, the less likely he is to stray in future, the better husband he will be for the dark-eyed daughter-in-law who inhabits her dreams. Tina chooses to ignore Andy's predilection for blonde hair and blue eyes. She is convinced he will return to the fold, even though events close to home should have taught her not to count her chickens. Andy has failed to nip Tina's dreams in the bud, allowing them to flourish, branch out and cast a shadow over both of us.

The 'Anna dream' and 'Anna's dream' share little common ground. The 'Anna dream' would have ten-pound notes trailing the hem of a bulbous wedding dress followed by a life of simple domesticity. 'Anna's dream' is of escaping the shop, breaking the mould, absconding to a place of higher education. The odds are stacked against me. The shop saps my energy, swallows up my time and provides no food for thought. Moreover, Tina has threatened to jump off Stretley Bridge if I leave home to study. She believes a woman should only leave the parental home for a fully furnished, four-bedroomed house with a BMW parked in the driveway. The best education a woman can get, she insists, is in the home and not behind a desk. 'What good is a woman who she no cook?' Tina says, as if culinary skill and a formal education are mutually exclusive.

Tina-the-child played in a fertile backyard with her sisters Mirianthy and Stavroulla, within a rectangular oasis where geraniums and oleander grew in terracotta pots and a sprawling jasmine dropped tiny white flowers like scented confetti. A prickly pear tree, punctuated with spiky fruit, grew alongside a vine, laden with heavy bunches of crisp black grapes. The girls played *koumeres* — maids of honour. They made tea-towel dolls and acted out the roles of housewives and mothers. They played hopscotch and rolled almond nuts at one another instead of marbles. They cartwheeled, skipped, plaited each other's hair and visited the homes of neighbours, whose doors were always open.

They watched their mother making halloumi in a small wooden outhouse. Heating goat's milk in a large copper pan, throwing in the rennet-rich stomach of a baby lamb and spooning out curds to be squeezed, wrapped in cheesecloth and set beneath a stone slab. Their stomachs rumbled in anticipation of the soft, white, ricotta-like cheese called *anari* that floated to the surface of the whey, which was served up warm with a spoonful of sugar and a sprinkling of cinnamon. Tina says nothing has or ever will taste better than the freshly made *anari* of her childhood. She makes her own version by heating milk in a large saucepan and adding lemon juice to produce a crumbly white cheese. She eats it with relish but admits it is a poor imitation.

Many of Tina's childhood neighbours were employed in the production of traditional foodstuffs. Her aunt was renowned for making *soujouko*, a rubbery sweet made by threading almonds onto a length of string and dipping the string into grape juice thickened with flour and flavoured with cinnamon, rosewater and mastic gum. Tina loved to watch her aunt dipping the strings, over and over again, and hanging them from the ceiling of her kitchen to dry. If she sat for long enough beneath the sweet-smelling rows that hung like knobbly brown salami, her aunt invariably offered her a slice. The sugary delicacies of Tina's childhood have nurtured a sweet tooth.

In spring time and early summer, when the dry earth gave way to a bounty of wild and cultivated produce, the village was a hive of culinary activity. Hard green olives were crushed with a flat stone and preserved in brine. Orange and lemon blossom was picked to make fragrant waters, used to flavour sweets and pastries. Women sat on their doorsteps shaping macaroni from a mixture of semolina and water. Orange peel, young walnuts, cherries, small aubergines and many other fruit and vegetables were simmered for hours in syrup to make preserves called *glyka*.

★ ★ ★

'Your usual, Elvin?' I ask, reaching for a tray.

'Yes please, duck,' he replies, delving into the deep pockets of his musty trench coat for change.

Elvin is the embodiment of lovable ugliness, as wrinkled and rubbery as a plastic troll, his teeth like shattered ramparts. He is otherworldly. A tall, spindly leprechaun. A creature to be swaddled in a fleecy blanket and spoon-fed rice pudding. His earthly manifestation lives on a staple diet of chips and peas and sometimes loses its grip on reality. On occasion, Elvin confuses the shop for a bus station and stares patiently out of the window, waiting for the 602 to Sherwood Forest. 'The poor man she's lost her marbles,' Tina says, shaking her head sympathetically, confusing the listener with her jumbled pronouns.

'Y'all righ, Elvis?' Tina shouts across the counter, her slip of the tongue elevating Elvin to a rock 'n' roll legend. I have tried to teach

Tina the correct pronunciation, through repetition and word association, but she refuses to learn, casually shrugging off her linguistic errors.

Elvin takes his tray of food and hands me a toffee, flat and round, in shiny gold wrapping. In his roomy pockets he keeps fudge for Tina, humbugs for Tony and strong mints for Andy, his humble offerings one almighty thank you for the simple acts of human kindness bestowed upon him. For the occasional tenner that Tony slips discreetly into his hand, for that bottle of sherry at Christmas, for the free piece of haddock every Friday and the genuine smile that greets him when he walks through the door.

Elvin sits down on the shop bench, his favoured perch for killing time. He spears chips with a tremulous hand and chews like a ruminant, his tongue cleaving to the roof of his mouth, a crusty green tidemark forming around his lips. Tina takes him a handful of serviettes and says, 'Eh Elvis, wipe you mouth,' which he does. Tina's forceful tone leaves no room for argument.

Tina can be very abrupt at times. Her natural tendency for plain speaking ('I say what I think, I not hide behind my thumb nail') is confounded by cultural quirks, abrasive to English sensibilities. Tina adheres to the following rules of social etiquette: personal comments are permissible ('You lookin fat today'); modesty is a waste of time ('This is MY shop. I'M the boss'); threats of decapitation and murder can be used affectionately or in jest ('you get back in the queue or I cut your head off' . . . 'if you don be quiet I kill you'); speaking loudly need not be an expression of heightened emotion ('YOU WAN SAL AND VINEGA'). Tina's rudeness provokes surprise, shock, amusement, but never anger.

Mrs Collins hurries across the precinct towards the shop, walking at a pace that would tax a person half her age and twice her height. Small and robust, she is carried on stumpy legs propelled by plump calf muscles. Tina, who admits to liking only a handful of people outside the family, is very fond of Mrs Collins. She likes the speedy way Mrs Collins moves, the slavish care she bestows on a sick husband and her expertise in the kitchen. A visit to Mrs Collins' house for afternoon tea clinched Tina's whole-hearted admiration. She was won over by the abundant array of homemade sponges and pastries. She stooped down to kiss Albert in his wheelchair and remarked on the fresh smell of his hair. 'What hospitality, what cleanliness,' she commented after the event, 'in that house I didn't mind putting a teacup to my mouth.' Tina has repaid the gesture a thousand times over, regularly plying Mrs Collins with her own cakes. Though she often gripes about the niggardly and inhospitable nature of the indigenous population, Tina cites Mrs Collins as the exception. Calling her a *nigogira*, a description used only sparingly to denote the most 'houseproud' of women.

'Y'all right, Elvin luv?' Mrs Collins asks, walking briskly to the counter.

'Welcome, Mrs Collie, I make you acapa tea,' Tina says, heading for the kitchen.

'Poor man,' Mrs Collins whispers, 'not a soul in the world to call is own. Makes y'realize just ow lucky you are, dunt it? So ow are you, Anna duck?'

'Fine thanks,' I reply, my feelings of self-pity suddenly dwarfed by the magnitude of Elvin's problems.

'You're better off in ere than out there,' she says, as if my only options are working in the shop or perishing in the cold.

Tina returns with a mug of tea and piece of *kateifi*.

'Y'spoil me, duck, really you do,' Mrs Collins says, eyeing up the cake.

'Someone he's goda spoil you, isenit?'

'It looks like shredded wheat,' Mrs Collins says.

15

'Is call *KA-TE-YF-I*, Mrs Collie. I make it miself.'

'I dint think you bought it from Pound-stretcher. How d'you find the time, luv? Workin ere and bakin cakes.'

'Where there's a willies a way.' Tina can transform the most innocuous statement into a double entendre.

'I couldn't agree more,' Mrs Collins says, starting to reminisce about the halcyon days, when women baked their own cakes, made their own jam and pickles, when no one had more than anyone else and wished for no more than they had. When a clip round the ear kept children in line, when her Albert still had two legs, before consumerism spread like cancer and cancer spread through Albert. Before pensioners started getting mugged for their milk money, before the local cigarette factory employing half the men on Fairfield estate closed down. When finally she pauses to swallow a clump of *kateifi* Tina takes up the gauntlet, eulogizing her childhood in the village, glorifying the simple life, a life of bread and olives, kinship, camaraderie and decency. Tina's life before the war, before division, before she came to England. The word England, synonymous in Tina's mind with immorality, sends her spinning off at a tangent.

'These gels they no av mathers.'

Mrs Collins, who has become attuned to Tina's wavelength over the years, knows the 'gels' in question to be the girl mothers — the growing number of teenagers on Fairfield estate, raising fatherless babies, who parade their children on the precinct like pampered poodles or drag them round the shops, snotty-nosed and screaming. Every morning the girl mothers gather beneath the Pound-stretcher awning, sharing cigarettes, sporting love-bites. Fairfield's older generation walk past them, shaking their blue-rinse heads, avoiding eye contact. The girl mothers don't like being looked at. The most innocuous of glances can unhinge the 'fuck off' that teeters on the tips of their tongues.

'It's those little uns I feel sorry for,' Mrs Collins says.

They examine the whys and wherefores of teenage pregnancy, apportioning blame, disparaging and condemning, without an iota of compassion or understanding. A child is a means to a council house, they both agree, spouting the party line. When their flood of critical commentary wanes, Mrs Collins turns to me.

'Hear your mum's tryin to fix you up with some Greek fella.'

'That's news to me,' I say, glaring at Tina.

17

'I don say that, Mrs Collie, you don understand me ... is my Engleesh is no good.'

'Mum, how many times do I have to tell you? I'm not interested.'

'I know you don interesting,' Tina replies defensively, curling her upper lip into a disdainful snarl.

Mrs Collins taps the plastic box behind her earlobe.

'Sorry, luv, I thought you said sumthin about a lad from Birmingham.'

'Bermiam? I don rememba sayin that. I must be getting old, Mrs Collie, these days I don remember nathin.'

'Got the same problem miself, luv.'

They discuss the trauma of memory loss, Tina confusing senility with invention, while I seethe at the indignity of having my future discussed across the counter. I have tried to nip the 'Anna dream' in the bud, by stating quite categorically that I will find my own husband. Yet Tina continues to try her luck and my patience, biding her time, believing I will grow out of my wayward sensibilities and forget that silly notion of falling in love. An inflated, overrated emotion, claims Tina, a zenith from which there is only descent and divorce. Start from the other end, 'grow to love someone', and the only way is 'up, up, up', she says. Up to where? A comfortable plateau with the peaks tantalizingly out of reach. I'd rather fall from a great height than nurture a seed that might never germinate.

'Cheer up, Anna, it's not like you to be so miserable,' Mrs Collins says, remembering the Anna who used to inhabit this body, the Anna who enjoyed working in the shop, who felt grown up standing behind the counter buttering bread rolls, who thought achievement was polishing the bains-marie until they shone like a new penny, before the shop became a ball and chain. These days dark, dank apathy and worse nestle behind my eyeballs, at the pit of my stomach, in my bone marrow. I look at photos of the 'happy Anna' cavorting in front of a camera lens, doing cartwheels with her knickers showing, smiling open-mouthed, flashing the teeth with the skewed incisor she has grown to hate. I don't recognize myself in her. I don't recognize the girl for whom happiness was a Mr Whippy with a flake and chocolate sauce. I know she didn't vanish overnight. She wasn't traumatized by a specific event. She trickled away, little by little, leaving only the memory of her existence. In the space she once occupied she left a restless gerbil on its play wheel, running nowhere, dreaming of escape.

I run from cameras nowadays, from Tony's

19

indiscriminate snapping, Tony who ignores any pleas to please point his lens elsewhere, who likes to take natural shots, immortalizing grimaces and flared nostrils. Tony frames these pictures and hangs them on the living-room wall, charting my development from Cabbage Patch baby to uninspiring teenager. Above the television is a black-and-white picture of Tina-the-adolescent, nubile and buxom, with luminescent hair and bee-stung lips. She was enviably pretty though never thin. In her day being thin was a disadvantage, it meant you were too poor to eat. Tina had a sizable bust, hips and a fleshy midriff, body parts now obsolete, waiting for the Rubenesque figure to make a comeback. Tina's curves have swollen, drooped, amalgamated. A tight corset keeps her loose bits reined in. Her face, though neglected and tired, is still pretty. Tina could have been — should have been — anything she wanted, something other than a slave to the counter.

Tina's *Kateifi*

Separate out the strings of a half-kilo packet of *kateifi*. Lay half the *kateifi* into an ovenproof dish, pour over a cup of melted butter and spread with ground almonds (1 cup) mixed with one teaspoon of powdered cinnamon. Cover with remaining *kateifi*, sprinkle with water and place in a hot oven for ten minutes. Reduce oven heat to low and cook *kateifi* for a further 20–30 minutes. Meanwhile prepare a syrup by combining four cups of sugar, three cups of water, three tablespoons of rose water, one teaspoon of lemon juice, one stick of cinnamon and two cloves. Heat ingredients until sugar has dissolved and allow syrup to cool. Pour cool syrup over hot *kateifi* and cover with a towel until liquid has been absorbed. When cold cut into squares and serve. Individual portions can be made by rolling nuts into small sections of *kateifi*.

2

Mercedes 450 SE. Squat and invincible. A metallic-gold tank, the epitome of luxury, flawed by its gaudy flamboyance. A flatulent sultan laughing in the face of the flimsy, economical and cheap-to-service. I sink an inch into the creamy leather, lean back against the headrest and watch the front door. I sit and wait in the no man's land between GMT and lackadaisical Greek time, a vast void of wasted hours. My hours. For I am a biorhythmic anathema in a family of tardy time-keepers.

I fled the house during the course of an argument about Andy's jeans, with the self-inflicted slash across the knee. 'What will people think,' Tina grumbled, 'if they see the son of Constantina Papamichael wearing torn clothes?' What Tina thinks they will think is that she is tight-fisted and a sloppy mother. Andy said he couldn't give a fig what people think. Supplication, bribery, threats and complaints of an impending hernia have all failed to dissuade Andy from wearing his favourite jeans. Whenever Tina starts a sentence with 'your brother's trousers . . . ' I make myself a large mug of tea and switch off, letting her grievances wash over me. I have learnt not to comment, not to get drawn in, not to fuel the fire, for I know Tina's wrath is fickle and swings like a pendulum.

Every Sunday I dress to please my mother, donning the clothes she feels appropriate for a lady: pencil skirt, silk blouse, black stilettos and ecru tights (bought in packs of twenty from the cash and carry). Tina's secondary flak has had the desired effect. Nurtured a daughter who is quick to compromise, eager to keep the peace, anxious to prevent Tina's abdominal cavity from rupture.

The stiletto-clad, beehived icons of Tina's youth have shaped her views on style. Whatever the weather, Tina stoically wears a knee-length skirt, court shoes and flesh-coloured tights. Stylistically, she is the bastion of stereotypical femininity. She does not approve of women clad in male accoutrements. She does not condone her daughter's love of trousers and clumpy shoes. Tina tells me I have the curves of a 'real woman' and should show them off. She likes to squeeze me into clothes a size too small, ignoring straining buttonholes and ripples of tightly squeezed flesh. Any excess girth is only 'puppy fat', she tells me, indicative of further growth spurts.

Andy never gets up before midday on a Sunday. He sleeps through the alarm clock, through Tina's shrill morning call. Only prolonged and violent shaking and the confiscation of his quilt cause him to stir, to open his bloodshot eyes momentarily and ask for a cup of tea, exuding stale morning-after breath. He spends an inordinate amount of time checking his scalp for baldness, using a hand-held mirror to carefully study the back of his head. Tony's rapidly retreating hairline keeps Andy in a state of constant fear. 'You don go baldy like your dad,' Tina says, reassuring him that his maternal grandfather had a thick head of hair.

Andy climbs into his car, turns on a pounding stereo, pulls out of the driveway and accelerates, boy-racer style, leaving a trail of exhaust fumes in his wake. On his days off, Andy likes to spend quality time with the Capri, racing through the city trying to beat the lights, checking out top speed, practising his handbrake turns. My brother is three points short of a driving ban. I envy Andy's freedom. His gender gives him licence to come and go as he pleases. To leave the table without moving his plate. To exit his bedroom without making his bed. To leave his socks in a corner of the room, to be picked up and sniffed by his mother before being deposited in the laundry basket. Andy is not a lazy man by nature. He simply utilizes the advantages bestowed upon his sex without question.

His efforts to help around the house are thwarted by his mother. I once saw Tina forcibly pull her son away from the kitchen sink and order him to sit down. Had he protested she might have slung him halfway across the kitchen. Tina is uncomfortable about any man, be it husband, son or male relative, partaking in 'women's work'. In Tina's mind, any husband who cooks and cleans is either henpecked or effeminate. 'Men have one role and women have another,' she says, citing a principle, which she has failed to live by. A more accurate reflection of Tina's life might be: 'Men have one role and women have many.' She matches Tony hour for hour behind the counter and comes home to a pile of dirty overalls.

Tony, smart and slick, looking like a 1930s card shark in his blue pinstripe, climbs into the driver's seat.

'Where are those women?' he says impatiently.

Tony smells of Old Spice and greenhouse, fruity, leafy, humid, of partially decomposed organic matter. He is an avid gardener and left to his own devices would spend the whole of Sunday cooped up in the greenhouse, turning the soil with his trusty trowel beneath a broad-leafed vine.

'At least Yiayia is ready,' Tony says, watching his mother-in-law descend the front step, holding on to the doorframe for support. Yiayia Annoulla waddles on arthritic hips towards the car, stopping en route to pick a sprig of bay leaves and put it in her pocket. A thriving bay tree grows in our front garden providing Yiayia with a constant supply of her favourite herb. Tina's mother loves to cook, as much as the rest of us love to eat. Tony's greenhouse produce and weekly access to Bambo's Mobile Grocery, selling Greek delicacies, keep her kitchen well stocked. Yiayia's monopoly on savoury dishes has forced Tina along a more dangerous avenue of culinary expression. Namely desserts. Greek, English, East European. Syrupy, spongy, chocolatey. Halouva, fruit cake, Pavlova. Boundless, countless, endless calories.

Yiayia's voluminous buttocks spread like silicone implants, filling her seat and encroaching on mine. She eclipses Tony's earthy smell with the scent of jasmine tonic, bay leaves and moth balls. Yiayia Annoulla, my namesake, lives in a granny flat, accessed through our living room. 'Onoma ge brama' — name and thing — she says of me, meaning same name, same thing, taking pride in our resemblance. Yiayia has a round, chubby, friendly-when-she-chooses face; when she chooses not to be friendly, you could cast her in the first scene of *Macbeth*.

Yiayia's lank grey hair is pinned at the sides with Kirby grips, the same grips she uses to clean the inside of her ears. There are traces of earwax, like the yolk of a soft-boiled egg, in the looped end of these grips. Yiayia fails to notice such minutiae. Her poor eyesight is compounded by the film of greasy fingerprints on the lenses of her NHS glasses. Luckily, Yiayia's other ways of seeing compensate for her visual impairment.

Tony sounds the car horn. Tina rushes out of the front door, sweat glinting on her forehead. It is not vanity that holds her up but domestic fastidiousness. She dresses in a matter of minutes and spends the rest of her time picking fluff off the carpet, straightening sofa cushions, polishing windows, eradicating all traces of dust. The house must look unlived in before she is happy to leave it. I have not inherited Tina's love of housework. I carry out my cleaning duties on a Sunday morning without dissent to lessen her load and circumvent her nagging. 'No one polishes like my Anna,' Tina says, exalting a skill born of frustration.

'Did you lock the front door?' Tony asks his wife as she sinks into the passenger seat.

'Will you do it, Athonis *mou*?' *Mou* meaning 'my'. 'My Adonis' she calls him, when she wants something, his mythical name in Greek pronounced with a rounded 'th'.

Tina turns to cast a critical eye over my outfit, which is ironic in the circumstances, since she is wearing a leopard-print blouse tucked into a zebra-print skirt. Tina can be frighteningly uncoordinated at times. Her top half need bear no relation to her bottom. Liking both halves in equal measure warrants a coupling. My preference for black, my tendency to play it safe, is not incidental.

'What species of animal is your mother today?' Yiayia whispers in my ear. I squeeze her doughy hand and we share a conspiratorial smile.

'Why haven't you combed your hair?' Tina asks, never satisfied by my efforts, refusing to accept that my hair is as unruly as her command of English. I have the head of Medusa. Curls, coarse as wire wool, tangled as a crow's nest, mock everything about me that is dutiful, the epitome of the inner me.

'I used to have lovely thick curls like my granddaughter,' Yiayia says, deflecting Tina's criticism, delicately lifting a corkscrew curl and inspecting it.

'It used to be lovely once upon a time,' Tina replies, remembering the good old days when I was too young to protest, when she used to drag a reluctant comb through my hair, tugging and snagging, like a rake through pond weed.

Tony turns the key in the ignition and the Merc growls into life. Tina spots the woman from next door staring at us from an upstairs window and casually sticks her Vs up, putting an end to the curtain twitching. The Polonovskis from number 66 keep a chronicle of petty misdemeanours committed by their neighbours. They hate anything that alludes to pleasure or recreation, anything outside the remit of 'functional': noise above a whisper, cars, children, music, teenagers, animals (four-legged, two-legged and winged). Every morning Mrs P, clad in her pink towelling sweat suit, scatters a caustic white powder on the front lawn to deter cats from defecating on the grass. I have seen Mr P chase a dog-walker two hundred metres down the road and drag him back to the crime scene: a dog turd lying among a clump of dandelion leaves on the pavement outside his house.

We prove a continual source of consternation for the couple. They send us letters of complaint by post to avoid the informality of walking along our driveway. No sooner has the sting of one letter subsided than the next brown envelope drops onto our doorstep, our name and address scrawled in diminutive print, a grudging acknowledgement of our existence. Our offences over the years have included loud exchanges on the driveway, the production of excessive exhaust fumes, barbecues in the back garden (air pollution and a fire hazard), shutting of car doors after the watershed.

The scene was set the day we moved in. Tina, betwixt unpacking boxes, managed to bake two coconut cakes. She took one to the Davis family living to our right, who graciously accepted ('with a hundred thank yous', according to Tina) and returned the gesture the very next day with an apple strudel. Tina offered the second cake to Mrs P, who opened her front door only as far as the chain would allow, looked at the cake as if it were a freshly discharged placenta and closed the door in Tina's face. Tina, thinking there had been some terrible misunderstanding on account of her English, knocked again. Mr P answered, looked at her as if she was 'a piece of sheet' (in Tina's words) and said in his anal, nasal, East European twang that his wife made her own cakes and, by the way, the removal van was blocking his carless driveway. Tina rushed back home and christened our neighbours *Becha* and *Pezevengis* (loosely translated as dry skin and cuckold).

There is no visible manifestation of the malice that eats them up inside. The Ps are grey haired and drawing a pension. Mrs Davis heard on the grapevine that Mr P, a civil servant for twenty years, lost his job over allegations of sexual impropriety. 'You mean e's one of them,' Tina remarked.

'What was he like before he lost his job?' I asked.

'Miserable,' Mrs Davis said, sending that theory up in smoke. 'No one really knows what goes on in that house, since no one's ever invited in,' she added.

'They just jealous cause they don't know how to eat,' is Tina's firmly held belief. Every dilemma has food as its root cause, or too many boiled root vegetables in the case of Mr and Mrs P. 'All that woman she cook is boiled cabbage and stinky swede.' Tina's motto is: 'Show me a person and I tell you what they eat.' If everyone had a rich and varied diet, she says, the world would be a better place. Perhaps it would. A slice of Tina's *galatoboureko* could tame the wildest savage, might even put a contented smile on Mr P's sorry face.

Civility has allowed the Ps' sickness to spread like gangrene, infecting all of us in some way, if only by recurring visions of Mr P swinging from the nearest tree. In this neighbourhood people turn the other cheek, fight fire with a water gun, wait for the Ps to get their natural comeuppance. Tony used to say, 'There is only one language those people will understand.' He put this theory to the test by grabbing Mr P by the scruff of the neck and threatening to kill him. Twenty minutes later the police arrived, hauled Tony off to the police station and questioned him for several hours before sending him home. These days Tony reads our neighbours' nasty letters with a look of mild amusement before throwing them in the bin or using them to light the barbecue. 'Don't the letters bother you, Dad?' I asked him once. To which he replied: 'Are mountains bothered by snow?'

★   ★   ★

I was four. The year 1973. I remember the sweaty kiss of grandmothers, the gentle hum of cicadas, the flavour of rose-scented ice cream and the taste of freedom. The freedom to roam, to walk without shoes, to eat with my hands, to chase lizards, to get dirty and to stay up late. I wandered Yiayia's village at will. I sucked honey from freshly picked carobs. I drank homemade lemonade with strangers. It was a magical place and I never wanted the holiday to end. To return to a flat above a shop that smelt of chip oil, to confinement within four walls.

I remember as if I dreamt him up, a tall, willowy man with golden skin and green eyes, who carried me effortlessly on his shoulders along mountain tracks, who walked with a staff, who took me mushroom picking and showed me an eagle's nest. I remember a magpie called Koko, who sat on Yiayia's shoulder and nibbled her ear. Yiayia found him on the floor below his nest, a flaccid bag of bones on the brink of death. She nursed him back to life and reared him on a diet of fruit and nuts. He never returned to the wild but made his home in a box above Yiayia's wardrobe. He used to steal knick-knacks and hide them beneath the eaves. He terrorized the neighbours, stealing their eggs and filling their car exhaust pipes with stones. He ate from my palm and pecked at my feet when I played dead.

If I close my eyes I can vaguely see the winding road that led to Yiayia's stone cottage, that passed through a village square and branched off to the right, that became a dirt track leading to Aunt Roulla's white-washed house. A bright and imposing single-storey structure that rose up like a highly polished tooth. A house with gleaming marble floors, sweeping verandas and iron rods rising from the flat roof, ready for the building of a second floor, a future home for my six-year-old cousin, Maria. It was the house of Tina's dreams and she planned to build a similar abode on an adjoining plot of land. Aunt Roulla's house took three years to build and was lost in the blink of an eye.

★   ★   ★

Tony parks the Merc next to Uncle Malcolm's Renault in the shadow of a three-storey Victorian façade. Andy screeches to a halt behind us. The Jamesons stand on their doorstep, looking like an advert from *Country Life*, watching us scrunch across the gravel driveway. '*Kalinikta*,' Malcolm calls out, greeting us with a Freudian 'goodnight'. Aunt Miriam doles out limp hugs as if we're made of vermicelli and might crumble on her doorstep.

Malcolm likes to boast that his finely crafted house with its high ceilings, sash windows and sweeping staircase was built by the renowned architect T.C. Hine, on sloping ground once owned by the Duke of Newcastle. He claims his living room, with its marble fire surround and ornate wood panelling, was once an elegant parlour where Victorian aristocrats received their guests. From his bedroom window Malcolm enjoys a panoramic view of Nottingham castle, squatting squarely on a verdant hill. 'I wouldn't live there if you paid me,' Tina says of Malcolm's handsome house. The ceilings are too high, the windows too big and the wooden floors too rickety for Tina's liking. There are too many trees in the vicinity, shedding a carpet of unwanted leaves in Autumn and inadequate light emanating from the gas lamps that line the wide streets.

Tina likes unlived-in homes, with PVC windows, fitted wardrobes and trees of manageable height. Tony, who likes a bargain and a playground for his DIY skills, bought our bay-fronted house at auction. He took his wife to see it, promising her a house with 'character', and was besieged with a hail of insults. Tina saw peeling wallpaper and soiled carpets and threatened her husband with decapitation. Tony set about gutting and extending, adding a granny flat and a conservatory, eradicating all signs of age, installing chandeliers with dimmer switches and fitting the finest quality shag pile. Six months later he took his wife for a second inspection and she grudgingly admitted that the house looked like a 'palace'. She promptly moved in but never entirely forgave Tony for buying a house with 'character'. Every time the floorboards creak or a pipe unexpectedly rumbles Tina accuses her husband of sabotaging her dream to buy a show home on a new estate.

Miriam leads us into the hallway where George and Charlie are racing wooden cars along the floorboards. Yiayia stoops as far as her arthritic hips allow, scoops them up like a bear catching fish and kisses the tops of their heads. Tina ruffles their curly brown hair, pinches their chubby cheeks and hands them a box of chocolates, intercepted as usual by Malcolm. The twins have not inherited the lean and lanky Jameson family genes. In spite of the strict no-chocolate diet imposed by their father they are plump and cherubic.

I perch on a green velour sofa, next to Tina, surrounded by an eclectic mix of Jameson family heirlooms: a desk in striated walnut, a heavy oak chest, mahogany chairs with skinny legs and clawed feet. A shaft of sunlight streams through the window, accentuating the white lustre of my silk blouse, making me feel as visible as a seagull floating on an oil slick. Athena strolls into the room, golden hair cascading in gentle waves down her back, wearing Levis and a baggy cardigan, intensifying my discomfort at being over-dressed.

'Hi,' she says through a lazy yawn. Athena has grey-green eyes that sparkle like bur-nished onyx. They consign all other eyes to the slagheap and give her inequitable power. Set in a plump-lipped, button-nosed, ethereal face, those eyes drag your ego down into the soles of your feet.

'*Ela na me filisis*,' Yiayia says, addressing her granddaughter.

Athena turns to her mother. 'What did she say, Mummy?'

'Granny wants a kiss, darling,' Miriam replies.

Athena moves hesitantly towards Yiayia and offers up a porcelain cheek. Yiayia takes her hand and kisses that instead.

Malcolm lowers the needle on the record player and sits in a crumpled leather armchair. Behind him the wall is lined with books; works of fiction, leatherbound ency-clopedias, antiquated reference books with gold lettering on the spines. Books passed down, with the rest of the house and its contents, from head teacher father to deputy head of the High School son.

'So how's the fish and chip business these

days, Adonis? Still making a fortune?' Malcolm asks, packing his pipe with tobacco.

'Things are OK,' Tony replies modestly.

'I think things are more than OK, old boy. You should try living on my salary.'

'You shoun try wekin twelve hours eday, six days eweek,' Tina interjects.

'I don't deny you work long hours,' Malcolm says, his tone faintly patronizing. 'All I'm saying is . . . your line of work is extremely profitable.'

'Not as profitable as it used to be,' Tony replies.

'You seen the price of potatoes these days?' Tina says, her voice rising in pitch and crescendo. 'How we suppose to make a livin? And they new potatoes they no good for fryin, they no cook probally and they fulla stones. The customers they don eat them, they bringem back and ask for a refan. Last week I toll Jimmy the potato man to take his damn potatoes and go to hell. Maureen Piper, they the best potatoes for fryin. The chips they cook nice and crispies.' Tina's impassioned commentary on potatoes contin- ues for some time and does not sit well with the Viennese waltz chosen by Malcolm as an auditory backdrop. Miriam listens to her sister with a frozen smile. Malcolm sucks nonchalantly on his pipe. Yiayia, lulled by the music, falls asleep, punctuating Tina's speech with a rattling snore.

* * *

We sit on dining chairs with plump embroidered cushions, spewing stuffing at their seams. Rust-coloured curtains, beneath tasselled pelmets, hang tired and unkempt. A circle of pink flowers on the overhanging glass lampshade is partly obscured by a velutinous layer of dust. Tina says her sister treats the grand old house like a chicken coop. Miriam is as lax about cleaning as Tina is obsessive. Miriam's life in general bears little resemblance to Tina's. 'My sista she's a ledy of lesha,' Tina says, disapproving of the fact that Miriam has never worked, exasperated by Miriam's inertia, saying her sister moves as if 'she's tired of living'. Miriam's speech is slow and considered, at times she has you perched on the edge of your seat, wanting to scream 'spit it out, Mirianthy'. In contrast, Tina does everything quickly. She moves with surprising agility for a fleshy woman, her mouth is one step ahead of her brain, she can gobble down two portions before most people are halfway through one.

Miriam parted ways with tradition when she married Malcolm, six months after stepping foot on British soil. Only the faintest hint of an accent links Miriam to her former life in the village. She is eloquent, formal, polite, rarely raises her voice above a whisper, seldom laughs too loud, too long or inappropriately. She plays bridge, reads the classics, glides through the house in cashmere sweaters and tailored skirts. With her straight black bob and pale complexion she looks more Parisian than Greek. Tina is dismissive of Miriam's transformation saying: 'You can't straighten a dog's tail.'

Athena and I sit opposite one another, two continents separated by an oceanic expanse of dinner table. As usual I am at the mercy of her mood and today she is in no mood to make conversation. My cousin has, for as long as I can remember, been going through a 'difficult patch'. Miriam attributes Athena's surliness to teenage angst.

The twins peek into the dining room from the doorway and Malcolm sends them to their bedroom with a barked command.

'The chudren they don gonna eat?' Tina asks.

The twins will get no lunch, Malcolm explains with a placatory smile, as punishment for kicking a football into his rhododendron. Tina glares at her brother-in-law with unveiled hostility while he casually sucks on his pipe and runs his fingers through his hair. Malcolm has a full head of thick brown hair, flecked with grey. He is a handsome man with a lightly suntanned hue and cheekbones that protrude like sand dunes. Except for the fine lines flowing like estuaries from the corners of his eyes, his skin is smooth and taut. Tina says his lack of wrinkles is a sign of the 'good life' . . . 'life behind a desk' . . . 'a life without problems'.

Miriam wheels a hostess trolley into the dining room and unloads its contents: roast beef, Yorkshire puddings, roast potatoes, boiled cabbage, garden peas and gravy. I have always admired the modesty of Miriam's Sunday lunch. At home we embellish a roast dinner with *koubebia*, pasticcio, a mountain of bread, dips and a mixed salad.

The roast beef is handed out refectory style, two wafer-thin slices to a plate. There is no noisy free for all, no collective scramble for food. The distribution of portions is serenely orchestrated, serving dishes circum-navigate the table in a tidy procession like synchronized swimmers.

'The meat is no cook,' Tina says, staring at the pink flesh on her plate, shattering the serenity.

'It's rare, Constantina,' Malcolm replies in

a haughty, didactic voice. 'Beef should never be overcooked.'

'*En omo to kreas*' — the meat is raw — Yiayia says, grimacing. Bloody beef is not part of our culinary tradition.

'What did your mother say?' Malcolm asks his wife.

'She doesn't eat beef, darling,' she replies.

Miriam often bends the truth to make it more palatable, misquoting her mother and sister without compunction to put them in a better light. It is an idiosyncrasy unbefitting a woman with Miriam's social graces. Her motives may be honourable but her unflinching ability to prevaricate in our presence is unnerving.

Miriam has not inherited our love of food. Her plate is more white space than sustenance. She eats to live while we live to eat. She drops a dollop of boiled cabbage onto her plate and rakes it with her fork, like a chicken scratching the earth with its foot, contemplating who-knows-what before putting the fork to her mouth and chewing for an inordinate length of time. Tina has a more tactile relationship with food. She sucks on bone marrow, soaks up plate juices with soft bread, crunches on well-cooked chicken skin, eats artichokes until her gums turn black and nibbles sunflower seeds until

43

she is constipated.

Malcolm opens a bottle of red wine and puts the cork to his nose. 'Ah wine that maketh glad the heart of man,' he says, getting up to fill our glasses. 'Just one glass for you, dear,' he says to Miriam. 'I know you're watching the calories.'

'You watchin the calories, wha for?' Tina asks.

'Malcolm says he'll leave me if I ever get fat,' Miriam replies, chuckling.

'And who would blame me?' Malcolm says.

'*Ti eipe o Englezos?*' Yiayia asks what the Englishman said. Seventeen years have failed to put her and Malcolm on first-name terms. Tina hurriedly translates.

'*Ton demona ton mavro.*' Yiayia calls Malcolm a 'black devil'.

'What did your mother say, Miriam?' Malcolm asks.

'She asked what the devil we're talking about.'

'What you mean you leave my sista?' Tina asks Malcolm indignantly, giving him a chance to redeem himself.

'I married a sleek racehorse. I wouldn't like her turning into a dumpy Shire.'

'Wha you talkin abou?' Tina says, genuinely flummoxed.

'If a woman lets herself go then she can't

blame her husband for looking elsewhere.'

Malcolm settles back in his chair and winks at Tony, a wink that could mean 'we men understand each other' or 'I'm only teasing'. Malcolm likes to get Tina worked up and watch her struggle to formulate a coherent sentence.

'So you think is all right for my Athonis to av e gelfriend cause I'm no Slimcia gel. If he do that I chop off is you-know-what and throw it in the chip pan.'

Tony shifts uncomfortably in his seat.

'I no be jokin,' Tina continues, 'I kick im out. Everythin is in my name anyhow. I get the house. I get the shop. I get the kids. He don get nathin.'

'Adonis, I think you made a mistake putting everything in the wife's name,' Malcolm says with an irrepressible smirk.

'I'm not planning to have an affair,' Tony replies.

'No . . . but she's a very wealthy woman by the sounds of it and some unscrupulous fellow could lure her away.'

'I don leave my Athonis for no one. He may av lost his hair and is no so good lookin as when I married him, bat looks is no everythin.'

'Anyone for more potatoes?' Miriam says, grabbing the serving dish and making her way around the table. I refuse her offer of second helpings. I could easily finish off the plate of Yorkshire puddings that lie tantalizingly in front of me but I won't give the Jamesons the satisfaction of calling me a glutton.

'Why you don eat today?' Tina asks, looking at my plate.

'I am eating,' I reply, hoping she won't pursue this line of questioning.

'You feelin sick?'

'No, I'm fine, Mama.'

Tina spears a Yorkshire pudding and drops it onto my plate.

'Then eat,' she says, 'you gonna waste away.'

★   ★   ★

Malcolm spoons a portion of custard tart into his mouth and surveys his guests like pawns on a chessboard.

'So, young man,' he says to Andy, 'what do you plan to do with your life?'

'Same as everyone else,' Andy replies casually, 'make a decent living, get married one day, have kids, what else is there?'

'Still working at the shop.'

Andy nods his head.

'You're a wise boy . . . stay where the bread's buttered. Why go it alone when you stand to inherit a lucrative business?'

'Too right,' Andy replies, refusing as always to be baited.

'You were never very keen on school, were you, Andrew?'

'Not the learning side,' Andy replies with a mischievous grin. 'Anna's the clever one in our family.' My brother speaks with the unflappable confidence of a man who is happy with his lot. He left school at sixteen with two CSEs. His main pursuits were not conductive to study. The shop, girls and football, the three inextricably linked. Playing football for the county supplied the groupies, working at the shop provided an income enjoyed by few boys his age, his tendency to splurge boosted his allure. 'Why bother with an education when I'm gonna end up in the shop anyway?' was his philosophy. A sense of duty and expensive tastes have sealed Andy's fate. 'What use is a sports car when I'm sixty and bald as a coot?' he says. The shop is a means to consumer durables.

Malcolm likes to belittle my brother whenever he gets the chance, citing 'academia' as 'God', an ideology somewhat at odds with Malcolm's obsessive fascination with Tony's income and assets.

'At least there's one bright spark in the

Papamichael household,' Malcolm says, turning to me with a Burgundy-gummed smile that induces a nervous flutter in my stomach.

'What do you want to be, young lady?' he asks, fixing me with an interrogatory stare, making me feel inadequate for having no burning ambition beyond graduation. My professional future is a sandstorm on the horizon. I am running from the yoke of tradition, to a hazy mirage in the distance, to an oasis promising personal fulfilment, motivated largely by the desire to leave home. Athena wants to be a lawyer. My cousin has time and space enough to explore her options. Higher education is a foregone conclusion, not a hurdle. It is a leisurely walk along a well-trodden path, a continuation of Jameson family tradition. I journey against the grain, contrary to the wishes of my mother.

'A psychoanalyst,' I reply, more out of desperation than conviction.

'I expect you're well acquainted with Freud then, and Wilhelm Reich. Now he was a clever chap. I think I've got a copy of his book in the study. *Die Funktion des Orgasmus*. I'll lend it to you. It's in German, of course, but I'm sure that won't be a problem for a clever girl like you.'

I don't bother telling Malcolm that I failed

48

my German O-level, that German makes as much sense to me as Morse code and that my psychoanalytic inspiration is the woman staring at him through the greasy lenses of her NHS glasses.

'My daughter doesn't have much time for reading these days,' he continues, 'she has her mind on other things. There's always some young fellow on heat sniffing round the house . . . Are you courting yet, Anna?'

'No,' I reply, feeling flustered, grateful that Tina has failed to understand the question.

'A lovely girl like you and no boyfriend. I find that very hard to believe.'

'Boyfren!' Tina splutters, custard flying from her mouth. 'My Anna he's a good gel, she don av boyfres.'

'Anna's a young, attractive woman, it's quite natural for her to start dating. Don't be so old-fashioned, Constantina,' Malcolm says. 'Only last week Athena brought her boyfriend Gordon home for tea. A cleancut, respectable boy. Son of a doctor.'

'*Aman apia i eyia apia gai to rifi*' — when the goat jumps the kid follows — Tina says, looking at her sister.

'What did your sister say, darling?' Malcolm asks.

'New Zealand lamb, lovely with mint sauce and new potatoes,' Miriam replies, starting to clear the table, a sign for Andy to express his thanks for lunch and make a speedy exit.

★   ★   ★

Miriam came to England, three years after Tina, on the pretext of marrying a fish fryer from Dudley, a match arranged by my parents. The eligible bachelor came from a well-to-do family with a chain of fish and chip shops. Eighteen-year-old Miriam agreed to the match on the basis of a Hollywoodesque photograph she was shown of a young man with thick wavy hair and a handsome jaw. Miriam kissed her mother goodbye and boarded the *Knossos* in Limassol, her crossing paid for by the fish fryer. On arrival in England a week later she was met at Heathrow by a barrel-like man with bushy sideburns and a receding hairline, who claimed to be her suitor. Miriam flatly refused to marry him on the grounds of deception. The man admitted the photograph sent to Cyprus was that of his better-looking cousin. Tina argued that looks were not everything and tried to persuade her sister to go through with the wedding but Miriam would not be swayed.

It was agreed by family consensus that Miriam should stay in England and work in the shop until a more aesthetically pleasing bachelor could be found. She enrolled on a language course, one evening a week, to help improve her poor English. Tina was unhappy about Miriam's unchaperoned excursions to the local college and her worst fears were realized six months later when her younger sister announced she was pregnant and planned to marry her English teacher. Tina was outraged and blamed herself for allowing Miriam too much freedom. Yiayia demanded Miriam's immediate return to Cyprus, arranging her betrothal to a widowed farmer in the village who was prepared to overlook her indiscretion and raise the child as his own. Miriam refused to go back and subsequently married Malcolm, to the con-sternation of both families.

Malcolm's father, an ex-army major who served in Cyprus during the EOKA conflict, accused him of bastardizing the family tree and disinherited his son. Mr Jameson senior had bitter memories of 1950s Cyprus when EOKA, fighting for the island's freedom from British rule, ambushed army patrols and blew up Government property. Major Jameson sustained a flesh wound when he was shot in the leg by a youth riding pillion on a motorbike. The victim's only consolation was watching the suspect swing by the neck from the gallows. The young man's parents appealed to the Queen, to Eisenhower and to Major Jameson himself for clemency. On the night before his execution the condemned man played Bach and Beethoven in his cell, to the surprise of jailers, and in the morning he bid farewell to his family without shedding a tear. Major Jameson felt justice had been done, although he couldn't be sure from his fleeting glance at the culprit that the right man had been apprehended. On his return to England he put the sordid episode behind him and lived quite happily in his glass house until Miriam appeared on the scene, like a curse, as if the spirit of the twenty-year-old man had come back to haunt him. Malcolm tells the story of his father's ambush with thick-skinned jocularity while Tina listens sour-faced, thinking how close her own father came to swinging from the gallows.

When Athena was born the rift began to heal. Mr Jameson senior fell in love with his golden-haired, emerald-eyed granddaughter and used to say with great satisfaction that she had inherited the Jameson family genes. No one bothered to tell him that Athena's maternal Grandfather Andreas had grey-green eyes and that his mother was reputedly a golden-haired beauty, a direct descendent of settlers from the Greek island of Mani, coming from a region famed for its fair-haired, pale-skinned inhabitants.

★ ★ ★

Miriam is uncharacteristically animated when she speaks Greek. Her measured, monotone voice goes up a pitch and sounds like a washing machine on spin cycle. Liberated by the absence of her husband, she listens with unashamed relish to Tina's incredulous stories, featuring Hambo's daughter and Kolokotronis' son, involving love, infidelity, bankruptcy, sexual impropriety and incest. Tina, the bard of tittle-tattle, a repository of titillating stories, knows how to hold an audience, littering her rhetoric with phrases like 'may I loose my sight if I'm telling a lie', 'there's no smoke without fire' and 'I swear on my husband's life that I speak the truth'. Tina never swears on the life of her children when embellishing her stories. Yiayia sits at the head of the table, portly as a China Buddha, drinking Greek coffee, listening to her daughters flush out trivia and exchange gossip.

Hambo's daughter Sophia, Tina tells us, has agreed to marry at least half a dozen suitors after a series of *broxenia* — introductions. 'She goes out with these men, gives her word to marry, her parents start making wedding plans and then she changes her mind. One was too sweaty, another had bad breath and a third had too much bodily hair for her liking. She's too fussy if you ask me.' Her most recent introduction to a solicitor from Southgate ended in scandal when she ditched the 'poor man' on account of a lazy eye she failed to notice until two months into their acquaintance. 'That girl is nothing but spoiled, rich and stupid,' Tina says in conclusion. My theory is that Sophia has no intention of getting married, that she is cleverly using the system to accrue a string of boyfriends and satisfy her sexual appetite.

Tina sips the last of her coffee and upturns the cup in its saucer. She crosses herself in rapid succession, asking the Father, the Son and the Holy Ghost to forgive her mother for what she is about to do. Yiayia reads coffee cups, an activity frowned upon by the Church. Tina calls it 'a bit of fun', assuaging God's wrath by proclaiming her total scepticism, insisting she does not believe a word her mother says. When all our cups have been upturned and the coffee sediment has begun to dry, Yiayia reaches for my saucer and turns it three times in a clockwise direction. Her readings, conducted in Greek, hold no fascination for

Athena, who disappeared upstairs after lunch complaining of a headache. She is as mocking of Yiayia's craft as Malcolm who calls it 'hocus pocus', refers to the sisters and their mother as 'The Three Witches' and would never agree to having his cup read. Yiayia says he has too much to hide.

In fingers plump as leavened dough, Yiayia picks up my cup and peruses the inside, looking for symbols, letters and numbers, which give clues to the psyche and forecast the future. Symbols tell of love, health and wealth, letters represent the initials of a person's name, numbers indicate how long an event will take to happen, in days, weeks or months. I stand behind Yiayia, looking over her shoulder into my cup, trying to decipher the grainy streaks, ignoring Tina who tells me to sit down, saying she doesn't want her daughter following in the fortune-telling footsteps of her grandmother.

'I see a bowl containing fruit in your cup. An apple, a pear, something resembling an aubergine,' Yiayia says, 'fruit represents family. A family closely connected, like the links of a chain, one dependent upon the other.'

'I must remind Athonis to buy a box of aubergines from the market,' Tina says, 'I haven't made moussaka for a while.'

'Mama, can we concentrate on my cup, not your cooking?' I say, anxious to hear what the future holds.

'*Oofou*. Am I not allowed to talk any more,' Tina complains.

'No one can beat you when it comes to talking,' Yiayia mutters, peeking at her daughter above the rim of her glasses.

'What's the use of a mouth without a tongue,' Tina replies.

'Aubergines, Yiayia,' I say, steering the conversation back to my cup and its contents.

'The aubergine is an uncommon fruit. Its appearance suggests that you view your family as being out of the ordinary, unusual in some way, a peculiar fruit. At odds with the families that surround you.'

'Is that what you think of us?' Tina says, shaking her head. 'Well I can tell you there is nothing strange about me.'

'You will learn in time to appreciate that which you now deem strange, to appreciate difference as a blessing not a burden.'

Yiayia points to an ill-defined symbol with her little finger, reminiscent of a Rorschach inkblot, and tells me it is a treasure chest, the sign of a good heart and a giving spirit. The lid of the chest is closed and bolted, she says, indicative of a closed character, unwilling to show their true self and face the world. She tells me I must find the key to open the chest and release the bounty that lies within. Then she points to a rounded clump of sediment, a recurrent theme in my cups, an accumulation of troubling thoughts.

'You worry too much, granddaughter,' she says, 'this is the downside of your sensitivity.'

'What has my daughter got to worry about?' Tina says dismissively. 'She has enough to eat, clothes to wear, money to spend.'

'Money does not feed a person's soul,' Yiayia replies.

'Don't you see any cockerels?' Tina asks, hoping for evidence of a suitor.

'No,' Yiayia replies, 'but I see a long road, straight and unwavering, that Anna is fated to travel. It will take her to the place she has to go. She will encounter obstacles en route, but her determination will win through. Here, along the road, is a rock blocking her path, a symbol of something immovable, perhaps an obstinate person. The rock cannot be shifted however hard she tries, she must go around it and continue on her way.'

'I wonder who the rock might be?' I say, looking accusingly at my mother, who is quick to supply her own interpretation.

'Perhaps the rock is there to stop her taking the wrong road.'

'In my granddaughter's cup there is only one road,' Yiayia replies, proffering her judgement like a trump card, as she puts down my cup and picks up Tina's. My readings are always short, characterized by troubled thoughts and happy endings. I am a closed chest but an open book. My grandmother's optimistic forecasts always lift my spirits and make the future I imagine seem possible.

Yiayia views the inside of her daughter's cup with interest. 'Ah, this is a very good cup. Here, close to the rim is a shoal of fish.'

'Haddock must be going up in price again,' Tina says, grinning, forever trying to lighten the mystical mood that descends when Yiayia begins her readings.

'No,' I say, 'you or someone close will be coming into money, Mama.' Under my grandmother's tutelage the mysteries of the cup are slowly unravelling.

Yiayia nods approvingly before elaborating. 'A lot of money, Constantina. Here beside the fish is a small seven. News of the money will come within seven days, seven weeks or seven months.'

'I have never won anything in my life,' Tina says dismissively.

'You will also be making a long journey,' Yiayia continues, 'travelling over land and sea. Here is an aeroplane, do you see it, Anna? The symbol is clear and unmistakable, the journey will be unexpected.'

'Perhaps Athonis has booked that holiday to Cyprus he has been promising.'

'Your cup is full of good fortune, you have nothing to worry about, daughter,' Yiayia says, plunging her thumb into the bottom of the cup and twisting it to produce a smudged print, which she claims to be the image of St Fanourios.

'Something you want will come to fruition, quicker than you expect. You must light a candle in honour of the saint and bake seven *Fanouropittes*,' she tells her daughter.

'Blessed be his name,' Tina says, crossing herself.

St Fanourios is said to grant a person's most heartfelt wishes after seven cakes have been baked in his honour and blessed by the priest.

'There is only one thing I pray for night and day,' Tina says with a maudlin air, 'to see one of my children standing at the altar and that would truly be a miracle. Neither of them shows any interest in settling down. Anna has her head in the clouds and Andreas . . . well he's a man and a man can't be rushed into marriage.'

Yiayia puts Tina's cup aside and picks up

Miriam's. She studies it for some time before shaking her head.

'Be careful, daughter, someone close to you has bad intentions.'

'How do you know?' I ask.

'Don't you see the snake, Anna?' she says, pointing to a wavy line with two bubbles at one end.

'I can't think of anyone I don't get along with,' Miriam says, shrugging her shoulders.

'The snake has two heads. The person in question does not show you who they really are. And you are easily fooled, Mirianthy. Here in your cup I see a pair of glasses, a symbol that suggests you have a tendency to ignore problems. In the past this has worked in your favour, allowing you to handle difficult situations with optimism. Now you are simply deceiving yourself and must take off the glasses that cloud your vision, in order to see clearly, to see things as they really are.'

It is hard to tell if Yiayia has struck a chord. Miriam, with her stiff upper lip and amicable smile, betrays no emotion.

'Why don't you tell my sister something worth hearing? Don't you see any cockerels for Athena?' Tina asks, unable to curb her fixation.

'I see a journey similar to yours. I see an aeroplane as big as my thumbnail — do you see it, Anna?' I nod my head, seeing something that looks vaguely like an aircraft. 'It is not a journey you have planned, it will come out of the blue.'

'Get your suitcases ready, Mirianthy,' Tina says.

'Such a journey is impossible,' Miriam replies. 'Malcolm is afraid of flying and I would never travel alone.'

'I can only tell you what I see in the cup. I cannot make you believe it,' Yiayia says, shrugging. She puts down Miriam's cup, takes off her glasses and wipes her watery eyes with the loose cuff of her sleeve. Without the small cup in her pudgy hand Yiayia seems to shrink in stature. The cup transforms her from amorphous mass into Mediterranean maharishi, able to translate an innocuous substance into a panoramic landscape of metaphorical roads to cross, rivers to forge and mountains to climb, into a world inhabited by saints, suitors and strange fruit.

The magic begins with the hallowed ritual of making Greek coffee or *Elliniko kafe*, when Yiayia fills a small copper pan called a *briki* with water and adds an instinctive measure of finely ground Greek coffee and as much sugar as requested by the drinker. She sits the pan on a gas flame, allowing her ingredients to float for a while before gently stirring, lifting the pan from the heat when the coffee begins to bubble up and rise to the rim. When Tina was a girl, new brides were often judged on their ability to make a good Greek coffee. In spite of countless lessons from mother, my coffee always boils over, soiling the cooker and throwing my domestic aptitude into question.

As we carry the empty cups to the sink Yiayia places a heavy arm around my shoulders.

'Do you see this?' she asks, pointing to an elaborate swirl of sediment on the inside of my cup.

'It looks like a person with wings,' I reply.

'Yes,' she says, 'this is a very good sign indeed. It means you have a guardian angel . . . someone watching over you, Anna.'

As she clumsily squeezes me against her spongy breast I feel incredibly safe, protected by her aura, glad to have her as an ally and privileged to be her granddaughter.

★   ★   ★

Yiayia does not openly admit to powers supernatural but claims to have keen intuition and clear vision. She can read a person's face, the set of one's features, decipher a frown or a raised eyebrow, interpret a smile or a crumpled shirt. I have seen her glance fleetingly over the top of her glasses to gauge a reaction before elaborating a point. She has better hearing than people give her credit for and only needs half a sentence from a whispered conversation to form a coherent opinion.

Yiayia has an innate understanding of human nature and makes poignant generalizations. She knows *per se* that most women have two important men in their lives, a partner and a father; she knows all teenage girls have a love interest and suffer some form of angst; she says a person in their thirties revels in their strength and sense of freedom from the past and that past traumas can return with a vengeance to haunt a person in their forties. She believes we are never truly free of our past, that it makes us what we are, determines the set of our jaw and the look in our eye. Often she uses the cup to offer her family advice, to bolster and support and warn of things they may be too emotionally involved to see. Using her sixth sense she tells them things they already know about themselves but have buried deep in their subconscious.

Yiayia has inadvertently schooled me in the art of intuition. By watching and listening, by daily exposure to insightful comments, I am learning the art of acumen. To trust the feeling in my gut, to pick up signs I would normally choose to ignore, to sharpen an indolent mind. At the expense of my innocence. I can feel a change fermenting inside me and the niggling disruption of my natural tendencies.

What I can never learn is Yiayia's ability to prophesy. She has accurately predicted a prodigious number of events, some inane, others quite dramatic. She predicted someone in the family would undergo an operation a week before Andy had his appendix removed, foresaw the visit of a relative from overseas three days before a distant cousin from Australia arrived unannounced on our doorstep, warned Tina of a road accident just hours before Tony wrote off his car. Tina calls it coincidence and good guess work but that doesn't stop her reaching for the incense burner when her cup heralds unwelcome news.

★ ★ ★

A narrow stairwell, cold and dank, leads to Athena's third-floor bedroom. The smell of old carpet inhabits the landing and continues, unabated, into Athena's room. I tread carefully over books, magazines and cereal bowls, coated with craters of aquamarine mould, to get to the bed. Athena views me with moody detachment, from the comfort of her Lloyd Loom, smoking a long, slim cigarette. I slump onto the bed, unsettling dust motes. Tenacious sunbeams penetrate the foggy window, illuminating a cloud of twirling specks. I search my brain for something to say. My cousin is quick to misconstrue and belittle, to yawn when the topic of conversation is not to her liking. Her body language renders me tongue tied and inarticulate. I need eye contact, hand gestures and a look of genuine interest to conduct a conversation.

'Your mother's prehistoric,' she says suddenly, inducing a hot flush of indignation. 'What does she mean no boyfriends? If Mummy tried to stop me seeing Gordon, I'd tell her to sod off.'

'She's just a bit overprotective,' I reply, feeling the need to fight my mother's corner.

'You'd think she would have changed after so many years in England. Someone should tell her this is the twentieth century, not the Stone Age. God, I don't know how you live with her. I wouldn't put up with it. Not for a minute. Mummy isn't like that at all. She lets me do whatever I want. I am sixteen, for Christ's sake.'

On and on she goes, suddenly finding a voice, while I quietly seethe, unable to think up a reply that will curtail the flow of judgemental rhetoric, choked by the intensity of my irritation. I am Tina's harshest judge and her staunchest supporter, a dissenter but no Judas.

' . . . tell her where to go . . . pack your bags and walk out,' she says unhelpfully, proving once again that she doesn't know me at all. I wouldn't have the heart to walk out; I'm not made that way. Athena's big words only serve to make me feel small and inept.

★ ★ ★

Tina stands in the front doorway, stuffing chocolate buttons into the twins' open mouths. Miriam makes no attempt to stop her. She has tried in the past, only to be accused of subjecting her sons to dietary hardship by colluding with the lunacy of her husband. Malcolm's edicts do not stop at chocolate but cover a whole gamut of sensory stimuli. Television, processed foods and high-tech toys are also banned from the Jameson house. Last Christmas Tina bought the boys a radio-controlled car, a hand-held electronic game and a stocking full of assorted chocolates. The twins love their aunt

66

and generally open her presents in the privacy of their shared bedroom.

Tony and Malcolm stand on the driveway, talking to a middle-aged brunette with heavy make-up and high heels, wearing a jersey dress drawn tight around a saggy bottom and heavy breasts.

'That's our neighbour,' Miriam says. 'She's the wife of a surgeon.'

Yiayia pulls a witchy, disapproving face. 'I don't care whose wife she is, she wears too much make-up for my liking.'

'They say she has slept with a legion of unsuspecting local men,' Miriam says matter-of-factly.

'Who can blame the men when she dresses like that?' Tina says, shaking her head, popping a piece of chocolate into Charlie's gaping mouth. My mother can be disturbingly misogynistic at times, quick to blame women for indiscretions requiring mutual consent.

'You enjoined yoursevs apstes?' Tina asks, turning to me.

'It's a shame the girls don't spend more time together,' Miriam says.

'You right,' Tina replies.

'Why doesn't Anna stay the night?' Miriam asks.

'I'd love to,' I lie, 'but I'd need a change of

clothes. Maybe next time.'

'Don't worry about clothes, Athena can lend you something,' Miriam replies, ignoring our obvious difference in size.

'OK,' Tina says, oblivious to the look of desperation in my eyes, 'Anna he can stay. Athonis she pick him up in the morni.' She kisses her sister and walks toward the car, grabbing her husband en route, rudely ignoring the surgeon's wife who turns to smile at her.

Miriam and Tina are keen for their daughters to get along. The sisters have a special bond in spite of their differences. '*To yema then yinete nero*' — blood cannot become water — Tina says, insisting shared ancestry is sufficient common ground for an emotional connection and that the bond between cousins is the next best thing to sisterly love. Athena and I are as connected as a severed nerve, firing impulses into a void. There was a brief period in our lives when we used to get along, when being a year older and considerably bigger gave me kudos. Athena actively sought my company because I had more toys and more pocket money, because in our house the sweet cupboard was a free for all. Then she sprouted breasts and changed into a sultry, sulky, prima donna.

With a heavy heart I watch my means of

escape backing out of the driveway. Left alone with the Jamesons, I feel like a goldfish marooned on a draining board, longing for nothing more than the predictable safety of its bowl and a scattering of food.

'Daddy, I'm going to Rebecca's,' Athena says, reaching for her jacket.

'What about your cousin?' Miriam asks.

'I'd rather stay here and play with the twins,' I say. I have no desire to meet any friend of Athena's.

'No, you'll go together,' Miriam says, taking off her cashmere cardigan and draping it across my shoulders.

★   ★   ★

We walk along the tree-lined street, more briskly than stilettos allow. Athena marches along while I hurry beside her, my skirt constricting my stride, feeling like a short-legged sausage dog trying to keep pace with its owner. I am painfully out of breath by the time we reach the far-flung reaches of Rebecca's door. A slim, strawberry blonde in tight black leggings and sweatshirt opens the door. She looks at me with deadpan eyes, in the same unreceptive way she might react at the sight of a milk bottle standing on her doorstep, then stands aside to let us in.

'Come up,' she says, not bothering to ask who I am, grabbing Athena by the hand and leading her up the stairs. On first impressions Rebecca is as churlish and undemonstrative as my cousin and I imagine, with fleeting pleasure, planting a crisp and resonating slap on her cold, pink cheek.

Rebecca's bedroom smells of sandalwood. A joss stick stuck in a ball of plasticine burns on her bedside table. Beside it, a small candle illuminates a joint as long and fat as my index finger lying in an ashtray littered with cigarette ends. Athena kicks off her shoes and stretches out on the bed next to Rebecca.

'Mummy and Daddy have gone out for the night and you're just in time,' Rebecca says, reaching for the joint, rolling it between thumb and forefinger, and passing it to me. It is a magnanimous gesture, a hash-scented olive branch, a symbol of Rebecca's generosity.

'No thanks,' I say, sinking into a spongy armchair, feeling vaguely guilty, knowing my refusal is a slap in the face, that I have annihilated any slim chance we had of getting along.

'She doesn't smoke,' Athena says, reaching for the joint.

I am too uptight to take drugs. My greatest

fear is losing the inhibitions that have kept me on the straight and narrow for so long. Who knows what I might do without the weight of reason, self-consciousness and guilt weighing down upon me. I like the smell of secondary smoke and often fight the urge to rifle through Andy's pockets for a cigarette. Some years ago I satisfied my need for artificial stimulation by smoking my way through a family pack of Johnson's ear buds, lighting one end of each bud with a match and inhaling quickly on the other end to achieve a momentary high. Then Tina replaced the Johnson's with the supermarket's own brand. The plastic was thin and highly inflammable and on one occasion an ear bud burst into flames scorching my eyebrows. I graduated to pot pourri, wrapped in coloured Post-it pads, smoking my roll-ups on the flat extension roof outside my window. I quit the day Tina discovered a burn hole in my carpet, forcing me to tell a treacherous lie about Yiayia and her incense burner. Smoking innocuous household products somehow seemed less of a crime. Tina would never have connected the rapid consumption of ear buds to anything other than dirty ears.

Athena and Rebecca blast away to planet hash, leaving me swamped on earth in a cloud of smoke, isolated and completely ignored. They chat about mutual friends while a voracious worm of malcontent gnaws at my stomach.

'I'd love a cup of tea, Becks,' Athena says lazily.

'I'm too stoned to move,' Rebecca replies, stretching out her long limbs.

'Anna,' Athena says sweetly, 'will you go?'

I drift through the dark house in search of the kitchen, feeling my way down the stairs and along a dimly lit corridor. The kitchen, vast and pine-filled, stinks of yesterday's fry up and soiled cat litter. I switch on the light and see a damp litter tray lying next to the back door and a corpulent tabby sitting on a chopping board licking its bottom. I scrub the tannin stains from three off-white mugs and make tea, while the fat tabby curls itself around my ankles and purrs.

I head back upstairs, on leaden feet, with a loaded tray and attempt to lever the bedroom door handle with my elbow. Rebecca pulls open the door and looks at me with a languid, almost friendly look in her eye, finally acknowledging my presence or so I think before she opens her mouth to say: 'Can you fetch some bickies?'

★ ★ ★

I approach a crowd of people standing in a square and tell them I can fly. No one appears to believe me, so I start flapping my arms like a bird. Slowly, I begin to rise up into the air and hover above their heads while they cheer and applaud. Then I fly away, over the crowd, over red-tiled rooftops, over a patchwork of cornfields, carried higher and higher by a stream of warm air, floating light as gossamer in a perfectly blue sky until a tap on the shoulder wakes me up and brings me plummeting to earth like a brick dropped from a motorway bridge. Back to the oppressive darkness of Rebecca's room, where the air is cold and stale and I feel as buoyant as a sack of Maris Piper.

'We have to go,' Athena says, heading for the door, while her friend lies sleeping beneath a thick blue quilt.

On the street outside a blast of cold air whips ferociously through my clothing. Athena grabs my arm and presses against my side as we hurry home, providing all the warmth of a sparrow. I want more than anything to feel warm, to collapse onto something soft, to cocoon myself inside a fresh-smelling blanket and sleep. The journey home seems tortuously long, the pavement extending as we walk, stretching before us like a sheet of grey rubber. I have the eerie sensation that I'm walking along Cowley Drive towards my house, then I lose all sense of time and place and allow Athena to lead the way.

Finally, after what seems like hours, we reach the Jameson house. Athena turns her key in the lock and pushes open the door. We walk into a pitch-black hallway and start to feel our way along the wall towards the stairs. A beam of yellow light suddenly zooms in on Athena's face, causing her to clasp a hand over her eyes. Malcolm sits menacingly at the foot of the stairs, flashing a lighted torch in his daughter's face.

'What time do you call this?' he asks.

Athena blinks into the light, then glances at her wrist watch. '4 a.m.,' she says calmly.

'Your mother's been worried sick. Where the hell have you been?'

Athena tries to walk up the stairs past Malcolm but he grabs her roughly by the arm and pulls her down.

'Look at your eyes, young lady. Do you think I don't know what you've been doing?' he says, in a voice that is cold and menacing. 'I warned you, Athena.'

'Piss off,' Athena screams, yanking her arm back and running up the stairs. I follow her, sprinting up the dark stairwell and dashing into her bedroom just before she slams the door.

'Bastard,' she shouts, tearing off her clothes and flinging them angrily onto the pile in the corner of the room, slipping her naked body into bed, burying her head beneath the quilt and starting to snore. I am amazed by her speedy transition from fury to REM. A thick skin has many advantages, allows one the luxury of sleep at times of crisis.

My mind spins, my legs throb from overexertion. I can no more relax than I can touch my toes. I perch on the edge of the bed and wonder where best to sleep: on a carpet clogged with superfluous keratin or next to Athena, naked and outstretched? I take off my shoes and curl up like a foetus on top of a musty quilt, a chill draught freezing my back. Too cold to sleep, I lie awake, watching daylight seep, ever-so-slowly, through the muggy window, my stomach swelling into a tight, hard, painful ball. Bohemian squalor is not conducive to restful sleep. For all its books, antiques and Victorian grandeur, the Jameson house has no warm, beating heart. It feels cold and sanitary in comparison to Tina's homely womb of sweet smells and creature comforts.

When I hear signs of life from downstairs I move to the Lloyd Loom and wait. Athena wakes up briefly and sits up in bed, golden hair partially covering her bare breasts, reminiscent of a Pre-Raphaelite Ophelia. She yawns, looks at me queerly, tells me I look 'god awful' and falls back to sleep. I stare impassively at my reflection in the bedroom mirror, at blotchy skin, red eyes, hair frizzed and matted, plump on top like a soufflé. The sound of the doorbell lifts my inertia and sends me rushing downstairs quicker than I came up. I find Tony standing in the doorway talking to Miriam.

'Good morning, sleepy head,' my aunt says cheerfully, before asking if I need a hairbrush.

* * *

I drink coffee from a hand-painted mug, large enough to hold the dose of caffeine required to shake off my sluggishness. Savouring an hour of Sunday-morning quietude before the tumult ahead, before the clatter of breakfast pots and pans crescendoes, shattering the peace. I lie on the sofa, as snug as a plump bug, in Tina's roomy sequined cardigan, breathing in the comforting smell of Chanel and cinnamon and caramelized onions, infused in the peachy woollen fibres.

I reach for the book that lies beside me and read a sentence that thrusts me back into an austere nineteenth-century landscape. To a sceptical protagonist whose sense of 'absolute stagnation' seems to mirror my own. To a wicked aunt and an oppressive institution, to a woman agitated to pain by her 'restlessness'. And somehow, in her misery, I find solace and lose myself entirely.

Reading is my balm, my comfort, a consolation for having no life. When frustration threatens to overwhelm me, I grab a book and find a quiet corner. And Tina looks at me as if I'm somehow dysfunctional, complaining that I spend too much time reading. The alternative is slamming doors, arguing until my throat hurts, addling my brain with television.

I like a finely crafted sentence, a dramatic twist of fate and a defiant voice. I like a book that draws me in and begs me to return when I leave it. I read when I should be writing essays, when I should be wading through the A-level texts lying on my desk. Through *The Canterbury Tales*, *Economics Made Easy* and *Introduction to Psychology*, through the subjects that will pave my way to a degree in combined arts. I work in short bursts, fitting academia between the shop, my own reading and family commitments, switching with difficulty from one mindset to another — from bread rolls to Freud, from shop banter to nineteenth-century verse. Tina thinks I am clever, too clever for a woman. I would describe myself as stubborn and determined. My mind is a slug, slithering slowly but surely towards sustenance, dodging salt grains on route. Tina is the salt. Threatening to fizzle me into oblivion.

Leaving home to study is my only path to freedom. Some have made the terrible mistake of equating marriage with freedom, of acquiescing for an easy life, of marrying too young. I see them in church on a Sunday, balancing children on their nubile hips, talking like their mothers, dressing like their mothers, looking as world-weary as their mothers.

'No daughter of mine will leave this house to live beneath a stranger's roof. You will study from home or not at all. We will buy you a car, any car you want, and you can come and go as you please,' Tina says, thinking she can buy me off. The promise of spending money galore and a student life of luxury come at the price of my freedom. The freedom to eat a humble ham sandwich, to enter my abode without an inquisition, to claim unfamiliar streets as my own, to assert my independence. 'Independence' is a dirty word in our house, akin to 'promiscuity' and 'debauchery'. 'We are not individuals but members of a family,' Tina asserts, 'we must draw together or else we will be pulled apart.'

'How will I sleep at night, worrying about your safety?' she says, tugging at the heart strings before voicing skewed ethics and misplaced priorities. 'What will people say?' 'What will people think?' 'So . . . when exactly do you plan to get married?' 'Who will replace you in the shop if you leave?' What Tina fears most of all is assimilation: that I will fraternize with English people and forget my Greekness; that I will meet a pale man with blond hair, a *kastrishi*, and shatter the dreams that are her life force.

Tony behaves like an impotent spectator in the battle between mother and daughter. He gives me a pained 'what can I do?' expression and seals his lips. He is a lamb with wolf's teeth. I have seen him conspiring with his wife, instructing her in whispered tones, fine-tuning her arguments. Yiayia has tried to overrule her daughter with maternal authority but she is largely ignored. 'Anna's a sensible girl. Let her go,' she says. 'What do you know?' Tina replies, negating her mother's unquestionable wisdom.

Andy walks through the epicentre of an argument like a spectral illusion. In through the middle of a high-pitched maelstrom and out again. Unscathed and unmoved. 'She'll never let you go,' he says dismissively, his tone suggesting I should give up. I reply with a stock, standard, 'she can't stop me', sounding like a petulant child, wishing with every grain of my being that things were different. That Tina would give me her blessings and send me off with pride. That she would boast unashamedly to the neighbours and share in my happiness.

Tina's voice quickly rises in pitch and volume when we quarrel. Loudness and frenzied gesticulation are her cultural inheritance. There is no malice in her booming voice, just crescendo. She rattles on about right and wrong, morality and amorality and the importance of tradition before resorting to emotional blackmail and crocodile tears. When I am drowned out by the power of Tina's voice I often say to myself: '*Anna skase gai kolimba*' — Anna shut up and swim — or '*skase gai fae*' — shut up and eat — if I happen to be sitting at the dinner table. And I close my mouth and swim silently against the choppy tide.

Forced to choose between acceptance and treachery I have opted for the latter. Applications have been sent to three universities outside my home town, without Tina's knowledge. I await replies and hope for a miracle in the interim.

Tina was a broad-hipped adolescent with a tiny waist who wore polka-dot scarves in her hair. The villagers called her 'shona' (snowy white) because she had pale skin and 'boureka' (a sweet pasty) on account of her full figure. Plump and pale epitomized beauty in those days, it meant you were well fed and able to stay out of the sun. A breed apart from the farmers, crop pickers and builders, with their brown, weather-beaten faces. Tina had plenty of admirers but fell with sixteen-year-old fervour for a youth with 'bright eyes and big dreams' who hurtled through the village on a motorbike, over-taking donkey carts, upsetting old ladies balancing kindling on their heads. Hair slicked back, cigarette dangling from the corner of his mouth.

Tony set his sights on Tina and wooed her with letters that spoke of 'love' and 'two souls becoming one'. He had an uncommon affinity with words for a boy with little schooling. Tina hid the letters under her mattress, which is the first place Yiayia searched when she recognized the tell-tale signs of young love: a poor appetite and Tina's refusal to have her coffee cup read. Yiayia did not consider Tony a suitable match since he had no proper job and owned nothing but a motorbike and the clothes on his back. She had set her sights on a young man with a Government job, a sensible haircut and a motor car.

The young man proposed formally through his parents and had Tina consented I would now be my uncle's daughter. Rejected by my mother, the civil servant went on to marry my Aunt Roulla. Being the eldest, Roulla had to marry first or risk 'having her fate stolen by a younger sister' and ending up on the shelf. Having envisaged life with a plump, syrup-coated pastry, my Uncle Michalis was cajoled into exchanging vows with a dark-skinned carob.

Roulla was still a child, a fact she continues to declare with bitterness. Sexually immature. Unlike Tina, she still played with dolls and plaited the hair that reached down to her waist. She dreamt of becoming an actress, the next Irene Pappas, and would drape herself in a white sheet and wander round the back yard like a muse. Michalis and Roulla were introduced on a Saturday, the following Monday (without Roulla's consent) their betrothal was announced in the personal column of the daily paper. A week later they were engaged. Roulla claims she ran screaming from the room when she first laid eyes on male genitalia. Though the wedding was brought forward due to her rapidly swelling abdomen, Roulla insists she never had sex before marriage, that Peter's conception was a complete mystery. When Peter was born, Roulla turned from aspiring thespian to drama queen, self-expression and theatrics confined to her living room.

Girls of Tina's generation got married before their hormones kicked in. Sex was a rude awakening, a trauma, according to Roulla, which left a sour taste. Tina has always stressed the supremacy of the virgin bride and believes chastity, that fragile strip of mucus membrane, is the finest quality a young woman can possess. But then, she grew up in an era when brides would save their bloody bed sheets to show their female relatives.

A year ago I developed thrush and the doctor prescribed a pessary. Tina had a shock when she spied the elongated tube of plastic and realized its intended purpose. She phoned the GP right away, saying, Docto, Docto, my daughta she's a vegin, you know.' I stood with mouth agape waiting for the punch line. She put down the receiver with a contented smile on her face, reassured that my course of medication would not rupture the hymen and my dignity would remain intact. I was livid and vowed never again to share with Tina personal details of an intimate nature. Her absurd puritanical streak has given rise to ridiculous secrets between mother and daughter. I have resorted to hiding my tampons in a college locker lest she telephone the makers and accuse them of deflowering her daughter. I discreetly dispose of the bulky, unusable pads she buys in carton loads from the cash and carry.

The day I started menstruating Tina behaved like a tragedy had befallen the house, dabbing her bloodshot eyes with a tissue and whispering to Tony in the kitchen. Neither parent could look me in the eye. I felt as if life as I knew it had come to an end. Tina gave me a pad the size of a small baguette, with a loop at either end, and sent me off without explanation. All she said was a cryptic, 'Now you're a woman you have to be careful.' I had no idea what I was meant to be careful of. Black cats, cracks in the pavement, airborne spermatozoon?

Yiayia lifted my mood of self-pity with a graphic account of the indignities suffered by women of her generation. Menstruating women, considered 'unclean', were forbidden from stepping foot inside a church. They pinned rags to the inside of their underwear to stem the flow of blood and boiled these

84

rags in water and vinegar before hanging them outside to dry. They toiled in the fields while blood trickled down their legs and couldn't take a bath because they feared their wombs would fill up with water. Yiayia's mother had slapped her hard across the face when she started her periods, to acquaint her with the pain of womanhood.

*　*　*

'Yes please,' Doreen says, flashing her Norma Jean smile. Harmless flirtation is Doreen's *raison d'être*. A young man with a ruddy face, oblivious to Doreen's charm offensive, orders a bag of chips and turns to watch the television above the fruit machine. Last weekend we celebrated Doreen's fifth anniversary at Tony's Fish Bar with a bottle of Dandelion and Burdock and an overdose of carbohydrates — a round of soft, white, thickly buttered rolls filled with chips. My parents have seen enough counter staff come and go to know they have a gem in Doreen. She is not afraid to get her hands dirty and seldom complains about the anti-social working hours. On occasion she locks antlers with Tina over matters pernickety, since my mother likes things done properly and Doreen sometimes cuts corners. The women exchange heated words, then return to their posts as normal.

While Doreen wraps she tells me matter-of-factly that she plans to leave her husband, to do a midnight flit to somewhere hot and humid. She routinely calls her spouse 'Alan the thief', saying he stole the life she was meant to have, the life she plans to reclaim just as soon as she wins the pools. Every Saturday, Doreen and Tina fill out their individual pools coupons, marking the score draws indiscriminately, while discussing how to spend their millions. Doreen plans to buy a luxury villa in Spain and never do another day's work in her life. Tina intends to repatriate, to build a house with a swimming pool and lead the Beverley Hills lifestyle of the nouveau riche.

Doreen clings tenaciously to the tangible reminders of her youth. To baby-blue eye shadow and a blonde, flick-out bob, unflattering on a woman of her age — style statements belonging to the time when she was queen of the dance hall, twisting in a wide skirt and winkle pickers, four kids and an unwise marriage ago. She blames Alan for her demise and calls Tina the luckiest woman alive having a husband like Tony. Whenever Doreen praises Tony too highly, Tina puts her straight with one of her favourite sayings:

'Every good man she goda a good wife beind im.' These words of wisdom are a fine example of Tina's inimitable gender-juggling, mind-boggling syntax, unhindered by logic, a law unto itself.

'Oi, what the ell are they doin?' Doreen says, staring out of the shop window. 'Andy, come an av a look son.'

The three of us stare out across the precinct, through early-evening darkness. Pale yellow lamplight illuminates the back of two hunched figures casually urinating on the bonnet of the Capri. Andy watches tight-lipped, emasculated by the presence of his mother.

'It's that Kevin an is mate,' Doreen says, shaking her head.

Kevin and Darren zip up and head straight for the shop, unperturbed by the sight of us glaring at them through the window. They walk in, cocky and defiant, visibly energized by their mindless act. Two familiar-looking girls with backcombed hair, large dangly earrings and heavy eye make-up follow them in. I have watched Kevin graduate from school truant to hard-core drop-out, from short, mean boy with a pretty face to disaffected youth. His lackey, Darren, misbehaves to get a laugh. He has the kind of demonic face you might see projecting from a

Victorian roof gutter. Misshapen lips and bulgy amphibious eyes.

'I'll serve,' Andy says, leaving no room for argument. I sit on the window ledge, antipathy painfully compressing my stomach.

The girls order two bags of chips and sit on the shop bench next to Elvin, throwing him withering looks, giggling into their hands as they watch him struggle to spear a soggy chip.

'Doner and chips,' Kevin says, viewing Andy with his customary hostility. 'And I don't want no rabbit food, just give us some extra meat.'

Andy serves in angry silence.

'All right, Dore,' Kevin says, winking at Doreen but receiving no greeting in reply. Kevin claims Doreen as one of his own. He thinks she has no place fraternizing with the likes of us. Them and us: the served and the servile; insiders and outsiders; white skin and brown with a hint of olive; the haves and have-nots, throwing the natural order.

'That your motor outside?' Darren asks.

Andy nods.

'Could do with a clean, mate,' Kevin says, inducing a hail of insolent laughter from his friend.

Andy calmly slits open a pitta, fills it with meat and hands it to Kevin.

'Put some chilli on, mate,' Kevin says.

Andy pours a spoonful of Tina's home-made chilli onto the meat. A mild chilli sauce made with tomatoes, fresh chillies, onions, garlic, ground cumin, cloves and turmeric. Tina insists on making her own chilli sauce, believing that in some small way she is enriching the quality of people's lives or as she would say 'teaching the locals how to eat'.

'I don't want that shite,' Kevin says, 'I want the hot stuff.'

I sense my brother's irritation, I see the muscles in his neck pulsate. The desecration of his car he can accept but not the merest, most indirect slight against his mother. He takes a bottle of extra-hot chilli sauce from under the counter (reserved for customers with a stronger palate) and dribbles it onto the meat.

'Don't be fuckin tight. I like it hot,' Kevin says, before glancing behind him at the girls and draping an arm around his friend's shoulders.

'You can shag the fat one,' he says.

'No problem, mate. I'm not fussy,' Darren replies.

'I wount touch her with a barge pole.'

'You've touched worse, mate.'

'Not without ten pints down mi fuckin frote.'

'Eh, mind yer language, there are ladies

present,' Doreen says.

'Mind y'fuckin snout,' Kevin replies, touching his nose and grunting like a pig.

The foursome eat their food at the back of the shop. The 'fat girl', more full-bodied than fat, only fat relative to her emaciated friend, hands her unfinished chips to Kevin. He wolfs them down, to ease the sting of chilli, his face as red as a maraschino cherry. Then he pulls the larger girl to her feet and puts an arm around her waist.

'Give him a kiss, Trace,' he says, gesturing towards Elvin.

'Get lost,' she replies, 'I ain't kissing no spaco.'

Kevin grabs the back of her neck and pushes her towards Elvin, while she lashes out with her arms, struggling to free herself.

'Aou, yer urtin me,' she cries out.

'Let her go . . . NOW,' Tony shouts from behind the chip pan.

Kevin yanks the girl's head downwards until her lips are pressed against Elvin's pea-stained mouth. Elvin stares vacantly ahead of him, seemingly unmoved by the commotion. I feel a sharp pang of anger and wish I could pluck the poor man from that scene and plant him somewhere safe and hospitable.

'Giv im a blow job while ye down there,'

Darren says, his laughter a seal-like honk.

The girl pulls away, cringing, wiping her mouth on the back of her sleeve.

'Y'dirty cow,' her friend says.

Trace runs out of the shop, sobbing, followed out by wolf whistles.

'Little bastard,' Doreen whispers.

★　★　★

Heather is more fern than her unkempt floral namesake, a backdrop over which the eye brushes before settling on a rose or lily. She is an undiscovered gem, as unaware of her assets as those who dismiss her on first impressions. Her elfin features and aquamarine eyes are lost beneath large glasses and a mop of strawberry blonde hair. We are comfortable companions, both of us riddled with hang-ups about our size, our shape, the dryness of our hair, both prefering one-on-one friendship to immersion in a group.

Heather sits on the window ledge, her long skirt tucked between her ankles, biting into a battered sausage. Heather is happy to spend a portion of Saturday night behind the counter, keeping me company, enjoying the banter and the tickle of Tina's quirkiness. She holds her long limbs close to her body, trying to keep her natural clumsiness at bay, tripping me up with her big feet on my way to the bains-marie. I have grown accustomed to Heather's obtrusive limbs and ungainly carriage and generally watch my step. Tina moves through the shop like a worker ant on acid and does not take kindly to dodging anyone. To keep my friend from getting in the way, I set her tasks in a quiet corner of the kitchen: buttering bread rolls, cutting salad, filling up vinegar bottles. Heather has a formal, somewhat fearful relationship with food. Her chopping and buttering skills are mechanical and painfully slow. She handles a bread roll with the care one might bestow on a hand grenade, slices cucumber as if it were Semtex. She insists I inspect her handiwork when she's finished. 'Well,' she says proudly showing me a dish of sliced cucumber, 'what do you think?'

'Fine,' I say lamely, unable to conjure up a more deserving accolade.

A waist with the circumference of my right arm belies Heather's hearty appetite. She gratefully fills her hollow legs with Tina's cakes and anything disfigured in the frying pan. 'The poor girl must eat nothing at home,' Tina says with unnecessary gravitas, calling her a 'renga' — smoked kipper — a vaguely derogatory description alluding to her slender frame. 'She's thin, mum,' I say.

'That's good not bad.'

'A woman should look like a woman, not a camel,' she replies.

Resolved to feed the poorly nourished and fatten up the human race, she bombards Heather with food. 'Your mum's great,' Heather says, viewing Tina with the doting eyes of a well-fed dog. Heather can enjoy the fruits of Tina's generosity without the stranglehold of conditions and expectations.

'Mum's been up to her tricks again,' I tell Heather, sitting beside her on the window ledge, taking advantage of the lull.

'What's she done?'

I describe an incident that occurred bright and early this morning, on the way to the shop, when Tina insisted on paying a visit to her new accountant. 'Recently qualified . . . one of us . . . new in town,' I heard her say with enthusiasm. Tony pulled up outside a bakery and looked up at a sign below the first-floor window, reading Pavlos Christoforou FCCA.

'I'll stay in the car,' I said.

'No, come out,' Tina replied, 'and we'll buy some custard pies after the meeting.' I should have twigged right then, but I didn't. Greed led me by the nose, up a flight of dingy stairs to a first-floor office, lit by a glaring strip light, where I came face to face with a dark, well-built man, wearing a heavy gold bracelet, waggling an elongated nail on his little finger. A trimmed moustache beneath his nose lengthened as he broke into a generous smile at the sight of my parents. I stood at the back of the office, shuffling my feet, wondering what particular purpose that fingernail served, while my parents and their new accountant talked with an artificial air.

When we got back in the car, with our box of custard pies, Tina turned to look at me.

'What did you think of him?' she asked.

'Nothing,' I said, 'he's your accountant, not mine.'

'But what did you think of him?' she asked more pointedly, her upbeat tone revealing the real reason for our visit. 'What a *leventi*,' she added, describing him as a 'handsome youth'. Tall and well built, in Tina's mind, equating to good looks.

'He was horrible,' I replied, shocked and affronted.

'What was wrong with him?' Tina said irritably.

'I didn't like his nail,' I replied, saying the first thing that came to mind.

'A nail can be cut,' Tina said. 'The poor man probably plays bouzouki.'

'And that chain on his wrist,' I said, grimacing.

'You're too fussy,' Tina said, 'who's ever heard of turning down a man because of his chain.'

Heather smiles and looks fondly at Tina. 'Your mum's so funny,' she says, diffusing my exasperation.

'Not when you're standing in my shoes.'

My friend is a rock and a pressure valve, a listening, non-judgemental ear. I can talk to her without feeling disloyal, about anything and everything, knowing nothing I say will be subjected to unhelpful scrutiny.

'Would it be so wrong to meet someone through your mum?' Heather says, with a cheeky smile, chafing my Achilles' heel.

'Ptou, ptou, heaven forbid.'

'What does 'ptou ptou' mean?'

'It means I'm spitting away the very thought.'

'She only does it cause she cares.'

'Yeh. To the point of suffocation.'

Heather's mother is a different breed of parent. A hands-off, *laissez-faire* kind of mother who has, in spite of her efforts, reared an awkward, unrebellious daughter. Heather's family co-habit in a house devoid of rules. There are no set meal times, no cleaning roster, no necessity to interact. On a recent visit to Heather's house I was entirely ignored by her younger siblings, who sat glued to the television. In our house the number-one rule of hospitality is that all family members should embrace a guest both physically and metaphorically. 'I hear your mother's a great cook,' Heather's mum said, donning rubber gloves to nervously chop an onion. She cooked a runny bolognese, served with overcooked spaghetti and I found myself, though I knew it was very wrong, judging the poor woman on her cooking skills.

Over dinner, Heather's father was taciturn to the point of rudeness. Her mother over-compensated with small talk that made Heather cringe. She complimented me on my spoken English and expressed her love of 'that pink stuff . . . tramoslata'. She was nice, well meaning, unworldly. I felt like a dark shiny aubergine set amongst Granny Smiths and when it was time to leave I breathed an ungrateful sigh of relief. Heather came back to my house to immerse herself in noise, greasy aromatic food and petty arguments. My friend is drawn to the warm, overpowering bosom of my family in the same way that opposites attract. She has acquired, through our friendship, a taste for peculiar fruit.

★ ★ ★

Bodies line the back wall and trail out of the door. A sea of hungry faces cast impatient glances across the counter, eager to be served before the start of the soaps. Tina stands beside me at the counter, scooping and wrapping at considerable speed. Where others inherit musicality, athleticism, a flair for painting, a head for numbers, my genetic make-up has graced me with an aptitude for wrapping chips. A skill that can also be applied to stuffing vine leaves. Chip paper — vine leaf — different stuffing, same roll.

Most faces are familiar. There is little through trade on the precinct. I have been serving the same faces for a decade, watched girls grow into women, women grow older and the old grow infirm. Witnessed drunken infidelity, sober infidelity, child abuse, verbal abuse, drug abuse. Couples date, marry and divorce. I have observed the intimate minutiae of people's lives without even knowing their names. Tina has developed a crude system for naming the nameless. Pseudonyms (mostly Greek slang) denote a customer's most striking characteristic: *thontes* — big teeth, *moutas* — big nose, *fkiagas* — big ears, *gilia* — big belly. *Bikris* (sour) — a man who asks for plenty of lemon on his kebab but never smiles or says thank you. Cowboy — a pensioner who refuses to age gracefully and models himself on Rock Hudson. *Pisis* (tight-fisted) — a miser who insists on chips and curry in a bag, refusing to pay 2p extra for a tray. *Brocomeni* (good girl) — applied liberally to loose women. Tina greets her customers in the same way she might welcome a guest with a cheery '*kalos ton fkiaga*' — welcome, big ears.

★ ★ ★

Irene's high heels click-clack as she walks across the tiled floor. Two grimy children as spindly as their mother's bare legs follow her in. She props a bony elbow on the counter and places the following order: six bags of chips and a chicken breast. Faint lines criss-cross her tired face, like the slashes of a demented flick knife. The shop's fluorescent strip lights accentuate in their glare a painted mouth and pencil eyebrows. Tina views her customer with a look of disapproval. Unkempt children are a source of acute distress for Tina. Irene has a brood of them, anaemic and fatherless. They amuse themselves by setting bins alight on the precinct and terrorizing pensioners. Last week Tony caught two of them spitting sputum across the forecourt, seeing who could project it the furthest, putting off potential customers. He threatened to tell their mother unless they moved away. 'Give us a bag of chips and we'll piss off,' one of them said. 'Aw,' Tina crooned, 'they only chudrun, give em some chips, Athonis,' which Tony obediently did. The 'chudrun' showed their thanks by waggling their middle fingers, calling my father an 'f'ing Paki' and running off. 'I am Greek Cypriot,' Tony called out after them, giving them an impromptu lesson in ethnicity.

Irene rifles through the gunk in her handbag and extracts a dog-eared purse. Her daughter looks up at me with eyes the colour of a clear blue tropical sky. Beneath the grime and matted blonde hair is a soap-ad child, a child that could stir the most frigid of hearts. I smile. She sticks out her tongue and wipes her runny nose along a crusty sleeve. A boy with cropped hair, hardier-looking than his dainty sister, pulls at his mother's tight skirt and demands a sausage.

'You'll get what y're given, you greedy little sod,' Irene says.

'I want a sausage,' the boy repeats, his bottom lip quivering.

Irene ignores what Tina cannot — a child asking for food. She skewers a sausage and hands it to the boy.

'It's in the house,' she says.

'Wha about me?' the girl asks, pouting.

'Don't be so fuckin rude. You can share the sausage w'ye brother,' Irene says, giving her daughter a lesson in manners.

The boy stuffs the whole sausage in his mouth.

'You greedy little sod,' Irene says, whacking him across the head.

He bursts into tears, showering his sister with chewed sausage meat. The dream child swipes at his face like a cat. He grabs a fistful of matted hair and pulls her to the ground. They punch and kick and gouge, rolling around on the greasy floor.

Tina intervenes: 'Chudren, chudren, you don fight. I give you nather sausage, ana fish cake, anythin you wan.'

'Let the little buggers kill each other,' Irene says, more interested in the state of her nail cuticles than in breaking up the fight.

Tina mutters a stream of abuse in Greek ' . . . poor children, stinking whore . . . ' while spearing two sausages on chip forks and waving them, like elongated lollipops, above the children's heads. Scratched and tearful, the children disentangle themselves and reach for the offerings.

'Bloody savages,' Irene says, looking at her dishevelled children, taking the bag containing her order and walking out. On the forecourt a grubby Alsatian waits, tied to the rubbish bin, his head slumped in a discarded polystyrene tray. Irene unwraps the chicken breast and throws it to the dog. He goes berserk, grabbing the hot meat and champing it furiously with his back teeth, while Tina stands at the window, shaking her head in disbelief, complaining that the English treat their animals better than their children.

Tina's sweeping comments are a source of irritation and a frequent cause of argument. I tell her not to generalize, not to tar everyone with the same brush. 'You can't argue with the evidence of my eyes,' she says. Tina has been exposed to the seedier side of life, to life on a depressed council estate, home to the unemployed and unemployable.

Tina's saving grace is that she is quick to criticize her own compatriots or any other race that happens to offend her. She has strong, mostly disparaging opinions about the human race as a whole. Tina's political opinions are equally uncompromising and riddled with inconsistencies. She is vehemently right wing in England, espousing the virtues of capitalism, bandying such comments as 'charity begins at home'. In her own country she is a supporter of AKEL, the Progressive Party of the Working People. In England she flies the blue flag of

Conservatism. In Cyprus she pledges allegiance to the red flag of a party founded on communist principles.

★ ★ ★

The granny flat is cluttered and cosy, a world of icons and doilies and gadgets born of wit and ingenuity. On the coffee table lies a fan, modelled from a wire coat hanger and a cereal box. Above the cooker hangs a Chalcolithic contraption used to brown sliced bread over a naked flame. Rectangular tins that once contained halloumi, now nurture mint, parsley and coriander. Orange and lemon pips germinate in margarine tubs before graduating to catering-size baked bean tins.

Yiayia is not forced by circumstance to recycle non-perishables. She is well provided for. A flamenco dancer fan, a collection of ceramic plant pots and a Russell Hobbs toaster are stored in the side drawer of her bed. Yiayia has a vast booty of unused possessions, which she calls her grandchildren's inheritance. 'I have no use for new things,' she says, making do with her homemade devices. She has taken this ideology to its extreme, refusing to use her washing machine, saving it for the dowry of her namesake, namely me. She insists on scrubbing her clothes in the kitchen sink, to save Tina's washing machine from wear and tear.

I sit on Yiayia's bed waiting for her to change out of one blue, A-line pinafore into another. An activity that always takes longer than you would expect, since Yiayia is easily distracted and often forgets why she went to her bedroom in the first place. I watch her rooting through the contents of a Frytick vegetable fat box, whilst singing simple heartfelt lyrics in a soft, melodic voice that makes the hair on my forearms stand on end. '*Yie tis lemonias tis elias, yie tis angalias, tis haras . . .*'

Land of Lemon tree and Olive
Land of Hugs and Joy
Land of Pine and Cypress
Of young men and of Love
Golden-green leaf
Thrown into the open sea

Land of dry meadow
Land of embittered Madonna
Land of hot-dry wind, of Hades and of
  loss
Of wild weather and volcanoes
Golden-green leaf
Thrown into the open sea

Land of laughing girls
Land of drunken boys
Land of dreams and welcome
Cyprus of love and dreams
Golden-green leaf
Thrown into the open sea

So engrossed is she in foraging and singing that I don't have the heart to tell her that we have to leave in ten minutes. A stack of assorted boxes stand in a corner of the room containing what Yiayia calls 'memories' and Tina considers 'junk'. Old clothes, broken toys, bags, purses, misshapen shoes and the odd irreplaceable treasure are thrown together.

She empties the contents of her chosen box onto the bed, picks from among the gunk a small white seashell, a green beret, the George Medal, pieces of a jigsaw that make up a life. The life of her husband Andreas. The man immortalized in black and white on her window sill, next to St Andrew, framed by lighted candles. The blurred image, lined and grainy like an old mirror, does little justice to the man with 'skin the colour of wheat' and the 'grey-green eyes of a cat'. The only picture in our possession (though there may be more somewhere, lying in an inaccessible drawer) shows a man with wavy black hair, swept back, and a 'Grivas'-style moustache tweaked upwards at the edges. Tina has his lips. Miriam his cheekbones. Roulla his nose. Athena his eyes.

He was a handsome, hardy-looking man. Yiayia says her life has been empty since she lost him and that 'one day' they will be reunited. 'In this world not the next,' she declares with such certainty that I almost believe her. You'd think her pain would have eased after so long, that age would have dulled her devotion. But she continues to cry and hope, saying her hope won't die until she's dead and buried. She belongs to a dying breed of women who live for their husbands, who attend to them in death as loyally as they served them in life. Who shroud themselves in black, religiously observe saint days and memorials and keep gravestones as gleaming white as they once kept their husbands' shirts. A grave would, ironically, be of some comfort to Yiayia. Her husband was officially deader in his twenties than he is now. At least then there was a gravestone (by default) with his name etched on it, where his mother could cry and pull out weeds, not a makeshift shrine on a window ledge with lighted candles ready to be snuffed at any moment.

Yiayia picks up the medal and rubs it between thumb and forefinger like a charm, to help her conjure up the distant past. She remembers 'as if it were yesterday' events that took place half a century ago, but can't remember what she had for breakfast. Who can blame her when the past is infinitely more memorable than the present? She talks to me about the man she won't allow to die, evoking his image, making him real to his descendants. I don't tell her I've heard it all before, I don't tell her we have to leave in five minutes.

Papou Andreas was the youngest of six children. He left school, aged twelve, to tend goats and help in his father's coffee shop, growing up in an era when boys became men when they earned their first shillings and girls became women at the onset of menstruation. Life in the village was frugal at best. People ate what they grew. They lived on olives, broad beans, lentils and bread baked in clay ovens. Chickens, rabbits and pigeons, kept in back yards, were slaughtered on special occasions. Meat was a luxury. Women had no time to question their lot, not when there was wheat to grind, goats to milk, cheese to make, clothes to scrub, floors to wash on all fours and chickens to behead — all before the light of day waned, since there was no electricity. Light was a burning candle. Fruit was preserved in syrup, halloumi in brine and salted pork could last for years stored in its own fat. Public transport was a cart and donkey. There was no running water. My great grandmother collected water from the village well, carried it home in a clay jug balanced on her head. She used the same jug of water to clean her children, wash the clothes and water her plants.

In spite of the hardships, Yiayia claims 'people were happy'. They didn't suffer from the modern affliction of 'wanting what they couldn't have'. No one had more than anyone else and 'happiness was a full stomach'. Yiayia talks about the taste of lamb slow-roasted in a clay oven and in the next breath she talks about riots, injustice, an island ravaged by conflict. People were happy on a day-to-day level and incensed by the bigger picture.

Yiayia has painted a vivid portrait of how it all began, providing a context, beginning at conception several million years ago when tectonic plates below the Mediterranean sea merged together forcing the sea bed to rise up and form an elongated land mass. Moving on to a time before Christ when the Romans invaded and the island was passed like a hot potato from Julius Caesar to Ptolemy and from Anthony to Cleopatra. Back to a succession of Arab raids spanning three hundred years during which the island was looted of timber, copper, its people. To a list of foreign invaders and conquerors as long as your arm: Byzantines, Lusignans, Venetians, Turks, British, who lost in battle, sold, bartered or gave away the island at will. To a boy who grew up as the struggle against colonialism took flight, whose young mind was shaped by the nightly debates he heard in his father's coffee shop. There the men aired their grievances against the colonial power for failing to develop an island it considered second rate, they voiced complaints about high taxation, long working hours, low wages, forced labour, the exodus of young people from the villages. They spoke of political liberty and their dreams of *enosis*, union with Greece.

Was he brave or foolhardy, Papou Andreas, aged twelve, when he set out on foot to the capital to listen to churchmen and politicians speaking of 'union and only union', the need for sacrifice and possible bloodshed? When he followed the crowd that surged towards Government House, looting a state-owned timber mill en route for sticks? When he shoved his way through police cordons to watch the wooden slats of Government House go up in flames? He applauded the violent protests that followed, that brought the might of the British Empire crashing down upon his people. New laws dissolved political parties, banned trade unions, censored the press, abolished municipal elections, outlawed meetings of more than five people. They exacerbated resentment against the colonial Government and turned muted calls for *enosis* into battle cries. These cries were silenced temporarily by the outbreak of the Second World War when old adversaries became allies. When Britain called to arms the people of Cyprus, issuing veiled promises that the island would be granted its freedom in return for help in the war effort.

Coffee-house chat was hushed by radio updates on the allied advance. When Greece resisted Italy's invasion, patriotic fervour soared. Papou felt duty bound to fight for Greece and for his own freedom and though he was only seventeen he managed to enlist by offering up the birth certificate of an older brother, who had died in infancy, with whom he shared the same name. He joined the Cyprus Regiment, was sent to Egypt for training and then on to Greece to transport supplies and munitions to front-line troops. His active service was cut short in 1941 when his regiment was overpowered by German troops in Calamata and loaded onto freight trains headed for Czechoslovakia — to a brick factory where four thousand enslaved men were forced to produce more than thirty thousand bricks per day. If they fell short of this target they faced torture. Many died on foreign soil, from beatings, from bullets, from sub-zero temperatures, from starvation. They fought over potato peel, ate bread made from sawdust, suffered the worst excesses of depression, misery and hopelessness, until four years later, they were liberated by Russian troops.

Papou Andreas was shipped back to the island. He took a taxi to the outskirts of his village and walked home via the cemetery to visit the grave of his late grandfather. He was shocked to find his own name etched onto the marble. After four years without word, his parents had assumed him dead. His mother fell to her knees and praised God when she saw him. Yiayia remembers. She lived next door. She didn't know then that they would be married before the year was out. Their betrothal was arranged of course. She didn't love him at first. She admits that. But she grew to idolize the man they nicknamed 'Lazarus'.

St Lazarus has a special place in Yiayia's spiritual psyche. The saint entered her life in dramatic fashion and left a lasting impression. As a child she was taken to the old stone church in Larnaca, named after him, and was struck by an overwhelming feeling of wonder and trepidation. She was acquainted with the miracle of his resurrection and knew that beneath her feet lay the bones of a saint that died on her island home. The seventeenth-century icon of Jesus commanding Lazarus to rise from the dead struck Yiayia as the most awesome sight she had ever seen. In that holy place, thickly scented with incense, adorned with gold, where thousand-year-old voices seemed to whisper, she felt closer to God than ever before and her faith was consolidated. She knew then, with a sense of foreboding, that she would come to rely on St Lazarus as a crutch.

Yiayia grew up at a time when the Church and its teachings formed the hub of village life. Her mother and grandmother raised her on a diet of stories about miracles and veneration, sacrifice and bravery, disturbing and exhilarating tales about religious persecution and triumph over evil. 'The lives of the saints and their miracles' is Yiayia's bedtime reading. These stories have become yardsticks against which she measures her own life and her sense of loss. St Lazarus is a symbol of hope, a comfort when she feels troubled, a higher power to whom she can pray for the safe return of her husband. 'Please help me, saint,' she says, kissing the foot of the icon on her window sill.

3

Tina has a poster beside the kebab machine depicting Botticelli's Venus in the foreground with the Rock of Aphrodite in Paphos as a backdrop. This is the place where Aphrodite reputedly rose from the sea, from the *aphros* — or foam — from which she took her name. 'I cam from the islan of lav,' Tina tells her customers, pointing to the poster. The island of love. Birthplace of Aphrodite, Goddess of Love, beauty, fertility. Her palace outside Paphos was a brothel of sorts, where virgins would sleep with strangers before marriage, in honour of the goddess. *Ierodoules* they were called — holy servants — the ancient word for prostitute. Tina would refute such unsavoury associations with her island home. She is the *aficionado* of our picture-postcard history.

'Our lives would be so much better over there,' she says, her mind two thousand nautical miles away. She has grown accustomed to harping back, to looking forward and negating the now. The present is an unwelcome interlude, a sacrifice, a necessary evil. In Tina's 'Cyprus dream', life is a veritable utopia. Tony tends fruit trees, Andy drives an open-top car and I work in a bank. 'A banking job,' she says emphatically, chin raised in haughty reverence. 'He's a banker' is a mighty accolade, a mark of eligibility. 'He's a banker' carries kudos and prestige. Tina will secure my job through 'contacts' and I will exchange one counter for another. In Tina's 'Cyprus dream' Anna meets a banker and falls in love and life is hunky dory.

In Cyprus the banking profession does not appear to attract happy people. A simple counter transaction, an exchange of traveller's cheques *per se*, becomes a sweat-inducing trauma. A smile is met with blankness or unveiled hostility. On our last holiday the mild-mannered Tony resorted to bellowing across the counter at a nasal assistant, a Barbie aspirant, an artificial offence to womanhood. She loved her modicum of power and was determined to use it, refusing Tony cash from his own account, accusing him of offering up a fake passport. Granted he had a moustache in the picture and stood before her free of facial hair but any fool could tell that the photo-booth image and the flesh-and-blood man were one and the same. Tony's identity would need to be certified, the woman said officiously, by a priest or a village muhktar.

It was Friday afternoon, the banks would be closed for the weekend, we needed money. Tony tried diplomacy. He pleaded. He put a finger beneath his nose, Fuhrer-like, to replicate a moustache, before turning several shades of red and exploding. I scowled at the woman, while my insides churned with embarrassment. The commotion attracted the attention of the bank manager who scuttled out of his office, stern faced and ready for trouble. He broke into a generous smile when he recognized Tony as his wife's second cousin. '*Koumbare*,' he said, 'come into my office and we'll quickly sort out the confusion.' After plenty of hand shaking and back patting we were offered coffee, Orangina, hot sandwiches and an invitation to dinner.

'*Sygnomi, kyrie Papamichael, then gnorisa BYIOS isoun*' — sorry, Mr Papamichael, I didn't know WHO you were — said the counter assistant on our way out, in a sickly sweet, disingenuous voice, covering her back. In a country where action is severely impeded by official procedures and officious civil servants, emotional outbursts and nepotism are the only way to get things done.

The enmity I felt for the woman in the bank lasted the day. While Tony got on with the business of holidaying, I seethed and fought from my mind visions of forcibly extricating clumps of brittle bleach-blonde from the aforementioned head. Nature should have branded rude people with a light covering of fungoid tentacles or a hint of verdigris. To eliminate the element of surprise. To lessen the sting of unnecessary comments.

Tina plans to repatriate when the time is right. When her children acquiesce, when her village is handed back, when she can afford to retire, when land has been purchased and built on. Many have tried and failed in this endeavour. Tony had a friend who followed his dream. He sold his fish and chip shop and built a whitewashed mansion on the outskirts of his village to house his wife and three grown-up children. He said goodbye to friends who had shared three decades of his life and turned his back on England. Three years later he returned, on a mission to replicate the life he had earlier renounced.

His sons had struggled to find work with their broken Greek, in a place where who you know is paramount and graduates are two a penny. They opened their mouths and the locals pumped up their prices and called them 'Charlies' — the nickname for English Cypriots — a name used both amicably and to denigrate. His daughter met a handsome man who professed his love and fitted the parental bill. In due course she discovered that the real object of his affections was her father's bank account and the lure of an English passport. His wife developed discoid eczema exacerbated by a combination of excessive heat and air conditioning. She would spend the day scratching and dreaming of grey skies and quilt-covered beds. Tony's friend lived frivolously for the first time in his life and frittered away a large chunk of his savings. And slowly he grew tired of sitting in the sun. 'How long could I sit with my feet up, *koumbare*, doing nothing, spending money like it was water? I love Cyprus but England is my home.' Over time a culture diffuses into your fabric, however much you fight it.

I don't feel at one with the country that purports to be my own. I feel like an outsider, an interloper, an unwelcome guest. An undercurrent of animosity exists between the indigenous population and those who left for foreign shores. Between 'them' and 'us'. 'They don't like us,' we say, 'they're only jealous,' comes the all-too-easy absolution. When I look at 'us' from afar I want to cringe. At the conspicuousness of the parental generation and the hybrids they have raised. We visit 'our' country and extol the virtues of

117

England, question prices, complain about the heat, the dust, the sewage system, the cockroaches. We are Greek when it suits us and English when it doesn't. We flash our money, wear our gold, barter with the natives, and walk with our pseudo-European noses in the air. We gatecrash a house we abandoned long ago and behave like we own the place, boasting of our riches, when riches are all we have to show. We think we can buy our acceptance, when all we really procure is derision. And while our obsolete 'lock up your daughters' mentality has endured the Cypriots have moved on. All we know is how to work and save and splurge on a two-week holiday. The natives know how to live.

★   ★   ★

Elvin orders a pea on a fork and feels for change and a toffee in the deep pockets of his overcoat. I have grown accustomed to the episodes of strangeness that punctuate his normal routine and generally take them in my stride.

'We're out of peas, Elvin,' I tell him, spearing a saveloy and handing it across the counter. 'Have this instead . . . on the house.'

'Thanks very much,' he says, handing me a toffee and retiring to his perch at the back of the shop to nibble his saveloy and disengage from the world. I watch him with heavy-hearted interest, wondering how much of his life he has frittered away in a vacant stupor. And whether such behaviour is the cause or effect of incarceration. Elvin used to live within the red-brick walls of Hamberly House, a psychiatric hospital on the fringes of the estate. Several years ago Fairfield locals launched a campaign to get the place closed down, stirred into action by the widely held assertion that 'people like that shunt live near decent folk'. Locals were particularly opposed to the hospital's open-door policy, which allowed mildly disturbed patients like Elvin to roam the neighbourhood at will. The group, calling itself NAIMBY — No Asylum In My Back Yard — held soapbox meetings, distributed inflammatory literature and collected signatures.

NAIMBY was more a self-help than a protest group, allowing the free expression of bigotry, giving the anonymous their fifteen minutes of fame in the local press.

When the council announced the asylum was to close, there was widespread euphoria. Members of NAIMBY greeted each other in the street with victory signs and calls of 'power to the people', believing they had brought the council to its knees. The closure had nothing whatever to do with an inconsequential estate and everything to do with The Mental Health Act and 'care in the community'. Considered a breeding ground for apathy and institutional dependence, the asylum was closed down ward by ward, over a number of months. Residents were returned to their families or moved to sheltered accommodation and private housing. A number of former patients were moved to vacant flats on Fairfield estate, not down the road from, but right next door to decent folk. NAIMBY reformed, adopted the slogan 'Patients Out Of Fairfield', campaigned with somewhat less enthusiasm, until the homophobes caught wind of their new acronym and deserted the group, leaving only a handful of stalwart members.

There are, admittedly, some very peculiar people living on the estate, engaged in a range of repetitive activities. A man with a Bavarian-style moustache walks four steps forward and three steps back, counting as he moves, his short legs working much harder than they need to. We affectionately call him 'Savva' because he resembles Tony's second cousin by the same name. Tina refers to his girlfriend as 'Julie Andrews' because of a tenuous link with Mary Poppins. Savva's girlfriend converses with pigeons and Julie

Andrews once sang a duet with a robin. Savva and Julie Andrews happily canoodle in the chip shop queue, oblivious to hostile stares and muted calls of 'disgustin'. Their behaviour is no more disgusting than the sexual antics of sane people on a Saturday night.

★ ★ ★

Irene throws a crumpled chip paper parcel onto the counter.

'I want mi money back,' she says loudly, unwrapping the parcel to reveal a battered shell, minus the fish.

Tony leaves the frying and comes over to the counter.

'What's the problem?' he enquires.

'This is the bloody problem,' Irene says, lifting a flap of batter to reveal a shiny black slug.

'You wanyour money back. Wha fo?' Tina asks. 'You eat the fish.'

'That thing was under the batter. I dint see it till I'd finished. I nearly puked m'guts out.'

'You buy tha fish las week,' Tina says indignantly.

Tony takes a closer look at the miraculous gastropod which has allegedly crawled its way up the counter, jumped into the fish tray and survived oil temperatures of 2,000 degrees.

'That thing hasn't been in the frying pan, Irene,' Tony says.

'You callin me a liar? I could report y'to the council for this.'

Tony capitulates, returns to the frying pan, telling Tina to give Irene the money. Tina slams a handful of coins down on the counter while reprimanding her husband in Greek: 'This is a shop not a charity . . . Why don't you put a sign on the door, Athonis, 'two fish for the price of one'? Last week she found a red finger nail. Do you see anyone in here wearing nail varnish? I keep telling you to throw her out but you don't listen . . . talking to you is like knocking on a deaf man's door.'

Irene takes the money and leans across the counter.

'Thanks, Tony luv. No ard feelings, eh? You know ow much we love y'chips,' she says, rewrapping the battered shell and putting it in her handbag.

4

We drive into a tranquil horseshoe of Wimpey executive homes with quietly ostentatious second cars gleaming on tarmacked driveways, into a perfect curve of Georgian windows, double garages, stunted trees and immaculate front lawns. This soulless zone is, for Tina, the epitome of good taste. Tony parks the car outside Theia Roulla's house behind my uncle's top-of-the-range, plum-coloured Sierra.

My aunt, Theia Roulla, stands at her door yapping her welcome like a King Charles spaniel, watching us climb out of the car and ascend her gently sloping driveway. '*Yeia sas, Yeia sas kalosorisete*,' she calls out, clasping me tightly round the waist and squeezing like a boa constrictor. My aunt does not believe in half measures of anything and would rather squeeze a person to death than give them half a hug.

Roulla's front room houses a suffocating menagerie. Bone China and Made in China hog every available surface: St Georges spearing dragons, child beggars, a troupe of pirouetting ballerinas, naked ladies and animals of every genealogical type. Painted plates hang on the wall, depicting the Resurrection, Constable's Hay Wain and the Queen's Silver Jubilee. A long settee in deep red Dralon dominates the room like a Chinese dragon. Painted vases, big enough to live in, stuffed with pampas grass and peacock feathers stand either side of a plastic log fire, glowing bright orange, exuding heat like crumpled sheets of cellophane. Leading the eye upward to an enormous colour photograph in a gold frame, of Aunt Roulla with an enigmatic smile, seated in a gilded chair, flanked by her family.

'What a beautiful top,' Tina says to her sister, commenting on a black jumper with a plume of silver sequins sewn onto the front, reminiscent of a sparkler at midnight in suspended animation. 'Where did you get it?'

'Bambo the grocer,' Roulla replies. 'It's the latest fashion from London.'

The silver-tongued, pot-bellied Bambo is obviously branching out, from artichokes to women's wear. 'Just wait until you see Maria's,' Roulla continues.

Cousin Maria walks into the room, a phoenix rising from the flames emblazoned on her torso. Tina embraces her niece and two thousand coloured sequins.

'You look marvellous,' she says, 'don't you think so, Anna?'

Being at odds with the general consensus I am forced to lie: 'Very nice.'

'Then you shall have one,' Tina says. 'I am sick of seeing you in black. Black, black, black, all the time black.'

'I like black, Mama,' I reply, feeling lost in the midst of sparkly people.

'Black is for the bereaved,' my aunt adds, 'not for a young, single girl.'

'These days black is the fashion,' Yiayia remarks.

'What does an old woman know about fashion?' Roulla says.

'I may be old, but I still have eyes and a brain.'

My aunt is a shrunken version of her mother. She used to be plump and huggable but events over recent years have taken their toll. Being thin does not suit her. Contrary to popular belief, being thin does not suit everyone. Aunt Roulla's face no longer bulges pleasantly when she smiles, where skin was once pulled taut there are lines and wrinkles. Her weight has departed with her looks in tow.

Cousin Maria is a pleasant caricature of Tina-the-adolescent. Their visual similitude has always been an irritation, making me feel like a baby swapped at birth. 'My niece, she's the spitting image of me,' Tina likes to say, elevating Maria's average looks, bequeathing her the undeserved title of 'beauty'. Maria's backcombed hair, her penchant for lipstick and her refusal to wear flat shoes make her what Tina would call a 'real lady'.

Maria, nineteen going on twenty-nine, recently announced her wish to get married. A theoretical desire, since the other half of the marriage equation does not as yet exist. She has given the mothers free rein to find her a husband, earning herself immeasurable parental respect. Maria's decision is a dream come true for Roulla and a source of pain for Tina who cannot help but ask herself where she went wrong. The mothers have trawled the locality and beyond for eligible bachelors. Maria is considered a 'good catch', a match for the *crème de la crème* of suitors. My cousin has had two introductions so far and turned both hopefuls down on solidly superficial grounds. One was too thin, the other had a receding hairline.

'You don't look well today, Mama. Sit down,' Roulla says, guiding Yiayia towards an armchair in a futile attempt to keep her from meddling in the kitchen.

'Ptou, ptou,' Yiayia replies, spitting away

the evil eye, 'you'll make me ill with talk like that.'

My uncle, Theios Michalis, steps into the lounge smelling of charcoal smoke.

'Welcome . . . how are you . . . ? God has blessed us with perfect weather for *souvla*,' he says cheerfully, walking further into the room to shake Tony's hand, trailing soil along the pink shag pile.

'Get out, you fool,' Aunt Roulla barks, the King Charles spaniel turning Rottweiler. 'Look what you've done to my carpet.' Michalis backs out of the room looking apologetic.

Roulla rushes off to the kitchen and returns with a dustpan and a good-natured smile, oblivious to the consequences of her angry outburst, to the dampening of our spirits and the embarrassment caused to her husband. We should have grown accustomed to her sudden switches from sweet and loving to vitriolic, we have witnessed it often enough. 'She's been through a lot,' Tina says, excusing her sister's behaviour. A succession of losses have left my aunt embittered, whereas her husband refuses to dwell in the past and lament his fate. He is amazingly composed, a happy-go-lucky sort of man who tends to stay mute when his wife erupts. 'The only answer one can give a fool is silence,' Yiayia says disparagingly of her own daughter. Aunt Roulla's moods swing from animated to morose, from laughter to tears, her repertoire of expression limited to joy and pain, with nothing in between.

★ ★ ★

Tina helps her sister prepare the *souvla*, threading large chunks of seasoned meat onto battery-powered skewers. A saucepan splutters on the cooker like Old Faithful, discharging a sweet-scented column of steam into the air. Yiayia lifts the lid, tastes the sauce with her finger and adds salt. She opens the oven door, peers inside and shouts across to her daughter. 'Roulla, the pasticcio is ready.'

'I was just about to take it out, Mother.'

'Hurry up before it burns . . . and your potatoes need turning,' Yiayia continues, blind to Roulla's sour expression.

'Mama, don't worry yourself. Everything is under control,' Roulla says, forcing a smile, exasperated by Yiayia's well-meaning advice, aggressively territorial in her kitchen.

Uncle Michalis pokes his head round the door. 'Are the skewers ready?' he asks.

'I'm not a machine,' Roulla snaps, projecting her anger.

'Not long now, Michalis,' Tina chirps,

trying to dissipate the tension, treating he. sister with kid gloves. Too much pussy footing around my aunt has nurtured the anti-social side of her personality.

'I don't know how that poor man lives with you,' Yiayia mutters.

'Where did you get that watermelon from?' Tina asks, spying a miniature version of the Hindenburg in a corner of the kitchen.

'From the marketa,' my aunt replies in Gringlish, that jumbled fusion of a language that we slip in and out of at random. A mix of English and Greek. A form of Greek that differs from the language spoken on the mainland, which is truer to the ancient, and evolved under the influence of successive invaders and conquerors. The Romans bequethed to Cyprus the word *moula* (mule), the French *barberis* (barber), the Ottomans *kasabis* (butcher) and the British *exos* (exhaust). In England we have taken English words and made them Greek. *Marketa* (market), *baso* (bus), *garache* (garage), *pinapo* (pineapple). An English Cypriot dropped in the centre of Athens asking for the location of a market at which to purchase a pineapple might say something along the lines of: 'Hello, *thelo na bao stin marketa na yoraso pinapo*.' The average Athenian would

.ook at them with lofty incomprehension, as if conversing with a Martian.

★ ★ ★

I help Maria set the table, passing china plates and silver-plated cutlery through the kitchen serving hatch into the dining room. I hand her one plate too many. I do it to be spiteful, to remind her of the brother that no one ever talks about. She hands the extra plate back without comment and lays the table. Polishing crystal tumblers, folding and fanning out napkins, positioning a row of wicker table mats. We chat about the events of our week while the unsaid hangs heavily between us. Maria exudes an air of unquestioning innocence. Her loyalty to me is as strong as it ever was. I am the one with the mean spirit who shuns contact and finds it increasingly difficult to accept our differences.

Maria used to have a dream. She planned to study beauty therapy and open up her own salon. We spent many lazy Sunday afternoons locked in her candyfloss bedroom, leafing through copies of *Woman's Own*, plotting our escape from the family business, planning our respective futures. Maria's dream vanished with Peter, displaced by a vision identical to her mother's, superimposed by a

desperation to please and a need to restor
the smile that left Aunt Roulla's face two
years ago. I want to shake her back to life but
I know she is too far gone, lost in the land of
self-sacrifice. I often hanker after the
closeness we once shared, when I would
loosen my belt, stretch out on her bed and
become her guinea pig. She would pluck my
eyebrows, wax my legs and massage my face
with scented oils. I enjoyed the firm touch of
her soft hands and the sound of her soothing
voice. We grew up together, and were as close
as sisters, until she made the sudden decision
to get married, leaving me in her shadow,
cementing her allegiance with the enemy
— our mothers.

★   ★   ★

The men are stooped over the barbecue in a
corner of the stone patio, watching a plume
of smoke rising from the centre of a funnel
that has been fashioned from a catering-size
baked bean tin. Michalis lifts the funnel out
with a metal fork, evens out the coals and
fans them with a piece of cardboard, before
loading up the barbecue. Tony pours out two
small glasses of zivania, a white spirit distilled
in the Troodos mountains, smuggled through
customs in Evian bottles.

I perch on a small wall surrounding an alabaster fountain — Aphrodite astride a giant scallop shell rises from the centre, puking water onto giant koi. Water gurgles, the sun warms my face, a cold breeze bites like tiny piranha at my legs. The men take off their jackets, roll up their shirtsleeves, their cheeks ruddied by the heat of the barbecue and the rapid consumption of 100 per cent proof. Cooking *souvla* is traditionally a male pursuit, providing an excuse to drink, escape the women and display one's prowess. Cooking a good *souvla* is a source of great pride, the sign of a *meraklis*, a man who does things well.

★　★　★

The dining table is spread with a feast befitting the kings of ancient Salamis, the first city of Cyprus, a place of great wealth and prosperity. Founded by Teucer, hero of the Trojan wars, the city's principal deity was Zeus, the God of Hospitality. On the table before us lie dishes of chicken, lamb and pork *souvla*; *yemista*; roast potatoes; rice with vermicelli; salad; pitta bread; hummus; taramasalata; tzatziki, and Roulla's speciality, *macaronia tou fournou*. Yiayia and her daughters have divided up the culinary map,

leaving no dish unconquered. They ar
lethal triumvirate, assailants of the waistli
Moderation, small helpings and dieting a.
unwelcome at my aunt's table. Tina's own
view on dieting is: 'I don drink, I don smoke.
I don go dancin. Nobody is gonna stop me
eatin.' I load up my plate, indulge my senses.
I throw caution to the wind and save feeling
guilty for later.

I eat in a hedonistic stupor, savouring the
tastes and textures, letting the conversation
wash over me. I hear Roulla complaining
about her ailments, Tina cursing the potato
man, Tony blaming Kissinger for the invasion
of 1974, Michalis blaming the island's
guarantors, Yiayia lamenting the absence of
her husband. The Cyprus problem is a
regular topic of conversation. Deliberation,
conspiracy theories, personal anecdotes and
impassioned rhetoric volley over plates of
pasticcio. 'They let us burn' . . . 'we put our
fingers in the fire' . . . 'we were pawns'
. . . 'we dug our own grave'. The Cyprus
problem overshadows all others. It has
scarred the generation that lived through the
war and tainted their children. Tina's voice is
particularly loud and passionate. She shouts
in spite of our proximity When Andy draws
this to her attention she continues unabated,
reminding her son that her temperament is

:ek not English, insisting that the only :ce deserving quiet is a church.

While my aunt complains vociferously to ner mother about the clamour of her husband's snore, Tina leans towards Maria and speaks in a conspiratorial tone.

'I'm sure you're going to like him,' she says.

I shut out the other voices around me to concentrate on my mother's.

'Do you think so, Thea?' Maria replies.

'He's tall, good-looking, a good boy.'

'Have you seen him?'

'Not with my own eyes. But that's what I've been told by my contacts in Birmingham.'

'When will he be coming?'

'In two weeks,' Tina replies excitedly, thrilled by the prospect of introducing the elusive man from Birmingham to her niece. The man meant for me will be meted out to her and a good catch will not be wasted.

★ ★ ★

Tina crosses herself and expresses her hope for 'good news'. Yiayia polishes her glasses with the loose cuff of her sleeve, reaches for Roulla's cup and peers inside.

'I see a table and ten chairs,' she says to the assembled group of women. 'You will soon be

playing host to important guests . . . besi—
the table is a cockerel.'

'A suitor,' Tina squeals.

'Did you tell her?' Roulla asks her sister.

'Not a word. I swear on my husband's life.'

'Carry on, Mama,' Roulla says smiling.

'On the table is a loaf of bread . . . this is a sign of good luck. A sign that something good is going to happen. Something that will change your life for the better.'

'I am going to see my daughter standing at the altar,' Roulla says, taking Maria's hand and stroking it.

Yiayia rotates the cup and brings it closer to her eyes. 'I see a tree, laden heavily with fruit . . . the future will continue to be bountiful, Roulla. You will want for nothing. You are blessed with plenty.'

'Blessed,' Roulla says, her voice laced with irony, 'how can I be blessed when I have lost the thing that is most precious to me?'

'You must beware, daughter,' Yiayia continues, 'for coiled around the branches of the tree is a serpent . . . gorging itself on the fruit . . . growing stronger by the day . . . spoiling everything in your life that is good.'

'You don't need to tell me who the serpent is,' Roulla says furiously, 'I know her name.'

Yiayia stares thoughtfully at her daughter over the top of her glasses.

'The serpent is a symbol, Roulla, it may not be a person. The serpent may be within your own heart, eating away at you, until nothing is left but an empty shell. By then you will be no good to anyone. You must find peace, Roulla, light a candle to the Virgin and ask for forgiveness.'

'Forgiveness,' Roulla shouts, turning red in the face, 'what wrongs have I done deserving forgiveness? I have done nothing in my life but give. My only wrong is giving too much.'

'Calm down, Stavroulla,' Tina says, 'we're just having fun. Don't take Mama's readings so seriously.' Tina the eternal peacemaker stops awkward subjects in their tracks when she would do better to let them run their uneasy course and reach a painful conclusion.

Yiayia puts down her daughter's cup, picks up Maria's and finds it stuck to the saucer. She taps it gently on the base until it loosens, each tap corresponding to a letter of the alphabet. 'The name of your loved one begins with M,' she says.

'What's the boy's name?' Roulla asks her sister in a whisper. 'Marco . . . Mario?'

'I don't know,' Tina replies, 'but his mother is called Maritsa.'

'There's the connection,' Roulla says, taking two and two and making five.

'I see a meeting, a handshake, an agrment.'

'The cup never lies,' Tina says, forgettin her scepticism the instant a reading is fortuitous.

'I have a good feeling about this meeting,' her sister says.

'I see a large three in the upper part of your cup, look here it is,' Yiayia continues, turning the inside of the cup towards her audience. 'These events will happen quickly, within three days, three weeks or three months.'

'I'd better start looking for a hat,' Roulla says.

Yiayia puts down the cup, rests her elbows on the table and looks intently at Maria. 'You have a void in your life, granddaughter . . . do not rush to fill it. Think two and three times before making a decision that will determine your future. Nothing and no one can replace that which is missing.'

'What are you talking about, Mama?' Roulla says, with a sour twist of her lips. 'Nothing is missing from my daughter's life. She has everything and more. And no one understands or appreciates your riddles.'

Yiayia looks inside Maria's cup once more. 'I see a large crowd of people . . . a meeting of old friends and strangers at a gathering to mark a significant occasion.'

That can only mean a wedding,' Tina says, r a baptism.'

'Not before the wedding!' her sister remarks, raising her eyebrows. 'Let's hope it's not a funeral.'

Tina collects up the cups and carries them quickly to the sink muttering, 'Ptou, ptou, heaven forbid.'

★   ★   ★

Last night I dreamt I was lying in a coffin, a glass panel positioned above my face. My eyes were shut but I could see the grief-stricken faces of my family staring down at me. I could hear Tina crying out and the priest's melodious liturgy. Through closed lips I could hear myself shouting, 'Let me out, let me out.' But no one did, because no one could hear me. A suffocating flush of fear washed over me. My insides raged, lashed out, fought to free a body that lay perfectly still.

When I woke up, Tina was sitting at my bedside, stroking my forehead with her sandpaper hands and I felt utterly relieved to be alive. 'You've been shouting,' she said, 'I was worried.' She looked at me in a way she rarely does: with deep concern and absolute love, her dark eyes betraying a bounty of fears. I wanted to reach out for her hand and tell her she was forgiven for steeping my life in overbearing rules and restricting my freedom. But she broke the spell. She looked away and pulled herself together. She quickly cast off the raw emotion that had her on the verge of tears, that might have thrown her off balance and impeded the progress of her day. 'Go back to sleep,' she said, matter-of-factly, 'we have work in the morning.'

Macaronia Tou Fournou
Roulla's Speciality

Boil one packet of no. 1 macaroni (big-holed variety) in plenty of water flavoured with a chicken cube. When macaroni is *al dente*, drain in a colander and toss in one cup of grated halloumi, two tablespoons of dried mint and a pinch of cinnamon.

Heat two tablespoons of sunflower oil in a saucepan, add one small, finely chopped onion and 1lb of minced pork. When meat begins to brown add one tablespoon of fresh or dried mint, a handful of finely chopped parsley, a pinch of powdered cinnamon, salt and pepper.

Make a white sauce by melting three tablespoons of butter in a saucepan and adding three tablespoons of flour and a drop of sunflower oil. Stir with an egg whisk until the mixture is smooth and begins to brown. Then slowly add five cups of warm milk and stir over a low heat until the cream begins to thicken. Take sauce off the heat and stir in two beaten egg yolks.

Lay a thick layer of the macaroni in a

baking dish, spoon over the meat and cover with remaining macaroni. Top with white sauce, sprinkle with grated halloumi (optional) and cook in a medium oven for twenty minutes or until golden brown.

5

'You'd better sit down, luv,' Mrs Collins says, throwing a copy of the *Stretley Advertiser* onto the counter.

'Why, someone he die?' Tina asks.

'No, luv, but you might be tempted to commit murder when you read this.'

Tina hands me the paper. Mrs Collins tells me to turn to page three, to a picture of Irene and four sallow-faced children seated on a precinct bench next to the headline: *Chippy Serves Up Slug And Chips.* Behind the family group looms the neon sign: 'Tony's Fish Bar — Pukka Pies.'

I read aloud from the newspaper: '*A woman claims she was violently sick after finding a slug in her fish and chips. Irene Rogers, 35, from Fairfield estate, made the gruesome discovery after buying lunch for her family of six from Tony's Fish Bar on the local precinct.*'

'Who's she tryin to kid?' Mrs Collins says. 'She's never thirty-five.'

'*. . . When Ms Rogers returned to the shop for a refund she claims she was verbally abused by the owner's wife, Mrs Papamichael . . .*'

'How they know my name, the bastes?' Tina shouts.

' . . . *Mrs Rogers said: 'My kids have been put off chips for life.' The owners of the shop refused to comment . . . '*

'That's a lie,' I say, 'no one asked us for a comment.'

'Someone he rang,' Tina says, 'he tol me he's e jernalis. He say sumthin ebouta foreigner's body in the fish. I don understand what he's talkin aboud.'

'What did you say to him, mama?'

'I was busy. The shop he had a queue. I toll im to sod off.'

' . . . *A spokesman for the council's environmental health department said the allegation would be fully investigated . . . '*

The story goes on to list other 'shocking' infringements: cats found in the fridge of a local Chinese takeaway, a vole found in a packet of crisps, a severed finger discovered in a beef vindaloo. Tina rages against the injustice of slander, predicts the destruction of her livelihood and ultimately blames Tony for refusing to throw Irene out of the shop.

'Your papa, she never listen to me. Now we gonna lose our costomers.'

'Don't worry,' Mrs Collins says kindly, 'no one round ere'll believe Irene.'

The lunchtime rush fails to materialize. Tina is livid. She sends Doreen home and spends the morning polishing, cursing Irene's mother with every agitated swirl of her Terri cloth. She buffs up the range, kitchen units, fridge doors, shelf tops, stools, the potato peeler, chicken machine, bains-marie, stops short of giving us all a wipe down. She's still fuming by closing time when a bespectacled man in a weathered suit walks through the door, approaches the counter with a clipboard and asks for the owner.

'Is me. What you wan?' Tina asks rudely.

The man doesn't manage to get beyond 'health inspector' before Tina starts running off at the mouth: 'My shop is spotless, tha woman he's lie, tha woman he's no good, I don av slags in my fish, is all lies.'

Tony quickly intervenes. 'What's the problem, sir?' he asks.

Tina continues her tirade. 'Tha woman he the problem, he lyin, he tryin to ruin MY business, I bin workin twenty year and nobody he complain bout slags in my fish before.'

'We've had a complaint,' the man says. 'I'm here to inspect the shop.'

'Come through,' Tony says, lifting up the serving hatch.

The man begins his inspection behind the counter while Tina curses in Greek and Andy sharpens the kebab knife close by. Tony is overly polite, gushing in his praise of the council, embarrassing in the extreme. He offers the health inspector a bottle of Cyprus brandy and a free meal for four. The inspector shakes his head politely, looking neither threatened nor open to bribery. He opens cupboards, runs his finger across worktops, inspects cutlery, scrutinizes the potato room. He scribbles on the paper attached to his clipboard, ignoring Tina's incessant comments: 'You see my sink how is shine' . . . 'I clean my shop with Mr Sheem you know . . . '

The health inspector turns to Tony. 'Not long now,' he says with a reassuring smile, before moving across to the fridge. He pulls open the freshly polished, stainless-steel double doors and the amiable smile vanishes as he looks into two bloodshot eyes that stare out of a sinewy head sitting on an oval platter.

'What's this?' he asks, taking a step back, looking disgusted.

'It's a goat's head,' Tony replies calmly, 'a Greek delicacy.'

Tina, thinking a cookery lesson is called for, explains that the head is wrapped in silver foil and roasted in the oven. The skull is then cracked open and the flesh and brain are eaten with 'plenty of salt and lemon juice'. Some people like to eat the eyes, she says, but they are too rubbery for her palate. She stops short of inviting him home for a goat's head dinner, since he looks ready to throw up. 'We no gonna feed this to our costomers,' Tina adds, 'they don know how to eat.'

The health inspector closes the fridge doors and scribbles furiously.

'Is there a problem?' Tony asks.

'There was a plate of ham next to the goat's head.'

'And?'

'And I'm sure you know the dangers of storing raw and cooked meat together.'

'Oh yes,' Tina replies, 'semolina.'

⋆   ⋆   ⋆

Malcolm walks into the shop with the air of a man surrounded by Lilliputians. Athena follows him in, hands thrust deep into her cardigan pockets. We exchange cursory greetings across the stainless-steel divide, while she glances up at the white fish fryer's hat perched on my head. I considered throwing it off when I saw her ambling radiantly across the forecourt but I feared my unpredictable hair might chose to defy gravity and sit in a heap on top of my head, as if shaped in a pudding basin.

'I have driven past a dozen similar establishments, to procure the best fried fish in the city,' Malcolm says, confusing Tina with verbosity.

'You wha?' Tina asks. 'Why you don talk like a normo peson, Malco?'

'Malcolm paid you a compliment, Mama. He said you sell the best fish in the city,' I say.

'Eh, food always tastes better when it's free,' Tina says in Greek before asking, 'Ow's my sista?'

'Oh, Miriam's fine as usual,' Malcolm replies. 'And how's the lovely Anna?'

The 'lovely Anna', wearing pale blue gingham and a fish fryer's hat, feels as lovely as a monkfish and all the worse for seeing the lovely Athena.

'This is what I like to see,' Malcolm says, 'children working for their living. Not like my lazy lot. Athena gets up at midday on a Saturday, lounges around the house until the evening and then goes out partying with her friends.'

The 'lovely Anna' has drawn life's short straw.

'As long as she keeps getting those As and doesn't get herself pregnant then I have no objections,' Malcolm says casually.

'Ptou, ptou,' Tina says, popping a square of Elvin's fudge into her mouth to sweeten the taste of Malcolm's acrid words.

'When was the last time you had a night out, Anna?' Malcolm asks.

'Not for a while,' I reply, feeling flustered and inadequate, hoping Malcolm won't ask me to be more specific. All hitherto attempts to get a Saturday night off and go out with Heather have been met with opposition and/or triggered a psychosomatic illness in one or both of my parents. I managed to negotiate a rare midweek night out with Heather six months ago, a night that required considerable forward planning and a fair amount of deceit. An innocent drink with my friend had to be disguised as a night at the theatre, 'a course requirement', I said, forcing my mother to acquiesce. I bought tickets for a performance of *Othello*, which I had no intention of going to see, and left them strategically beside the telephone on the table in the hallway. Before going out I equipped myself with perfume to mask the smell of smoke and mints to obscure the scent of vodka lime and an alibi in case I was spotted by prying Greek eyes. I went out with a knotted stomach and too desperate a desire to enjoy myself, to a small basement club, where I sat in a private nook with Heather, waiting to acclimatize, wanting to dance but feeling too self-conscious. As soon as I began to loosen up, midnight struck and my night came to an unsatisfying end. I walked through my front door, passed Tina's sniffing nostrils, into what felt like airport security, wondering why I had bothered going out at all. The night was too rushed, too planned, too fraught. I should have used my wasted tickets and gone to see *Othello*.

Tina has watched *Animal House* and claims to know what goes on at parties. 'Anything could happen to you,' she says, 'girls are taken advantage of, their drinks are spiked, drugs are forced into their mouths.' And I can't deny that bad things happen but Tina's 'what if' scenarios call to mind Yiayia's story of the *skebarni* — the lath-hammer — a tale exemplifying the pointlessness of 'what if' about a newlywed couple enjoying a celebratory meal with their in-laws. The bride goes off to the cellar of her new house to fetch a bottle of wine. When she fails to return her mother goes in search of her, then her father, then all her relatives disappear, one by one, into the cellar. Finally the groom goes to investigate and finds the family sitting on the cellar floor crying. When he asks his wife what she is crying about she says: 'I must never have a child.' 'Why?' he queries. 'Because if I have a child, I may one day ask that child to go to the cellar to fetch some wine. And what if the child reaches up for a bottle and dislodges the lath-hammer on the top shelf. And what if the lath-hammer falls onto the child's head and kills the child, then I will be inconsolable . . . ' Yiayia often reminds her daughter of the lath-hammer story when she starts to fret about her children.

'Don't you have a birthday bash to go to next week?' Malcolm asks his daughter.

Athena nods.

'Why don't you take your cousin?'

'I'm sorry, Athena, your cousin she av to wek,' Tina replies.

'Constantina, the girls are going to a birthday party,' Malcolm continues unabated, 'and I won't take no for an answer. It's high time this young lady started having some fun.'

Why does Malcolm feel a duty to emancipate me? To pluck me prematurely from my cotton wool cocoon and command me to fly?

'We see,' Tina replies.

'I won't leave until you say yes,' Malcolm says with a sly wink, thinking he is doing me a favour.

'OK, OK,' Tina replies, throwing me to the lions. 'Anna he can go.'

★ ★ ★

On Boxing Day it is customary for the Jamesons to visit. They stand at the door in their long winter coats and adeptly tied scarves, looking like characters blown off the front of a Victorian Christmas card. With exaggerated charm and facetious commentary, Malcom hands out presents that never live up to their elegant wrapping. They are edifying gifts that aggrandize the giver and belittle the recipient. Andy, who has no interest in books, receives anthologies of verse and Russian classics. 'I wish they'd give up trying to educate me,' he says, discreetly handing me his unopened parcels. 'Why don't they buy books for you?' Andy queries. A curious enigma indeed. And one I have spent many hours puzzling over. Malcolm's aesthetic leanings would never allow him to stoop so low as to buy something Andy would really like — a gadget or something for the car. Miriam has intimated that her husband controls the purse strings. He examines receipts and takes an uncommon interest in the purchase of gifts.

I receive quirky, invariably charmless small collectibles, picked up at antiques fairs and car boot sales. I am the stupefied owner of a horse brass depicting a windmill, a toby jug with fractured arm and a Victorian lace shawl. Books would make sense. Books might give me ideas above my station and make me a viable threat to Athena's intellectual supremacy. I have become an unwilling competitor in a race against my cousin, adjudicated by Malcolm. The race began when we took our first steps and will continue throughout our lives, to encompass careers, incomes, husbands and offspring. Malcolm boasts about his daughter's scholastic success, he is the king of one-upmanship. His talk of healthy competition has fostered an unhealthy relationship between cousins. 'There is no place but first,' Malcolm tells his children, in a self-professed effort to shape them into leaders. To make them strong and independent he denies them tactile love. To instil discipline he lashes out. 'A good old-fashioned clip round the ear never did me any harm,' he says, perpetuating the cycle of mild abuse, forcing an emotional wedge between himself and his children.

On Boxing Day the Jamesons let their hair down. Tina, the swami of Yuletide, fills her house with an assortment of rose-scented sweets and moorish savouries. Nutty biscuits coated with icing sugar or dipped in orange-flavoured syrup. A Christmas cake, thick with dates; dried figs; and a variety of *glyka* — fruits preserved in syrup — including Yiayia's *kitromilo*, made by simmering bitter orange peel in syrup after it has been soaked in water and sprinkled with asbestos powder bought from a local builder's merchant. This ominous additive, used for generations in the making of Cypriot preserves, guarantees crunch and reduces bitterness. Tina refuses to believe it may be harmful. 'I have been eating *kitromilo* for years and no harms has come to me,' she says, insisting taste should take precedence over any spurious risk to health.

Othello, Aphrodite and Commandaria jostle for space on Tony's wine rack. Tony buys Cyprus wines by the crateload in a conscious effort to support the Cypriot wine-making industry. Commandaria, he tells his guests after a glass or two of the sweet red wine, was responsible for the occupation of Cyprus in 1571. The Sultan Selim II was so taken with the tipple offered to him by a wine dealer, that he ordered the invasion and seizure of the island.

Crystal tumblers, highly polished, sit alongside bottles of whiskey, brandy, port and sherry. The house is festooned with thick gold tinsel and gaudy lopsided decorations, bought in bumper packs from the cash and carry. A large tree, synthetic and overloaded, is the centrepiece of an Aladdin's cave. For Tina-the-child Christmas was marked by a new pair of shoes, an orange and a shilling from her Godmother if she was lucky. Her tree was sparsely decorated with tangerines and cotton wool. Now she has the means, Tina wants the whole caboodle. She works for the joy of indulging her family and bombarding their senses, whether they like it or not.

The Jamesons eat like camels stocking up for a long trek, throwing caution and temperance to the wind. The women gather round the kitchen table and indulge their fondness for sweets. The men guzzle whiskey and nibble *mezedes*, Cypriot hors d'oeuvres, exotic finger food. *Chiromeri* — smoked ham, *zalatina* — pig's head preserved in a vinegary jelly, *patates antinaktes* — potatoes fried with red wine and crushed coriander, *okdapodi krasato* — octopus in red wine, *pastourmades* — beef and garlic sausages, *koftethes* — fried meat balls. The twins eat with unchildlike zeal, enjoying the strong, salty flavours. 'Those boys are definitely Cypriot, they know how to live,' Tina says, equating a passion for food with an appetite for life.

Tina calls her niece *astomi* which means

'fussy eater' but directly translates as 'no mouth'. Athena grimaces at the sight of an octopus tentacle or a pig's ear suspended in jelly. Anxious to please every palate and fill every stomach Tina roasts a chicken for her niece and defrosts a Black Forest gateau. Athena balances a plate on her bony knee and picks apathetically at its contents. She is more self- than food-centred. Eating for Athena is a pedestrian act, the means to a full stomach. I eat with uncommon restraint and stifle the 'mmm' that rises to my larynx with every mouthful. When the atmosphere between us becomes unbearable I play my trump card, pouring her a generous measure of zivania and telling her to knock it back, knowing it will slide like fire down the length of her oesophagus and thaw her frostiness. Her eyes water, her cheeks take on a crimson hue and slowly I discern a flicker of warmth in her bearing.

The Jamesons are never in a hurry to leave. Malcolm requests 'Zorba's dance' before the night is out and dances with his arm draped across Tony's shoulders. Kicking up his legs, shouting like a true compatriot, he drops cigarette ash on Tina's carpet. Then Tony puts on his favourite tape, the 'heavy stuff', and dances to the moody laments of Stelios Kazantzides, to a *zeimbekiko*, the traditional dance of the drunken man. Stooped over, arms in the air, face taut with emotion, Tony lurches forward and back, slapping his heels as he goes.

Yiayia's *Oktapodi Krasato*
Octopus In Red Wine

Cut a large octopus into small pieces, wash well and drain. Place in saucepan, add half a cup of olive oil and half a cup of red wine, two bay leaves, a stick of cinnamon and three cloves. Bring to the boil, cover pan and cook on a low heat for around an hour, until the octopus is tender and the sauce thickens.

6

'I bring you apieca cake, Mrs Collie,' Tina says, going through to the kitchen to fetch a slice of reject *Fanouropitta*, baked in the morning. The cake had come out of the oven lopsided, forcing Tina to bake a second perfect specimen to take to church, to be blessed by the priest, according to the bidding of her coffee cup. It is the first of seven cakes, made with seven ingredients: oil, flour, sugar, cinnamon, baking soda, orange juice and lemon zest. A cake baked in the memory of St Fanourios's mother, a sexually promiscuous woman, who spread idle gossip and was quick to criticize others. To teach her a lesson her son took the form of a handsome stranger with whom his mother quickly fell in love. When St Fanourios revealed his true identity his mother realized the error of her ways.

'I bake it jas for you, Mrs Collie,' Tina says, returning with the cake and a white lie.

Mrs Collins takes the offering appreciatively and hauls herself up onto a stool behind the counter, her short legs dangling, the hem of her velour dressing gown peeking below her overcoat. The shop has become an extension of her home, as familiar as a trip to the kitchen to switch on the kettle.

Tina spots Dodgy Dave hovering in the doorway with an assortment of plastic bags, and makes a beeline for the counter. She quickly lifts up the serving hatch to let him through, leading him past Tony's disapproving stare to a private nook behind the salad bar, where he can display his wares: a collection of leather jackets, minus labels. I have warned Tina against the purchase of stolen goods to no avail. 'They no stolen,' she insists. 'Dave he tell me they fall off the back of a lorry.'

Tina's hand is in her purse before Dave has named his price.

'I take one for Anna and one for Andreas,' she says, picking out the worst of a bad bunch for me: a burgundy leather box jacket with padded shoulders.

'I don't think it'll fit,' I say, eager to halt the transaction.

Mrs Collins suggests I try it on. Dave unzips the jacket and holds it up so I can slip my arms into the sleeves. Mrs Collins leads the cavalcade of compliments, peppered with such phrases as . . . 'real lady' . . . 'slimming' . . . 'very stylish'. I take off the jacket and hand it back to Dave, knowing Tina will buy it however vehemently I protest.

I own a collection of bargain jackets and a variety of bottom-drawer chattels, which Tina believes I will one day 'grow' to love. She hopes that the coming of age will transform my aesthetic sense as dramatically as a frontal lobotomy alters one's personality, that maturity will bring in its wake an appreciation of burgundy leather, crystal decanters and gold-plated cutlery.

'That jacket'd look lovely with a short skirt,' Mrs Collins says, chafing Tina's raw nerve.

'My daughta he don wear skets. He's got lavely long legs and he don dress like a lady, not like er casin Maria . . . Maria she's know how to dress . . . '

Mrs Collins buys a black leather jacket with a studded collar for Albert, 'to make him feel young again' she says. In his heyday Albert was reputedly a dashing six-footer and a ladies' man. Mrs Collins drapes the jacket over her shoulder and hurries home to her husband.

Dave orders doner kebab and chips and stands at the counter, flashing a gold incisor, trying in vain to make eye contact. Dave is the only man who pays me overt attention and the last man on earth I could think of in a romantic capacity. He is vaguely attractive in a scrawny, anaemic kind of way but he oozes desperation and thieves for a living. I keep a tight lid on my romantic and coital needs and have channelled all my unrequited desires into an obsessive fascination for a fellow student, an undernourished, baggy-trousered boy with a stunted red Mohican and an assortment of save-the-planet T-shirts. He heads a group of similar-looking students, who hand out leaflets outside the college canteen about animal rights and the dangers of radioactivity. In lieu of a name I refer to him as 'Papagalos' — parrot — on account of his erectile crest. I am happy to view him from a safe distance, to let him live solely in my imagination and feature in the X-rated ruminations that carry me through Saturday night, while I'm scraping dried peas off the bains-marie or plunging my hands into hot soapy water. Papagalos is a pointless preoccupation discussed ad nauseum with Heather.

'He'd never be interested in me,' I said to her one day, as we sat in the conservatory, overlooking Tony's manicured lawn.

'Why not?' she replied, entering patiently into a circular argument.

I sipped my coffee and let out a lovelorn sigh. 'I'm not his type.'

She tutted and arched her eyebrows. 'No,

you're too good for him. Have you looked in the mirror recently?'

'Yes, this morning and I saw a sour-faced frump staring back at me, with a big forehead and crooked teeth. I saw the ugly sibling.'

'Don't be ridiculous,' Heather said, shaking her head. 'I'd love to have your hair, Anna, and your complexion — it glows.'

'That's grease, Heather, from the chip pan and too much of Grandma's oily food.' Self-deprecation is the means by which I entertain myself and make light of my paranoias.

'You can't take compliments, that's your problem,' she said, a remark applicable to both of us. 'I know you won't believe me if I tell you, but a few days ago in the college canteen, I saw Papagalos staring at you.'

'You're mad,' I said, 'and you're right, I don't believe you and, what's more, I'm sick of talking about myself.'

I tried to steer the conversation away from me, to delve the depths of her romantic preoccupations, but as usual she clammed up and refused to talk, hiding behind the curtain-like fringe that obscures her prettiness.

Andy walked into the conservatory with a lighted cigarette. 'What are you two gossiping about?' he asked, sitting beside me on the bamboo sofa, acknowledging Heather's presence with a formal nod of his head. Andy treats my friend in the same way he treats me: with a paternal air, as a girl who needs protecting, preserving, shielding from the harsh realities of life and any pleasures involving the exchange of bodily fluids. He pricks up his ears and stiffens his back when suggestive comments aimed at Heather fly across the counter.

'We weren't gossiping. We were discussing Hermann Hesse actually,' I said in a haughty, Malcolm-like tone.

'Who's he then? Anyone I know?' Andy said, playing along, flicking his ash into a gilt ashtray shaped like a hand.

'I don't know what anyone sees in my brother. He's not exactly the brightest spark, is he?' I said, to get a laugh, but instead Heather looked uncomfortable.

'You got the brains and I got the looks, sister,' came Andy's retort.

'What did I tell you, Heather? Ugly sibling.'

★ ★ ★

'You don't want to be an old mother,' Tina says, speaking in the language that is natural to her, standing beside her kitchen cooker, deftly spooning a mixture of ricotta, sugar

166

and cinnamon into squares of homemade pastry, to make *bourekia*.

'Why?' I ask, licking clean her wooden spoon.

'It's better to have a family while you're still young and full of energy. You can always live your life once your children have grown up and left home. And it's so much easier to find a husband when you're in your prime. Your father's sister — '

'Yeh, I know. She waited too long and now she's on her own.' Tina often cites Tony's black-clad, sixty-year-old, unmarried sister as the worse-case scenario.

'You have her stubborn streak,' she continues, quickly folding over each piece of pastry, using the prongs of a fork to secure the edges.

'I have a mind of my own.'

Tina talks while dropping her finished pastry parcels into a pan of boiling sunflower oil. 'I don't know where you get your ideas from. Certainly not from me. One day, when you're a mother, you'll understand. You'll look back and say, that mother of mine had a point. If you ever have children.'

'Why shouldn't I?' I ask, bewildered by Tina's premature fears that she will never see me standing at the altar, never hear the laughter of Adonis junior, never share a plate

167

of pastichio with her in-laws.

'Every mother has her fears and I have more than most. I didn't want to tell you about Loulla. I didn't want to worry you.'

'Who's Loulla?' I ask, watching the pastry parcels fatten and begin to brown.

'An old woman in my village, who could make a person ill just by looking into their eyes.' Tina turns ashen as she recounts the story of an unfortunate woman who lost her father and two siblings to a mystery illness. To make sense of the senseless her fellow villagers turned to superstition, blaming Loulla's evil eye for the deaths. Once branded, Loulla was ostracized and spent her life wandering the village, being avoided, mumbling curses under her breath.

'I felt sorry for Loulla,' Tina says, flipping her pastries over with a slotted spoon. 'One day I stopped to talk to her. How I wish I'd kept my distance like everyone else. Loulla reached out, took my hand and offered to tell me what the future held.'

Loulla studied Tina's palm and told her she would one day be a wealthy woman with a big house, that she would leave the village for a foreign land, that she would marry for love and that two of her three children would survive. Then she placed a bud in each of Tina's hands.

'One of them opened into a beautiful white flower, the other seemed to wither. Loulla told me the open flower symbolized a son who would marry young and father many children.'

'And the withered bud?' I ask, fearing her reply.

'She said my daughter would never marry and never bear me a grandchild.'

Tina-the-girl was not overly concerned by the prediction but thirty years on, Loulla's words have come back to haunt her.

'We must try to avert the unthinkable by taking steps to find a suitable man, before it's too late,' Tina says, spooning the *bourekia* out of the oil and dropping them into an adjacent pan filled with clove, cinnamon and honey flavoured syrup.

I stand up and casually shrug my shoulders. 'You want me to base my life on the prophecy of a disturbed woman,' I say, feigning bravado.

In making her point Tina does to me what Loulla did to her all those years ago. She cruelly implants fears in my mind about the future. I feel deflated by the gloomy prophecy and comfort myself with a plateful of Tina's warm *bourekia*.

★ ★ ★

On muggy nights, when thick mist hovers like dry ice, the precinct reminds me of a sinister Dickensian landscape. Dark shadows and blind alleys provide cover for real and imagined foes. Mrs Collins was mugged once, just yards from her home. A man wearing a balaclava pushed her to the floor, put a knife to her throat and escaped with a handbag containing five pounds, a few pence and a week's supply of milk tokens. Mrs Collins ran to the shop for help, shaken and bruised and looking upsettingly frail. Tony rang the police. Tina made tea and cursed the day that mugger was born. I locked myself inside the storeroom and shed angry tears before returning to the counter with a forced smile. Horrible scenarios have since taken root in my head, about midnight encounters en route to the car after work, featuring fists and flick knives and unanswered calls for help. If a man's prepared to maim for five pounds and a handful of pennies, what would he do for the thick wad of cash that Tony pulls out of his back pocket to pay suppliers, peeling off notes like the layers of an onion.

Thieves used to force entry through the kitchen window to wreck the fruit machine, empty the till, steal a few bottles of pop and urinate in a corner. The police were sympathetic but ineffectual so Tony took matters into his own hands, connecting the kitchen window latch to a live electric current. An unwitting thief who tried to break in got a 2,000-volt shock. He was thrown halfway across the back yard and knocked unconscious. When he came to, he reported the incident to the police. Tony narrowly escaped prosecution by claiming that a loose wire had accidentally wrapped itself around the window latch, like the tendril of a vine.

★ ★ ★

A noisy crowd drifts across the precinct from The Royal Oak, the first wave of the pub rush. Within minutes the empty shop is bustling. Fluorescent strip lights illuminate sweaty skin and bleary bloodshot eyes. We serve at top speed to clear the queue. Drunken good cheer can turn nasty in a second. I'd like to stuff cotton wool in Tina's ears to block out the filthy banter that criss-crosses the shop like a pinball. Tina scoops and wraps, oblivious to the nuances of the English language, impervious to profanity, immune to the threatening ambience. She refuses to tread carefully, to stifle her abruptness, to be anything other than herself. 'I say whaneva I wan,' she declares, 'and if the costomers they swear at me I don understand anyway.' The problem is, Andy and I understand all too well — the said and the unsaid — and Andy's got a stomach full of old scores to settle. For slights against his mother and his sister, for the disrespect that is part and parcel of the job. Whenever Andy takes offence Tony says: 'Let it go, son. It's the drink talking.' The offenders look you straight in the eye the next day and you know they can't remember what they said the night before. But you can't forget and the indignation sits like a dollop of cement in the pit of your stomach.

Irene leans her elbows on the counter and stares up at the menu board through glazed eyes. Tina tells her husband in shrill Greek that he'd better throw 'this woman' out before she grabs a 'fistful' of Irene's hair and flings her out of the door.

'Right now I don't have the energy for a fight,' he replies, telling his wife to take a closer look at the man standing beside Irene, a burly, pug-faced man with a collection of blood-drenched tattoos running the length of his forearm.

'Wha you wan?' Tina asks curtly.

'Sausage and chips,' Irene replies.

'How you wan it? Open or wrap?'

'Up the arse,' replies the tattooed man.

'I'll give her one up the arse,' shouts another man.

Her boyfriend laughs. 'Join the queue, mate.'

Andy takes the chip paper out of Tina's hand. 'I'll serve,' he says, sending his mother into the back.

'What's wrong, son?' she asks, as if roused from a pleasant dream, behaving like all three wise monkeys rolled into one.

Irene inspects the contents of her purse and turns to her companion. 'Got no money, luv. Will you pay?'

'Pay yourself, you cheeky cow.'

'I ad a fiver. I must av dropped it,' Irene says, searching the floor around her feet.

'Pay next time,' Andy says, to save her further embarrassment.

The tattooed man orders chips and gravy and stares out of the window. 'That your motor outside?' he asks.

Andy nods.

'You Pakis are doin all right for yourselves,' he says.

Andy puts down the tray, his jaw flinching and walks into the back.

'What's wrong with im?' the burly man asks, shrugging his broad shoulders, looking confused.

I sit on the window ledge, sharing a tray of chips with Heather. My friend is a warming antidote to the dull ache left by the pub rush, a calming, kindred soul to whom I can expose my inner self. She is refreshingly unpretentious, monumentally kind and endearingly clumsy. I have seen her trip up on invisible impediments, choke on a sip of water, bump into a whole manner of immovable objects. A dipterous insect in a crowded room will choose Heather's eye as a landing pad. A pigeon will drop its augury of good fortune on her thin shoulder. Unassuming Heather is a straight A-student, quietly ambitious, determined to study dentistry.

'When's it gonna happen, Heather?' I ask, shaking a plastic bottle and smothering our chips with ketchup.

'What?' she mumbles through a full mouth.

'Romance,' I say, staring out across the darkened precinct, itching for a taste of life. I used to be in step with my peers until we all hit puberty and went our separate ways, before boys and parties became the norm and I became an anomaly. I have had to withdraw from the mainstream, to distance myself from more outgoing friends, to conceal my 'situation' and avoid the embarrassment of declining invitations. As I have drifted away from others I have grown closer to Heather. Her innate sensitivity and lack of social confidence have made her an outsider too.

'Things happen when you least expect them, Anna,' Heather replies with a pensive air.

'Not in here they don't. In here there's only Dodgy Dave and his rusty Cortina.'

The sight of Andy walking towards us cuts short my self-indulgent ruminations. 'What are you two talking about?' he asks.

'Nothing that concerns you,' I reply, 'get back to your potatoes.' My romantic yearnings are not a subject I would ever discuss with my brother. For Andy there are three gender types, male, female and his sister.

'Go on,' he says, 'tell me.'

'We were talking about Heather's love life,' I reply, watching my self-conscious friend struggle to dry-swallow a ball of food.

'Oh really. Tell me more,' he says, coming closer.

'We were discussing her lack of love life actually.'

'That's all right then,' Andy says, turning to leave.

'What's Heather's love life got to do with you?' I shout after him. 'You're my overprotective brother not hers.' And as the words leave my lips I turn to my friend, expecting to see an expression of mild amusement but instead I see a red face and a look of pained embarrassment that tell me Heather is no longer immune to my brother's charms.

'He's as bad as Mum,' I say, to detract from her discomfort, hiding my own disappointment with a smile.

'Eh, Elvis, we gonna close up. It's time to go home,' Tina shouts across the counter, as Kevin and Darren walk through the door, full of beer and bravado, red veins streaking the whites of their eyes. I relinquish my window seat to serve, piling chips and batter bits onto a tray, spooning on the last of the beans. They eat outside on the forecourt, heads stooped over a shared meal, shovelling the food into their mouths with wooden forks, before flinging the tray like a boomerang into the distance and coming back inside.

'I gev you a tenner,' Kevin says, approaching the counter, 'and you only gev me change for five.'

'I'm sure you gave me five,' I reply, feeling flustered, struggling to keep the intonation of my voice on an even keel.

He sucks his teeth and speaks in a tone spiked with malice. 'I said I gev you a tenner.'

Tina tells me in Greek to give him change

for ten and let him go to the devil. I decide to ignore her and stand my ground. 'If you'll just let me check the till roll, then we'll know for sure if a mistake's been made.'

Kevin leans so far across the counter I can feel his hot, beery breath in my face. 'I don't care what the fuckin till roll says I want mi money.'

He reaches out as if to grab the front of my overall when all of a sudden Elvin yanks him backward by the hood of his jacket.

'Fuck off, y'bastard,' Kevin shouts, pushing Elvin against the back wall. 'They shunt av let you outta that place. You're mad, you are, fuckin mad.'

Alerted by the noise Andy comes running into the shop front.

'Eh, you. Your sister short-changed me and that twat attacked me for no reason,' Kevin shouts before looking into my eyes and saying in a cold, deadpan voice, 'Giv me m'change, you fat cow.'

Andy grabs the metal scoop from out the chip pan, reaches it across the counter and whacks Kevin on the head, showering him with hot fat. The dull thud of metal on scalp is followed by an angry cry and a barrage of expletives. Kevin clutches his head and kicks wildly at the front of the counter with his heavy boot until Darren drags him out of the door by the arm, across the forecourt and into the night, his threats of vengeance resonating across the precinct.

Tina makes Elvin a cup of tea and Andy checks the front of the counter for damage. I head for the storeroom and sit down on a pea sack. The words 'fat cow', hissed with such vitriol, start swimming round my head. 'Fat cow', a throwaway phrase, used to describe a range of body shapes, a casual expression that can pulverize a fragile ego in a split second. I feel wretched and unsightly, all the more self-piteous for discovering my friend's guilty secret. Heather comes into the storeroom and finds me crying. She sits beside me on a neighbouring sack and rests her hand lightly on my knee, her silence a greater comfort than words could ever be. Distractedly, she fiddles with a hole in her pea sack cushion, picking off bits of paper, poking her finger through the tear. Then she wriggles around trying to get comfortable, the sack taking shape like a bean bag, before ripping down one side, shedding its load and toppling Heather from her perch. The sight of my friend splayed ungraciously on a pile of peas, makes me smile, in spite of myself.

★   ★   ★

Last night I fell into a nightmare. I felt myself spinning upwards through the centre of a whirlwind, towards a raging fireball. A terrible heat began to scorch and blister my skin as I moved closer to the conflagration. My screams were drowned out by the deafening roar of flames that lashed out like hundreds of reptilian tongues. It felt so real: the heat, the noise, the fear of death, the burning desire to live. Just when I thought the fire would obliterate me, the spinning stopped. I found myself sitting at my grandfather's feet, crying into his lap while he stroked my hair. Bathed in bright white light and looking otherworldly he reminded me of a saint.

I woke up feeling sweaty and breathless. I threw off the duvet and stared at the ceiling, trying to decipher my dream. I wondered how Yiayia's book — the *oneirokritis* — would interpret what I saw. The *oneirokritis* makes no attempt to fathom the subconscious, to unravel the psychological meaning of train tunnels and flowing rivers. It uses symbols to starkly predict the future. If a dream is left untold until lunchtime the prediction will not come true, the *oneirokritis* asserts. To dream of bread means something good will happen. A couple seen kissing will imminently separate. To see oneself holding a suitcase symbolizes a trip to the other side. To see a deceased person means someone close will soon join them. It was this thought that made me jump out of bed in a panic and rush to the granny flat, consumed by the irrational notion that Yiayia had died in her sleep.

Light from the candle on her window sill weakly lit the room. I peered into her face and heard not the faintest exhalation. I discerned no movement and convinced myself she was dead. I froze, not knowing what to do. Should I wake up Tina? Phone for an ambulance? I took a closer look at her face and, to my relief, I saw her eyelids flicker. A second later she pulled the duvet over her head as if she knew she were being watched. I pulled it back down before I left, to avert the risk of suffocation.

In the morning I felt exhausted and achy as if a whirlwind had actually spun me skyward the night before. A headache bubbled behind my eyeballs. I knew I looked awful without confronting a mirror. Tina saw me slumped self-pityingly on the sofa and asked if I was OK. 'Fine,' I replied, more aggressively than I intended. What could I say? I'm fed up of living. I'm fed up of the shop. I desperately want to be small. Tina made an instant diagnosis of 'bad mood' and left the room. 'Bad mood' is too innocuous a description for what I feel. Debilitated would be more appropriate.

Tina could never understand. She feels good or bad for an appropriate length of time and an acceptable intensity. She never wallows. She bakes or polishes her way out of a disagreeable mood. She understands a headache can be treated with aspirin. What she doesn't understand she trusts time and a wide berth will heal. I wish I could talk to her. But I fear I might say something she would rather not hear, that I would hurt her feelings in the process of healing my own.

I went back to bed and lay cocooned inside my quilt thinking how different my life would be if I were small and lithe of limb. Dwelling miserably on Kevin's insult. At lunchtime Tina shouted up the stairwell. 'Come down, Anna, Yiayia he's made moussaka.' Her assumption that fried aubergines could lure me out of my bedroom made me feel infinitely worse. I refused to go downstairs, spurned lunch, in spite of my hunger, in order to make a point. To make them understand this was more than just a 'bad mood'. After lunch Andy knocked on my door and asked if he could come in. I didn't reply. He loitered on the landing for a while, before padding softly downstairs. He should have made more of an effort.

An hour later Yiayia walked into my room

without knocking, armed with her incense burner. I lay on the bed pretending to sleep, while she filled the room with smoke, stroked my hair and chanted incoherently. Through half-open eyes, I saw her making the sign of the cross and wafting smoke in my direction. She finished off with a chorus of: 'In the name of the Father, the Son and the Holy Spirit . . . may evil leave this child', before kissing the top of my head and departing. The mention of evil woke me from my lethargy. I could not stay in my room a second longer, with the prospect of something evil lurking in my wardrobe, under the bed or doing the rounds of my circulatory system.

Yiayia called me into the granny flat and made me a cup of tea, brewed with cinnamon sticks and cloves. An English beverage enhanced with a Greek twist. I sat on her sofa, my legs covered with a blanket, while she talked about life in her village. About the man who used to park his van in the village square and beckon the children with shouts of: 'Come and see the wild monster, come and see the wild monster.' And Yiayia-the-child would run up to him with three pennies to pay for a look at the giant crocodilian creature in the back of his vehicle. Only when she was older did she realize that the creature was a lizard, viewed through a magnifying glass. While Yiayia talked in her sing-song voice, my thoughts were diverted from my unhappiness, to a dusty village square and a cluster of awe-struck children and a hapless monster-lizard.

★ ★ ★

Tina has cabbage whites fluttering happily in her stomach. She feels a sense of excitement akin to the ending of her Harlequin novels when the guy gets the girl, when she falls into his arms and unrequited love is finally satiated. She is a romantic at heart, a believer in pre-arranged love at first sight and today holds such fictional potential. Today could lead Maria to the altar, where a parent's duty ends and a husband's begins.

★ ★ ★

Roulla has had a new doorbell fitted. Tina presses it, setting off a tinny rendition of 'Zorba the Greek'. Her sister opens the door.

'What do you think of my new doorbell?' she asks.

'Where did you get it?' Tina asks, suitably impressed.

Roulla's reply is laced with familiar

phrases: 'new from London' . . . 'two-for-a-tenner' . . . 'special deal' and Bambo's chubby, side-burned face floats like a spectre before my eyes.

'I might get one myself,' Tina announces.

'*Ohi*,' Tony says, his 'no' pronounced with gusto.

'Who do you think you are, Metaxas?' Tina says dryly, alluding to the Greek premier's famous '*ohi*' uttered in resistance to advancing German troops.

'We already have a doorbell,' Tony says.

'If I listened to you I would never buy anything!'

'Don't worry, sister,' Roulla says, 'I purchased two for the price of one.'

Roulla takes us through to the living room, treading the tightrope between calm and hysteria.

'They'll be here soon,' she says, nervously pacing the room. 'We have to make a good impression.'

'I don't intend to put on airs for anyone,' Yiayia says, slumping ungraciously into an arm chair. 'We're not desperate for anyone's son.'

'Zorba the Greek' announces their arrival. Aunt Roulla, forgetting her varicose veins and arthritic knees, sprints to the door. Greetings are exchanged in the hallway. A woman with a deep voice compliments Roulla on her doorbell, her good taste in home furnishings and her choice of carpet. Roulla, all smiles and affectation, leads her guests into the living room.

'This is Mrs Christofide,' she says, introducing a short, plump woman with a small head and wattled neck, who walks with the air of a peacock but resembles a turkey. Her husband is tall and gaunt, reminiscent of a stick insect rearing on its hind legs. The fruit of this curious union is Panicos, a surprisingly normal-looking man of average height and girth, with a trimmed Errol Flynn moustache and short curly hair, who has a pleasant face but reeks of mother's boy. He looks me up and down fleetingly and I discern in the subtle contortion of his features a tinge of disappointment.

'You didn't tell us she was so tall,' the turkey-mother says awkwardly, sizing me up, mistaking my identity, making me feel like a fairground sideshow. Has she ever taken a good look at her husband?

My aunt laughs artificially and quickly clears up the confusion. 'This is my niece, not my daughter . . . THIS is my daughter,' she says emphatically, as Maria enters the room dressed in peach silk and shoulder pads. The turkey-mother's expression screams of her approval. Maria blushes and lowers her head with the humble servitude of a geisha. Panicos looks at her, then at me, then back at her, smiling involuntarily. I feel involuntarily snubbed.

Roulla spends the evening shamelessly extolling Maria's virtues: her culinary skills, her immaculate dress sense, cleanliness, homeliness, love of children, speed on the counter, unblemished reputation. The turkey-mother nods her head approvingly, saying few Greek girls have such credentials nowadays. 'They're not interested in housework', most have 'previous histories' and once a girl has had a 'boyfriend' she is not fit for marriage. No one sees fit to comment that this outlook is somewhat old-fashioned. She tells the assembled group that Panicos has had a few English girlfriends — 'what Greek boy hasn't?' — but is now ready to settle down with a 'good Greek girl'. A girl who dresses like a lady, cooks like his mother and will work by his side in the family business. Perhaps he should consider purchasing a bride by mail-order.

The husbands skulk off to the dining room to drink whiskey and play backgammon. The clatter of die thrown on wood and animated shouts of 'dorsa' (double three), 'dortcha' (double four) and 'doubeshi' (double five) filter through to the lounge. The mothers gossip about mutual acquaintances, compare and contrast ailments and discover, not so startling, coincidences. Both are refugees, lived in neighbouring villages, both had fathers called Andreas. 'Nothing in this life happens without reason,' the turkey-mother says, suggesting the twists and turns of fate were part of some divine masterplan to bring together Panicos and Maria.

My cousin pours tea, serves cake, is content to hover in the wings and let others do the talking. Panicos smiles like an affable clown, glances intermittently at Maria, makes all the right noises, addresses the mothers as 'theies' (aunties), agrees with his own mother's misogynistic summations and talks about wanting the 'simple things in life', a nice house, a good car and satellite television. He praises the Government's hard-line stance against the unions and pronounces his firm belief in Tina's oft-quoted saying that 'charity begins at home'. I listen with increasing anger, a demented smile cemented on my lips. Anger aimed more at Tina than Panicos, for wishing such a man upon me, for looking more impressed than she ought, for seeing only what she wants to see.

Yiayia, uncommonly quiet, face like a

sunken meringue, refuses to be drawn into conversation with the turkey-mother who calls her 'old woman' and speaks to her as if she's hard of hearing. Her monosyllabic replies are embellished by Aunt Roulla who feels the need to make excuses for her mother's uncooperativeness. The sound of Andy's car horn wakes Yiayia from her vegetative state. 'I'm going for a drive with my grandson,' she says, making her way to the front door, ignoring the look of fury in Roulla's eyes. Every Sunday Yiayia insists on squeezing herself into a cramped leather passenger seat, pulling a tight-fitting seatbelt across her belly and going for a drive in the Capri.

Tina defuses the tension by exalting the benefits of a 'conservative'. The turkey-mother talks about her plans to build a 'conservative' at the back of her house and Aunt Roulla tells them she will definitely vote 'Conservative' at the next election, which naturally leads on to a discussion about *kohlrabi*. Such dialogue exemplifies a form of lateral thinking unique to Greek mothers, or as Yiayia would say: 'One talks about broad beans and the other about marrows.'

★   ★   ★

As soon as the front door closes on the Christofide family the sisters demand a verdict.

'I liked him,' my cousin says, 'I really liked him.'

Roulla, elated by her daughter's reply, says: 'He was a real gentleman.'

Tina, a big fan of a hairy upper lip, compares him to 'Omar Cheriff', 'Englebet Humberdin' and 'Bet Renos', leaving me to question the accuracy of my own perception.

'What did you think?' Maria asks, forcing me to lie.

'Yeh, he looked nice.'

'You could meet a boy like that,' Tina says.

Later that evening, in the time it takes to drive back to Birmingham, the telephone rings. The turkey-mother speaks to my aunt, giving her the thumbs up for a first date. Maria and the mothers chatter excitedly about the future while I sit tight-lipped, my stomach knotted, feeling guilty, unable to share in their happiness.

★   ★   ★

I am lying in a cornfield beneath a starry sky. I am not alone. Beside me lies Papagalos, red hair erect, one hand nestling his head, the other holding mine. We don't talk. The touch of his hand excites me. Sensuous warmth turns to feverish expectation. I lie and wait for him to make his move, to roll over and put his lips to my neck, to kiss the soft skin just below my ear. A high-pitched screech, an intrusion of reality, scuppers the moment and returns me to the kitchen sink and a pile of unwashed saucepans. 'ANNA . . . you make Greek coffee for Mr Frank. *YLYKI*,' Tina calls out. I try to keep hold of the image, to put my arousal on pause, but Tina's voice smothers it like a fire blanket. I wonder where my ardour goes when it tries to escape but finds a bolted exit. Does it accumulate? Is it flammable? Am I in danger of spontaneously combusting?

I make coffee as requested and go through to the front. 'Mr Frank' is propped on a stool, eating steak pie, chips and gravy. Officer Frank Harrington patrols the estate. Tina calls him 'Mr Frank' as a mark of respect and an act of diplomacy. Whenever he comes in, Tina insists on feeding him. 'What you wan today, Mr Frank? Pie, sausage, a lidlobida dona?' Tina knows the way to a man's heart. Mr Frank is a devotee, a man who would gladly lay his waterproof jacket over a grease patch to prevent Tina from slipping. I hand the officer his coffee.

'The coffee is *Y-L-Y-K-I*, Mr Frank,' Tina

says, accentuating each letter. 'In my language thas mean 'sweet'.' Mr Frank acquired a taste for Greek coffee on a recent trip to Cyprus. He came to see us on his return wearing a 'No Problem' T-shirt and lugging a five-kilo tin of halloumi, as requested by my mother.

Tony tells Mr Frank about a recent spate of attacks on our property. About Andy's slashed car tyres and the brick thrown through the shop window during opening hours, about the arson attack on our bins that left a smouldering mound of charred green plastic.

'I know who he done it,' Tina says, 'is that boy, the one who he make trable in my shop. That Kevie.'

'Did you see him?' Mr Frank asks.

'No. Bat I know is him.'

'There's not much we can do if you dint see him.'

Mr Frank tells Tina that Kevin has been causing trouble for years. Joyriding, vandalizing, shoplifting.

'There are problems at home, domestic violence,' he says, lowering his voice.

'You mean his parents they hit im?'

'Not exactly. I was called out to his house last week when the neighbours heard screamin. I ran in. Found the lad beatin up his mother. She dunt want him anywhere near her. The social services are lookin into it.'

'Is a shame,' Tina says.

'Anyhow, I shunt really be telling you all this. It's confidential.'

'You don worry, Mr Frank. Me . . . I don gossip.'

★ ★ ★

Tina launches into a tear-jerking account of Maria's love life, telling Mrs Collins that a week-long acquaintance has blossomed into 'lav'. Two candlelit dinners and a night at the movies has convinced both parties they are perfectly matched. The 'boy he lav gardenin' and what's more he looks like Omar Sharif, Tina declares for the tenth time this week, provoking the anticipated gasp from Mrs Collins, who confesses she only watched *Lawrence of Arabia* for a glimpse of Sheik Sherif Ali Ibn el Kharish.

'This one he no ride a camel,' Tina replies, 'he drive a verynice car.'

Never having owned a car, Mrs Collins looks suitably impressed.

'Oh yes, he's a veryrich boy,' Tina continues, listing his immovable assets: a house, rental property, the busiest shop in

192

Birmingham. Tina, who started out with nothing, firmly believes that financial security at the outset guarantees marital bliss. 'When poverty comes through the door, love flies out of the window,' she says. Yiayia has a different saying: 'Better in a hovel with the man you love than in a palace with your mother.'

Tina predicts Maria's engagement will be announced within a matter of days.

'But she hardly knows him, Mum,' I say, unable to restrain my contempt for Tina's rosy vision.

'She know evrythin she need to know.'

'What does she know exactly?'

'That he's cam from c good family.'

'Why don't they wait a little longer, perhaps live together first?' I say, voicing the unacceptable. Tina opens her eyes wide in disbelief, switching to Greek to avoid offending Mrs Collins. 'Like the English,' she says, 'who live together without commitment. Who change partners as if they were underpants.'

'That's better than marrying a virtual stranger.'

'You can live with a person all your life and never really know them,' Tina says, smiling apologetically at Mrs Collins for excluding her from the conversation, before reverting to English and looking self-pitying: 'I will never av my sistas appiness.'

'Why not?' Mrs Collins asks.

'Because my daughta he's got fanny ideas. My daughta he's don interesting in men. He's only interesting in books. I jas don undastan my daughta.'

Doreen, who catches the tail end of Tina's woe-betide-me rhetoric, says: 'Let the girl live a bit before she settles down. Don't you know a woman's like wine, Tina, the older she gets the better she is.'

'And wine it can tern to vinega,' Tina replies, determined to get the last word.

Doreen is not an advocate of early marriage. She blames her own for curtailing her potential. As a teenager Doreen dreamed of fast cars and got fast food instead, she got five nights behind the counter and a part-time cleaning job. She works to support her family, to supplement the sporadic income of a husband who was made redundant two years ago, when the local cigarette factory closed down. Doreen complains about her husband's failure to find regular work but routinely says he has a heart of gold. I suspect she loves him, warts and all, and blames the system, not Alan, for their inability to make financial headway. If you catch Doreen off guard she admits to being proud of her achievements, of watching the pennies and raising four boys, of being married for thirty years to a man who meets her every night after work, to drape his coat over her shoulders and walk her home.

★ ★ ★

My heart sinks when I see him. The events of that miserable night come flooding back. The name-calling, tears in the storeroom, my feelings of self-loathing. Kevin stands at the counter and coolly orders a bag of chips. His head freshly shaved, a brown, lattice-shaped burn glinting on his forehead like a misshapen swastika. Heather, scated on the window ledge, tries to bolster me with a smile. To my relief Andy pops up by my side, like Mr Benn's shopkeeper, and takes the chip paper out of my hand. 'Sit down, leave him to me,' he says, before turning to Tony.

'*Sirt ton exo, Papa*' — throw him out, Dad — he says.

'Serve him,' Tony replies.

'*Papa, en ton serviro*' — Dad, I'm not serving him.

'Serve him,' Tony repeats, doggedly refusing to be swayed.

Kevin leans towards Andy and whispers: 'You heard your daddy, pig's arse. Serve me.'

Andy calmly forms a paper cone and fills it

195

with chips. He adds salt and vinegar and hands it across the counter.

'That'll be forty pence, you fuckin cunt,' he says.

Kevin grabs the bag, flings the hot chips into Andy's face and runs out. My brother tries to jump over the counter but Tony yanks him back by his belt strap and yells at him to calm down. Andy goes berserk, swearing and kicking the kebab machine, punching a hole through the Perspex display board before regaining his composure. In stupified silence we watch Andy lose control and vent his fury. Heather's slim hands, slumped in her lap, tremble as fiercely as my own.

'Wha is happen?' Tina asks, coming into the shop front with a steaming jug of curry sauce. She shakes her head as she listens to Tony's account before turning to her son with a disapproving look. 'If you ask me,' she says, 'you turned a flea into a camel.'

★   ★   ★

Two feisty hens and a mangy cockerel have taken up residence at the end of our garden, in a wooden coop surrounded by a barbed-wire fence. Tony had been hankering after livestock for quite some time to recreate the back garden of his youth. Tina vetoed any such acquisition saying she would leave Tony if he came home with a live animal. When he came home with three Tina merely huffed and complained about the potential smell. She was won over by Tony's persuasive arguments. The chickens, he said, would 'supply fresh eggs', 'give Yiayia a sense of purpose' and 'provide Anna with the pet she has always wanted', not one but three. I had been hoping for a cat. Tony believed the chickens would lure his children into the garden and bring them closer to nature. Two wet mornings trudging through sludge to search for eggs proved sufficient exposure to the natural world for me. I am content to watch the chickens from the comfort of a conservatory recliner. Andy has not yet ventured beyond the patio.

Tony's mother used to keep chickens, rabbits and pigeons, which were slaughtered on special occasions to supplement a staple diet of vegetables and pulses. As a boy Tony admits he never took much interest in animal husbandry, but four decades on he has been struck by the latent desire to rear animals of his own. Given a choice Tony would gladly give up work and live off the land. He is never happier than when trudging through freshly ploughed soil, applying manure and scatter-ing seeds. Tina would never exchange court shoes for wellies, never restrict herself to using only fruit and vegetables in season.

The chickens of Tony's youth did not live in a luxury coop, they were free to wander the back yard and sometimes the village, eating whatever scraps they could find. They were skinny creatures with little meat on their bones. Our chickens feast each day on a mountain of grain and the remains of our lunch. Tony takes great pleasure in going out to feed them, attracting the hens with a 'bak, bak, bak' and the cockerel with a *kikirikou*. Yiayia lacks Tony's sentimentality. She is happy to see our leftovers going to good use but would have no qualms about decapitating the chickens and frying them in wine and coriander. Tony has warned her against such action, telling her that in England killing a pet is a criminal offence.

★ ★ ★

I drink coffee in Yiayia's bedroom while she roots through the contents of a Frytick box. Smiling, she holds up a small white seashell.

'This is from the top of a mountain,' she says.

I don't tell her that I already know. I don't thwart her eagerness to tell me again the root of this enigma.

'He gave it to me,' she says, looking across at the picture of her husband on the window sill, 'he found it on his travels.'

I stretch out on the bed and listen to a story I have heard many times before about my Grandfather and his involvement in the Independence movement. Yiayia's stories are told with flair, each rendition littered with fresh gems. Her tales are like much-loved songs. Sometimes I request the one I want. I am consciously hoarding her stories to retell. My life can be nothing but commonplace in comparison.

★   ★   ★

Papou Andreas was a quiet, undemonstrative man. He led the solitary life of a goat herder, leaving home at dawn with his animals and returning at dusk, with only a dog for company. He was as hardy and nimble-footed as the goats he led up the mountain tracks of Troodos to feed on wild grasses. On his rambling walks he liked to collect seashells to take home to his children. He did not have to dig deep to find them, some lay scattered on the earth like spring blossom. The higher up he went the more he found — the legacy of an island that rose out of the sea like Aphrodite. Papou was most content when he was perched on a rocky outcrop overlooking the village, with no one to answer to. He used to say nothing was more important than a man's freedom, a tenet for which he risked his life many times, fighting for the liberation of his island.

The island's Independence movement, EOKA, was inaugurated on 1 April 1955, and called on the nation to fight for its freedom from British rule. Papou, then in his late twenties, played a significant role. He knew the location of potholes and caves where food, munitions and guerilla fighters could be hidden. He knew where to find fresh-water springs and could survive for many days on mountain produce. His vocation gave him licence to roam when others were subjected to curfews and lock-ins.

Clerics, students and peasants joined forces to fight a 30,000-strong British army, with homemade bombs and relics from the Second World War. Government buildings and military bases were attacked, army personnel were repeatedly ambushed. The violence intensified when Archbishop Makarios, the nation's leader, was exiled to the Seychelles. The British tried to curb EOKA's acts of violence by imposing a state of emergency. Villages were subjected to

early-morning raids and many EOKA sus-
pects were imprisoned without trial. The
possession of firearms and explosives carried
a maximum penalty of death.

As the penal measures on Papou's village
intensified so did his involvement with the
EOKA movement. He disappeared for days
on end, never telling his wife where he was
headed or where he had been. She knew
better than to question his whereabouts.
Secrecy was EOKA's staunchest code. A
decade passed before he spoke to his family
about his involvement in the Independence
movement, about how he led guerilla fighters
to safe houses and transported explosives
from one secret location to another. He once
accompanied EOKA leader General George
Grivas ('Dighenis') up the mountain to a
network of caves where men were trained in
bomb-making and guerilla warfare. Grivas
moved around the island incognito, dressed
as a shepherd. He was thought invincible at
the time, a demigod. A popular story told of
how he once cut open the stomach of a
donkey and climbed inside to evade capture.
Grivas and other EOKA protagonists were
immortalized in a song that Yiayia always
sings on 1 April to the tune of 'My Darling
Clementine':

Itan proti Apriliou, tis EOKA's e archi
Bou agoustike stin Kibro, e foni tou
  Digene
Marcos Drakos, Afxentiou, Zakos kai
  Karaolis
Thosane me tosous alous, tin neanigi zoi
Ma abolous tous leventes, bio tranos kai
  thinados
Eitane o Afxentiou, tis EOKA ibarchiyos

It was the first of April, the start of
EOKA
When in Cyprus was heard, the voice
of Digenes
Marcos Drakos, Afxentiou, Zakos and
Karaolis
Gave with so many others, their young
lives
But of all the brave young men, the
greatest and strongest
Was Afxentiou, EOKA's second in
command

Troodos provided a safe haven for many of
EOKA's protagonists. The British targeted
the mountains using sniffer dogs and
uncovered a vast quantity of munitions and
wanted men. With the help of an informer
they discovered Grivas' second in command,
Grigoris Afxentiou, and burned him alive in

the cave in which he hid.

Soldiers were parachuted into mountain villages under cover of darkness to carry out lightning raids. During one such search in October 1957 Papou was found hiding beneath the hearthstone of a safe house. Two soldiers entered the house where Papou was taking refuge and found his host sitting in front of a burning log fire with his wife and children. The soldiers questioned the couple at gunpoint and searched the house but found nothing. They were about to leave when one of them noticed the fire had not long been lit. He ordered the family outside, brushed the burning wood aside with his foot and prised open the hearthstone. Papou was found crouching beneath it, in a narrow hole just wider than his hips.

My Grandfather's capture was one of many that night. He escaped the hangman's noose but spent two years in detention, two years of hitherto unknown hardship for Yiayia. She sold the animals to survive and when money ran out she relied on the charity of family and friends. There were days when the children went to bed on empty stomachs, when Yiayia would fill a saucepan with stones and pretend to cook beans, lulling her children to sleep with a gentle rattle and the promise of food.

When Britain finally agreed to grant the

island its independence Papou was released from detention. In a dramatic turn of fate, a number of the men with whom he was detained exchanged prison cells for seats in the newly formed Parliament. Papou, a humble goat herder with little schooling, went back to the village to rebuild his life.

★ ★ ★

Gordon drives close to the steering wheel, peering through the front windscreen like Mr Magoo. He stalls at traffic lights, crashes the gears, drives along a dual carriageway in second. He hampers his pitiful driving skills still further with regular tokes on Athena's joint. I discover during the course of an erratic journey that Gordon has only a vague idea of where he is going, that we are heading for the party of a friend of a friend, to an address faintly scribbled on a crumpled tissue. After a series of five-point turns we end up in a cul-de-sac. Gordon climbs out of the car and cocks his ear skyward.

'I think it's over there,' he says confidently, pointing to a direction he calls 'due east'.

Gordon is healthy and athletic-looking, as handsome as Athena is pretty. I study the back of his sandy-coloured head, thick with well-groomed hair that glints in the darkness.

A pure white cricket jumper is casually slung across his shoulders. Gordon is content to drive along the quiet streets at a leisurely pace. There is no clock ticking away in his head. He can squander a night out. There will always be another one next week. I must get to the party, squeeze in a good time and return home before my parents finish work.

Gordon stops the car again beside an open playing field. He and Athena get out, look around and suddenly run off, across the field, into a clump of trees. I know they haven't found the party, unless it's in a tree house, because surely they would have taken me with them. Half an hour later they saunter back and climb into the car, covered in twigs and dry leaves, offering no explanation, having had a warming romp. Gordon crashes into first and pulls away from the curb. I fight the overwhelming urge to strangle him with the sleeves of his jumper or to boot the back of the driver's seat and send his flushed face through the windscreen. A tension headache bubbles behind my eyeballs, in spite of the aspirin I took as a pre-emptive measure. I am on the verge of asking Gordon to stop the car and let me out when we stumble upon a 1960s semi with a motley crew of bikers squashed into a small patch of front garden.

★ ★ ★

The dark house is packed and smoke-filled, smelling of sweat and beer. We find a small space in the living room and have a conversation of sorts, over an electronic beat. Planet hash calling earth, come in earth. Earth is not an enviable place to be. In spite of his classic good looks, Gordon is woefully lacking in sex appeal. His smile is too broad, his public school confidence bordering on pomposity. He has learnt to fraternize outside his social circle, but does so with an artificial air. There is nothing mysterious about Gordon, no depths to delve beyond the minor traumas of his skiing holiday.

Gordon fills a lull in conversation by sucking on Athena's neck, and I am suddenly surplus to requirements. I consider cutting my losses and going home by taxi but am loath to waste a precious hour's worth of freedom. Instead, I head for the only room with light and space and drink enough to numb my feeling of discomfort and claustrophobia. En route to the fluorescent kitchen I cut across a makeshift dance floor and stop to watch a small group thrashing about to 'She Sells Sanctuary'. Flailing their arms and throwing back their sweaty heads. And in amongst them, to my joy, is Papagalos, wearing combat trousers and a loose-fitting T-shirt, playing air guitar to a thumping bass. Even though he looks absurd, moving like a string puppet, disjointed and out of time, my heart pounds in celebration. When the music stops he looks straight into my eyes, acknowledging my presence with a smile, setting my cheeks ablaze. His look lingers, beyond the friendly. Its meaning is unequivocal, even to me. And just when I dare to believe in miracles, to imagine a clinch in a dark corner, of squeezing him like putty in my arms, a girl with spiky hair and a pierced nose puts her arms around him and he looks away.

And still I don't leave, in spite of my disappointment, so strong is my need for a 'good time'. I continue my journey to the kitchen and extract a bottle of Othello from my bag, procured from Tony's wine rack. Standing in a vacant corner, drinking from the bottle, I wonder whether party-going requires a certain amount of practice to perfect. A red-faced boy wanders in and stands beside me.

'Hi, what's your name?' he asks, craning his neck upwards, standing his pre-pubescent body too close for comfort.

'Anna,' I reply, feeling too aggressive to chit chat, hoping he will leave without my having to be rude.

'What did you take tonight?' he asks, rubbing up against me.

'What do you mean?'

'Drugs, man,' he says.

'Aspirin,' I reply.

'They're wicked in a can of coke. Your head must be spinning,' he says, putting a spindly arm around my waist. I push him away, more forcefully than I intended, sending him reeling on unsteady feet into a corner of the kitchen.

'Relaaax,' he says, stretching out his arm once more.

'Please go away,' I say firmly, employing the patience and control I have acquired in the service industry. He does as I ask, leaving me alone with the dark and full-bodied Othello.

★   ★   ★

I feel an urgent tapping on my leg and wake up feeling achy and disorientated. I look up and see a ceiling of stripped pine, the under belly of the kitchen table. Beside me lies the sleeping red-faced boy, his heavy head slumped on my arm.

'What have you been up to?' Athena asks, her tone faintly disapproving.

'Nothing,' I reply, crawling out from under the table and struggling to stand, catching sight of the kitchen clock, on the stroke of 3 a.m.

'I should have left at one,' I say, panicking. 'Where's Gordon?'

'Flat out on the living-room floor I'm afraid,' Athena replies casually.

'I have to go,' I say, searching in vain for my bag. 'I need some money, Athena. I need to get home.'

'Sorry. I don't have a penny on me. Daddy's a tight bastard.'

Andy is my only hope of rescue. I find a telephone in the hallway and ring the shop, hoping my brother will still be there, entertaining in the potato room. When he picks up the receiver I reel out a vague address and tell him to hurry. I sit on the bottom step and wait, my head throbbing, my throat as dry as a salt lake in summer. Glancing upwards I see a human vine stretching the length of the staircase. Lying amongst the concentration of bodies is Papagalos and the pretty dark-haired girl. While she nibbles on his ear, he looks at me through glinting eyes and blows a kiss. And in response, feeling angry and insulted, disappointed that his principles don't extend below the waist, I stick up my middle finger. A momentary sense of satisfaction subsides into a dull ache.

*   *   *

There are shouts from outside and the frenzied barking of a dog. I open the door a crack and peek outside. A burly biker with tousled hair holds a smaller man's head between his knees, while a mongrel barks excitedly at their heels. The assembled crowd urges the larger man to break his captive's neck. The smaller man jerks his head upwards, catching his captor where it hurts, causing him to drop to his knees and cry out in pain. The skinny mongrel licks the injured man's face while a vampish woman lunges at the victor, screaming hysterically. The smaller man looks directly into my eyes and shouts: 'ANNA, RUN!'

I see the Capri parked at the end of the driveway and run blindly towards it, jumping quickly into the passenger seat. Andy climbs in beside me, slams his door shut and accelerates quickly down the road, escaping a hail of beer cans. I feel too ill to talk. I open my window and take deep breaths of chill air, trying to calm the churning in my stomach. When Andy stops at traffic lights I stick my head out of the window and throw up, down the side of the car. My brother's stony silence on the journey home is oppressive. I have slipped from my pedestal into the gutter, all for the sake of a disastrous night. I sense his disappointment and read his uncharitable thoughts. Andy has the mistaken impression that his sister can't handle freedom and that his parents are right to keep a tight rein. He thinks he has a right to judge when he has no right at all. As I have no right to question his lifestyle, his sexual antics in the potato room or the thick smell of patchouli oil ever present in his car.

* * *

'Thank God you're alive,' Tina says, crossing herself, her eyes resembling bloated redcurrants, rattling away in her mother tongue: 'I called Mirianthy . . . she didn't have a clue where you were . . . my sister doesn't know where her daughter goes . . . what have we come to in this country? . . . I sent your dad out looking for you.'

'Where?' I ask.

'Everywhere, all over the city. I told him not to come back until he found you. And what happened to you?' she asks, suddenly noticing Andy's bloodshot eye.

'I walked into a tree,' he replies irritably, leaving the room.

'So why are you so late?' Tina asks angrily.

I offer a garbled explanation about getting lost and losing my bag.

'Oooofou . . . you reek of smoke,' Tina says. 'Did the people at the party smoke?'

'A few did,' I reply, astounded by the naïvety of her questioning.

'You don't need to tell me what kind of people they are,' Tina says, shaking her head, 'and don't think of asking me to go to any more parties.'

* * *

A brown paper envelope lies on the doormat, addressed in minuscule print to Mr A. Papamichael. I wonder what terrible offence could have caused Mr P to forsake the Royal Mail, leave his house at daybreak and cross enemy territory on foot. The whiff of foreign food wafting from our kitchen into his, the sight of Yiayia's undies billowing like windsocks on the back washing line. I carry the letter into the kitchen where Tina and Yiayia are dunking morning-coffee biscuits into Greek coffee.

'Open it, open it,' Tina says, spotting the letter.

I do so, at the risk of losing my appetite for a full English breakfast, and read aloud, to a chorus of 'the bastes, the bastes, the bastes' from Tina. Yiayia carries on dunking in blissful ignorance.

'What have we done this time?' she asks, when I've finished reading.

I explain that it is not 'we' but her alone that is the subject of a bizarre allegation. According to the letter, she was spotted yesterday evening throwing an animal skull over the privet hedge into the back garden of number 66. That this *despicable act* has traumatized Mrs P who is a vegetarian. *The police have been informed* as well as all other *relevant authorities* and, though he fails to quote the relevant law statute, Mr P claims such behaviour is a criminal offence and *WILL lead to prosecution*. So incensed is Mr P that he resorts to the use of capitals. The letter cites the *elderly woman's previous offences* as throwing potato peel and rotten vegetables over the hedge and pinching apples from the garden of number 66 with the use of an *elongated device*. Yiayia, who has denied all of the above, refutes the current accusation.

'They're mad,' she says. Feeling no further comment is required, she reaches for another biscuit.

'What lies!' Tina adds. 'Whatever will they think of next?'

My indignation is somewhat diluted by a guilty conscience. I saw Yiayia carrying the remains of a goat's head dinner through to the granny flat and wondered at the time what recycling plans she had for the skull. No one can say the neighbours don't deserve it, but I wish Yiayia would confess and Tina would accept the truth and laugh about it. Yiayia often resorts to white lies to cover her misdeeds. Last spring she uprooted the marigolds Tony had carefully planted along the length of the garden and threw them on the dung heap, planting potatoes in their place. Tony, managing to control his anger, asked his mother-in-law why she had done such a thing. She swore on her life that she hadn't and Tony was forced to let it drop. The next day I overheard Yiayia telling Tina that planting anything inedible in the garden was a waste of soil.

7

Tina says my chosen path is troublesome. Allowing one's marital future to chance is a mistake, she insists. Only by controlling the variables at the outset, and handpicking a partner, can wedded bliss be guaranteed. 'And who knows a daughter better than a mother?' she says, arguing the case for intervention. And all this from a woman who fell in love, who defied the wishes of her parents and married an unsuitable man. 'At least I fell in love with my own kind, not a marmalade-eater,' she says, referring to the English by the name assigned to them during colonial rule, on account of their eating habits.

Tina could not handpick a pair of shoes I would approve of, let alone a husband. Her choices are egocentric, based on her own aesthetic values and her preconceived ideas. Unquantifiable variables that I hold dear would be entirely overlooked. A quick wit, a generous spirit and street-wise charm do not enter into the introduction equation.

★ ★ ★

Tony and Panicos talk about vegetables. Runner beans and cherry tomatoes excite an inordinate amount of enthusiasm from our guest. Tony boasts he had a bumper crop last year and puts it down to spreading the soil with manure. He advises Panicos on the prudence of a dung heap in the corner of the garden.

'Doesn't it smell?' Maria asks.

'Not when it's dry, it's only grass and hay,' Tony explains, before extolling the therapeutic properties of manure. 'When I was a boy,' he continues, 'donkey dung was used for healing wounds.'

Yiayia, excluded from a conversation conducted in English, asks: 'What is Athonis talking about?'

'*Yia scada tou yarou*' — about donkey shit — Tina says ungraciously, before remembering she has guests and must be on her best behaviour.

Panicos' enthusiasm for gardening is matched by his active interest in Greek community affairs. He expresses particular concern about the erosion of family values, the increasing incidence of divorce and the growing number of children born outside wedlock. He cites the example of a young man in Birmingham who set up home with a black woman, subsequently fathered two

216

mixed-race children and was 'naturally' ostracized by his parents and the community as a whole.

This case and others like it inspired a public meeting in the church hall where solutions were sought to stem the flow of degeneracy. After three hours of fierce debate, during which two women fainted and a fight broke out, a vote was taken on a number of recommendations, two of which were agreed unanimously: the purchase of a table tennis table for the youth club, followed (if sufficient funds could be raised) by an all-expenses-paid trip for Greek youth to Drayton Manor Park.

A visiting priest, known for his emotional outbursts and booming voice, blamed parents for irregular church attendance. He expressed his shock on hearing children at the Greek school arguing evolution over divine creation (worse still, arguing with a priest!) and accused parents of raising a generation of atheists. He accused fish fryers (90 per cent of the community) of worshipping money before God and said: 'A donkey is still a donkey even if it's hung with gold,' before asking parishioners to put their hands in their pockets and give generously.

'Most boys of your age,' Tina says, 'my son included, take no interest in Church affairs.'

'Andreas has other interests,' Yiayia chips in, refusing to accept any slight against her grandson.

Tina goes on to praise Panicos' 'maturity' and her tear ducts moisten as she speaks, because this is another Harlequin moment come to life, because this is what she wants more than anything in the world. A community-minded son-in-law with an interest in runner beans and cherry tomatoes. And I know in my heart that I will never be able to deliver, that Maria's life is the closest she will ever get to her dream.

Maria and Tina discuss engagement party plans. I feel excluded, unable to share in the joy of an event that feels hurried. If Maria had any doubts at all, how could she pull out now with the hall booked, the dress half-made and three hundred invitations already printed? With her aunt in raptures and her mother floating on a cloud? When no one is prepared to take her to one side and tell her to slow down, take stock, get to know him first? Such a person would be lynched for sure, for killing the joy this family needs. Roulla most of all. After losing Peter.

Panicos leans forward in his seat. 'I suppose you'll be getting married next?' he says to me with an annoyingly presumptuous air.

'My cousin's not getting married yet. She's gonna study,' Maria replies, viewing me with doting eyes.

'What you studyin?' Panicos asks in his thick West Midlands drawl.

'A-levels.'

'And then?'

'University.'

'Wooo university,' he says, 'bit of a brain box, are ye?'

'Yeh. Anna's always been clever, not like me,' Maria replies, in her most helpless, girly, infuriating voice.

'You are clever, Maria,' I say. 'Don't say things like that.'

'Don't worry, babes, you don't need brains. I can do the thinking for both of us,' Panicos says, smiling, and everyone laughs. Ha ha. Hi hi. Except Yiayia who doesn't understand.

'What's the point of an expensive education,' Panicos continues, 'when you're gonna end up at home, raising kids? I mean yer never gonna be the breadwinner, are ye?'

I always flounder in the face of rampant chauvinism. My mind clouds up like a cerebral cataract. I have plenty to say but nothing comes out. But there must be some visible manifestation of my irritation because Yiayia asks, 'What's the matter with Anna?' And Tina, feeling vindicated, explains to her

219

mother that I am simply 'angry' because I am unable to accept the truth, the way of the world, the laws of nature, that a woman's place is in the home and a university education is simply a distraction before the inevitability of marriage and motherhood.

Yiayia listens thoughtfully, agreeing that motherhood is the worthiest of roles, before beginning a slow recitation.

> *Mana krasi to bethi, mana o nios, kai mana*
> *   o yeros*
> *Mana akous se kathe meros, ach ti onoma*
> *   yligo*
> *Tin hara sou kai tin libi, me tin mana*
> *   tin mirazis*
> *Trifera tin angaliasis, then tis krivis*
> *   mistigo.*

> 'Mother' calls the child, 'Mother' the youth, and 'Mother' the aged
> 'Mother' you hear in every place, Oh what a name so sweet
> Your joy and pain with Mother you share
> Tenderly you embrace her, from her secrets you don't keep.

Yiayia's dulcet tones are a calming prelude to an acerbic comment that follows. 'I am an uneducated woman and what do I raise? An ignorant daughter.'

'What do you mean, Mama?' Tina asks indignantly.

'If I had been educated, perhaps I could have saved you from a life of toil behind the counter.'

'I'm happy with my life.'

'That's because you don't know any better. Your daughter is lucky enough to have the chances you never had. Why should she waste them? I can be forgiven for my mistakes. I knew no better. But you? What excuse do you have?'

'I won't have my daughter leaving home. I won't let her forsake a family life to have a career,' Tina says, pronouncing the word 'career' with disgust, as if it were a sexually transmitted disease.

'We can't always dictate what our children do and don't do,' Yiayia continues.

'No, but we can guide them, advise them.'

'And they can reject that advice. Did you listen to me when I told you not to marry Athonis?' Yiayia says, winking at her son-in-law, while Panicos shifts uncomfortably in his seat, as if the 'old woman' has let slip a dark, family secret.

'What's that got to do with anything?'

'Time has shown that I was wrong and you

were right to follow your heart. Let Anna do the same.'

I have heard similar exchanges between mother and daughter — Yiayia championing my cause, Tina fighting her corner, too blinkered to see beyond her own convictions. Invariably she emerges from an argument unmoved and unconvinced, deflecting reason, sending it shooting back to her opponent like a ping pong ball.

'I'm sure Panicos hasn't come to hear us argue, Mama,' Tina says, with no hint of animosity in her voice. Tina forgets an argument the second she draws it to a close. She never takes offence, is never disconcerted by a snub or a raised voice. A successful marriage, claims Tina, requires one or both parties to possess this quality, this ability to throw off feeling as if it were an overcoat. Tina fails to understand anyone whose feelings have a longer shelf life. She thinks emotional immunity is a matter of will rather than disposition, that clearing one's mind of confusion is as easy as polishing dust from a mantelpiece. She says I take after Tony's sister who was quick to take offence and slow to offer forgiveness — a woman who never married, never 'flourished', cut herself off from family and friends. And what am I supposed to conclude from Tina's cautionary tale? That I could end up the same way if I continue being 'over-sensitive'.

* * *

The contents of the 'Tina box' lie scattered on Yiayia's bedspread. She fingers the jumble (platform boots, a stack of airmail letters, bus tickets, a red purse, a yellow bootee impaled on knitting needles) and finds the object she is looking for: a sugar-coated almond, dirty pink. Yiayia found the forgotten sweet in a side pocket of her handbag more than a decade after she put it there, on the day of Tina's wedding. It is the only memento she has of that day, though she wrapped the lacy dress in paper and stored it in the ottoman at the foot of her bed. What has become of these things? The dress, the ottoman, the four-poster bed built by her grandfather. Are they lying where she left them when she fled? Undisturbed, covered with dust and cobwebs. Or were they eaten by moths and used as firewood?

'Maria seems to be in love,' I say, taking advantage of a private moment with my grandmother to draw her out on the subject of Maria.

'Your cousin wants to be in love,' Yiayia replies with her usual perspicacity.

'Mama thinks they're well matched,' I continue, trying to provoke a contentious response.

'Your mama sees what she wants to see.'

'They were very touchy,' I say, knowing her answer before she has opened her mouth to reply: 'Love is a private thing. Not a public performance.' Along with big feet, I have inherited my grandmother's cynicism.

She swivels the sweet distractedly in her fingers and looks thoughtful. 'Your mama forgets what she was like at your age. She was stubborn and married your father against my will.'

Yiayia could no more prevent my mother from marrying Tony than she could stop a landslide. Tina and Tony met in secret, promised themselves to one another, fuelled the gossip mills and were married to circumvent a scandal (though hand-holding was their only crime, according to Tina). My grandparents reluctantly gave their blessings and even offered to give up their home for the newly-weds. Tony, too proud to take up the offer, sold his motorbike, borrowed money and bought a ticket to England, determined to prove his worth.

He joined the mass exodus leaving the island in search of a better life. Cyprus was in transition, from crown colony to independent nation. Jobs were scarce, wages low. Radio broadcasts invited former subjects of the crown to take up work in Britain, where jobs were said to be plentiful. Tony suffered many hardships during his first few months in Britain. He spent his first night sleeping in a telephone box and was repeatedly refused work (EOKA was still fresh in employers' minds). He tasted hunger and longed for home. He worked on a bicycle assembly line by day and in a restaurant kitchen at night. Six months passed before he sent for Tina. She disembarked at Dover with a trunk full of pretty dresses, hungry for new experience, abdomen rounded as a football.

Tina fell from the clouds when she arrived in the city that became her temporary home. Oppressed by the greyness, the dank air, the filthy, litter-strewn streets. Tony worked fifteen hours a day while she stayed padlocked inside a cramped bed-sit, too scared to venture onto the busy street outside, populated by immigrants: Indians, Irish, Jamaicans. She felt fear and loneliness for the first time in her life, acute and unremitting, in a country where the sun never seemed to rise.

In the first letters she sent home Tina spared her mother the truth of her predicament. She wrote instead of her hopes for the future, of Tony's promise to build her a house on a plot of land overlooking the village. She wrote about the baby *growing heavy* inside her, *kicking like a footballer*, of how she knew the child was a boy from the elongated shape of her belly and the pudginess in her cheeks. This boy would take the name of her father, he would change her life, he would wear the yellow bootees she was knitting. Yiayia read between the lines and made half-truths whole.

'You can't imagine how many times I cried for my daughter,' Yiayia says, 'knowing she was alone in a strange country, with no one to help her, with no one for company, knowing she could barely boil an egg. Stavroulla was the one who used to help me with the cooking. Your mother was more interested in dreaming.'

Yiayia picks up a crumpled, airmail envelope and carefully removes the letter from inside.

'I have kept this letter from you,' she says, 'your mother didn't want you to know its contents.'

'To know what?'

'About the fate of her first child.'

'She told me she had a routine miscarriage.'

'Her son was due in a matter of days when

she lost him. His death was not a natural occurrence.'

She unfolds the blue paper and reads from a letter in which Tina doesn't hold back to spare her mother's feelings. A letter in which she describes pacing a first-floor landing to stretch her legs, tripping on loose carpeting and tumbling down the stairs. She blacked out between trip and fall, came to as she lay in a crumpled heap at the foot of the stairs. She describes crawling her way back up, climbing into bed, mopping up the blood *that flowed like a river* with bed sheets. She writes of excruciating pain and of feeling too embarrassed to cry out for help.

'Your father found her when he got home from work. Lying in a pool of blood. He ran to a telephone box to call for help while she haemorrhaged.'

Tina was rushed into hospital, hanging on to life by a thread, the baby boy already dead inside her. Her labour was induced. Her son was stillborn.

I would give my life a hundred times over, Tina writes, *for the baby to have lived. What I feel now is worse than death.* In a flurry of tear-stained prose she demands to know the whereabouts of her son. *Why was I not allowed to bury him? Was he thrown out with surgical waste and other women's placentas?*

What will happen to his unbaptized soul?
She blames England for the baby's death. She blames Tony for failing to protect her and for not being there when she needed him. She blames the evil eye and Loulla's curse. She blames herself for wanting the baby too much, for walking on the landing, for tripping, for failing to cry out, for getting married, for refusing to listen to her mother.

'Constantina has never fully recovered from that loss,' Yiayia says. 'Every year, on the day her son should have been born, she comes into my room and we talk about what could have been.'

'Why hasn't she told us?'

'My daughter insists on hiding her emotions for fear of upsetting anyone else. Especially Athonis.'

I am on the verge of tears, on the brink of understanding my mother a little more. Of understanding why her rhetoric is riddled with complacency. 'I never had a teenage' . . . 'I don't know what it's like to be young' . . . 'life has been hard' . . . 'I grew up before my time'.

⋆ ⋆ ⋆

Andy knocks on Yiayia's bedroom door and walks in, wearing his leather *Top Gun* jacket,

228

smelling of frosty night. He finds us slumped on the bed, rummaging through memorabilia, lost in a reflective stupor.

'What's this?' he says, picking up the sugar-coated almond.

'It's a sweet given out at weddings. Single girls put them under their pillows to dream of the man they will marry,' Yiayia replies. She collects up the Tina artefacts strewn on her bed and puts them carefully back into their box. My brother has little interest in the past and no head for stories. 'A tale told to Andreas is like a seed sown on a mound of rock,' I have heard my Grandmother remark.

'Come into the kitchen. I will make you both a Greek coffee,' Yiayia says, 'and then I will read my grandson's cup.'

'I would love a coffee, but you know I don't believe in that fortune-telling stuff,' Andy replies, looking tired and preoccupied.

⋆ ⋆ ⋆

We sit at Yiayia's kitchen table, sipping coffee and eating homemade biscuits, surrounded by clashing accessories and Yiayia's creations. We sit on mismatched chairs, saved from the skip, with comfy cushions, made out of moth-eaten curtains. Yiayia's kitchen, albeit small and cramped, is cosier than Tina's roomy farmhouse affair, with its pristine worktop and its fruit bowl tiles, where dropping crumbs feels like a crime. Yiayia keeps her kitchen outwardly clean but ignores the finer points of cleanliness. Inside her cupboards there are tins of stale biscuits, ancient packets of Cyprus delights and several bottles of *triantafilo* — rose cordial — with sticky lines of red syrup trailing down the sides.

Andy sips the last of his coffee and upturns his cup in its saucer.

'I thought you didn't want a reading?' Yiayia says, pursing her lips.

Andy looks at the upturned cup, sitting in a shallow pool of coffee. 'Did I do that?'

'Well it wasn't me,' Yiayia replies, taking hold of the cup and rotating it three times, before lifting it up, blotting the rim with kitchen towel and inspecting the inside. Her concentrated gaze is broken by transient expressions of pleasure, concern and amusement.

'You read it,' she says, handing me the cup, folding her arms and leaning back in her chair.

'Is that a good idea?' Andy asks, looking a little shocked.

'You don't have anything to hide from

your sister, do you? And anyway you don't believe in fortune-telling.'

I take the cup from Yiayia's hand and study the contents. At first I see nothing but indiscriminate streaks and grainy splodges, my nerves getting the better of me. I feel under pressure to perform, to get the reading right and justify my grandmother's confidence in me.

'Try to forget everything around you,' Yiayia says, issuing an instruction that helps me to relax and focus on the cup, until the symbols begin to jump out at me like the three-dimensional images in a hologram.

'There's a heart,' I say, 'close to the rim of the cup.'

'Matters of the heart will imminently come to the fore,' Yiayia says, interpreting the symbol.

'And beside the heart I see something that resembles weighing scales.'

Yiayia nods her head approvingly. 'Love has my grandson in a quandary. He is unused to such troubling thoughts. Affairs of the heart have always been clear-cut in the past, but not any more. Now his heart tells him one thing and his head another.'

'What should I do, Yiayia?' Andy asks, sitting bolt upright, forgetting his scepticism.

'I can't tell you what to do. All I can say is,

the heart is large and clearly defined, which means the feelings are genuine. If you follow your heart and trust your instinct, you will make the right decision.'

'I wish things were that easy. There are complications,' Andy says, glancing awkwardly at me, reluctant to elaborate in my presence. He gets up to leave.

'Sit down,' I tell him, 'there's more in the cup. A kind of rocket thing with stars shooting off it.'

'Well done. You're learning,' Yiayia says, 'you recognized the comet. It is a sign of big trouble ahead. Trouble that has been brewing for some time, that will soon come to a head. I would advise you to avoid confrontation, Andreas.'

Yiayia gets up and goes into her bedroom, returning with a blue stone threaded onto a safety pin.

'Keep this with you at all times,' she says, 'it will protect you from the evil eye.'

* * *

A coach driver comes into the shop and asks for directions to the M1. Tony draws a diagram on chip paper, while the coach sheds its load like a bloody nose. Liverpool FC supporters fill the shop, singing football songs, boasting of their victory over Nottingham Forest. Hearing the commotion Andy comes through to the front and casually fiddles with the peppers in the salad bar, standing guard over his family. Tina accuses her son of being too ready for a fight and says, 'If you don ask for trable, you don get trable.'

'*Kalos tin gilia*' — welcome, big belly — Tina says, serving a man with a watermelon gut, who orders a mixed fry and breaks wind. '*Ton yaro*.' Tina calls him a 'donkey' while serving with a smile.

'You married, luv?' the man asks in a thick scouse accent.

Tina glances playfully at her husband. 'Me . . . no . . . I no marrie.'

'Fancy cumin back to Liverpool with me?'

'*Faousa na fkalis*,' Tina mutters, wishing upon the man a bout of Black Death. 'I no think my boyfriend he lie that,' she replies, before telling me in Greek that she wouldn't go near this man if he was made of gold. The customer orders a diet coke and blows Tina a kiss before leaving.

My generously proportioned mother has more than her fair share of sex appeal. Men of middle age and above frequently stare at her across the counter. She generally treats them with contempt, muttering outrageous insults under her breath. In her own unique way, Tina knows how to use her feminine wiles: engaging in mildly flirtatious exchanges with the fishmonger to secure the best haddock, sharing playful banter with her customers to keep her husband on his toes, hurling dominatrix-like commands at Jimmy the indolent potato man to spur him into action.

'Nex plees,' Tina shouts out, her voice loud and piercing.

A lanky man, flushed with drink, orders chips and gravy. Tina tells him the chip box is empty and he will have to wait. The man stretches a long arm across the counter, reaches into the chip box and grabs a handful of scraps. Tina instinctively slaps his fingers with the chip scoop and in his haste to extricate his hand he catches his wrist on the boiling element inside the chip box. He reels backwards, clutching his seared wrist, discharging a shrill cry. The shop falls silent. The smell of burnt skin rises up from the chip box. Andy stops fiddling with the peppers and stands stiffly like a thick-set pit bull. We stand in the midst of a precarious situation that could go one of two ways. Mercifully, the injured man starts to laugh.

'Dickhead,' his friend says. 'Thrashed by an al woman.'

Tina waves the chip scoop triumphantly in the air and says: 'Anyone else he wanna put his hand in the chip box?'

The shop fills with laughter and good-humoured banter and the queue quickly clears.

'Where's the pickled onion jar?' Tony asks, suddenly noting its disappearance.

'They must'av nicked it,' Doreen replies.

'You'd better go and fetch it,' Tony tells his son.

'Forget the blady anions. Who he care aboud anions?' Tina says, shaking her head, as Andy shoots out of the door.

We watch from the shop window as he climbs up the coach steps and speaks to the driver, who stands up and waves an accusing finger at his passengers. A burly man on the back seat gets up and holds aloft the pickled onion jar. He unscrews the lid, fishes out an onion and puts it provocatively into his mouth. Andy walks further into the coach and then disappears as if through a trap door. Tony grabs the kebab knife and runs towards the coach. Tina and I follow him out and watch as he leaps up the coach steps, brandishing the knife like Zorro at two men who have Andy pinned to the floor, one of whom is the man with the scorched wrist.

'Let go of my son or I'll kill you,' Tony yells, his wild eyes betraying the fire that lurks in his soul. Stunned by Tony's ferocity, the men let go of Andy.

'And give the man his onions back,' the driver says, waiting with hands on hips for the jar to be passed along the row of seats.

We are mooned at as the coach pulls away. Tina sticks her Vs up and curses the mothers of an entire coachload. Back in the shop Tony throws the pickled onion jar in the bin and fetches a steak from the fridge for Andy's bruised eye.

'Now you've got a matching pair,' Doreen says sympathetically.

'Your dad she cause all this trable jas for anions,' Tina complains, fishing the jar out of the bin, giving it a wipe down and reinstating it on the counter.

★ ★ ★

Mrs Collins rushes into the shop, brandishing a copy of the *Stretley Advertiser*.

'Wha they find in our chips this time?' Tina asks.

'If only,' Mrs Collins replies, 'this is much worse, duck.'

'Who he's die then?'

Mrs Collins reads aloud from the front

page. "'A sixty-five-year-old man was *attacked and left for dead*. Two assailants wearing balaclavas attacked him yesterday as he walked along Fairfield canal. He was found *lying in a pool of blood* by a woman walking her dog. The man, *a former resident of Hamberley House*, is named as Elvin Jones.'"

'Elvin Jones,' repeats Mrs Collins, when we fail to react.

'Who is she?' Tina asks.

'It's Elvin, Mum, Elvin,' I say, as the bad news sinks in.

'Oh no,' Tina says, her eyes filling up.

Mr Frank is quoted in the paper, calling the attack '*ferocious and cowardly*' and appealing for information.

'Elvis he gonna die?' Tina asks.

'Elvis died in 1977, luv,' Mrs Collins replies. 'Our Elvin, on the other hand, he's gonna be all right. I phoned the ospital this mornin.'

Tina rushes into the back to tell Tony. Her voice is loud and high pitched, her curses more virulent than usual. Mrs Collins' angry rhetoric washes over me. I see a mouth moving, spouting words that fail to penetrate my consciousness. My mind is elsewhere, mulling over Kevin's threats of vengeance and Elvin's plucky intervention. I wonder if I was the catalyst for Elvin's attack, feel the

237

eggy contents of my stomach rising up into my mouth.

'Y'aright, luv?' Mrs Collins asks, looking concerned.

'Tha poor man,' Tina says, returning from the kitchen, her cheeks ablaze.

'Anna's lookin very pale,' Mrs Collins says.

'Is no wonder,' Tina replies, shaking her head disapprovingly, 'she no eat brekfas this morni.' As usual, every dilemma has food as its root cause.

Tony hurries into the shop front and suggests a visit to the hospital.

'Oh no,' Tina says, wincing, 'I no have the stomach. You go with Anna.'

★   ★   ★

The white corridors of Stretley hospital smell of disinfectant and boiled root vegetables. The unhealthy air leaves a sticky acrid taste in the mouth. Tony walks beside me, too stoical to bother about bad smells. While he follows the signs, intent on finding Elvin, I take in the sights and sounds of human fallibility, observe the consequence of mishaps and renegade cells.

Elvin has a private room, stark and uninviting, with a policeman sitting outside and a vase of carnations wilting miserably on the window ledge. The white walls, exposed to dank, hospital air have yellowed like oxidized paper. Elvin lies perfectly still beneath a starched white sheet, his back to the door, more estranged from the world than ever, his thin limbs barely discernible beneath the folds of the bed sheet.

A young nurse standing at the foot of the bed greets us with an amiable smile.

'Elvin, you've got visitors,' she calls out.

We walk around the bed to view head-on a face disfigured by bruises. Coarse black stitches score Elvin's cheek and one eye weeps inside a purple eyelid. His face is a sobering sight. My need to vomit is supplanted by a sudden rush of blinding anger. Elvin stares blankly at the wall, ignoring our presence.

'Looks worse than it is,' the nurse says, tucking in Elvin's bed sheet. 'It's mostly bruising. A couple of weeks and he'll be back to normal.'

'Did you hear that, Elvin mate?' Tony says, touching him gently on the shoulder. 'A couple of weeks and you'll be back at home.'

'I didn't say that,' the nurse says. 'It's unlikely that he'll be going home at all. There's talk of sending him to sheltered housing.'

'Why can't he go home?' Tony asks.

'He's a vulnerable man. He needs looking after.'

I summon the strength to look into Elvin's eyes and force a connection. To my surprise he turns his head and looks directly at me, smiling weakly, for just a second. And in that second his wounded face is so tender and full of love I want to cry. I smile back and hope my eyes will speak for me too and return the gesture. Elvin's look is one I will never forget. It tells me I am far more to him than just a girl behind a chip shop counter, that I am the closest thing to family he will ever know. I sense his utter helplessness and have the sinking feeling that I will never see him again.

★   ★   ★

My eyes feel heavy in their sockets, my throat dry and sore. Last night I hardly slept. I dreamt that Andy and I were being chased by something unknown through a dense forest. I kept tripping over branches and creepers, grazing my legs on clods of frozen earth. Andy ran like a gazelle, dodging over-hanging branches, running nimbly through the under-growth, only stopping to pick me up and urge me to run faster. I kept telling him to leave me, to save himself but he wouldn't listen. I woke up and felt intensely relieved to find

240

myself in bed but was unable to erase the image of the forest from my mind.

When finally I fell asleep I found myself back in the forest, stumbling breathlessly, cold air chafing my throat, Andy pulling me by the arm until I could run no further. Doubled over with a stitch, I begged him to let me rest. The second we stopped running, the trees began to mutate, to turn from gnarled brown oaks into spotted, jeering hyenas baring bloody fangs. Andy picked up a stick and jabbed all around him to keep them back, fighting though he knew we had no chance of escape. 'RUN,' I shouted but he just kept on jabbing, until a hyena lurched forward and sank its teeth into my brother's throat. I covered my eyes and screamed so loud I woke myself up. Tina ran into the room and sat on my bed for a while. 'You could have woken the dead with those screams,' she said.

★ ★ ★

The doorbell rings several times in succession, interrupting my Saturday morning snooze. My legs feel leaden and uncooperative, after an evening behind the counter and a midnight dash through the forest. The doorbell rings again, the buzzer pressed down and held. The urgency of the ring forces me out of bed and across the landing to Tina's room. Gently, I nudge her awake and tell her there is someone at the door. She sits up, looking confused, still half asleep.

'Your brother, where's your brother?' she asks in a panic, as if a horrible scenario, the worst of her fears, has just flashed through her mind.

I look out of the window and see Andy's car parked in its usual spot on the driveway.

'He's at home,' I tell her, 'don't worry.'

'Thank God,' she says, planting her head back down on the pillow.

'But, Mama, there's someone at the door.'

'If your brother's alright, you go back to bed . . . 't's only Jehovah's.'

Tina's natural rudeness increases tenfold at the sight of a Jehovah's Witness. She knows all she needs to know about their practices to dismiss them outright. Some weeks ago a well-dressed couple were talked into silent submission by Tina's impassioned rhetoric about the joys of Christmas which ended with 'I'm sorry bat you no human beans' and a slammed door.

The doorbell rings again, more urgently than before. Tina reluctantly climbs out of bed and puts on her dressing gown. She runs a comb through her fine hair and heads downstairs. I hurriedly dab my face with loose powder and follow her, curious to discover the identity of our early-morning visitor.

We find Yiayia standing at the front door, fiddling with the key, her hair in disarray, her glasses askew, a vision of senility, though she has more sense than all of us put together. She opens the door to a familiar-looking man in an ill-fitting suit.

'YES,' Tina shouts from behind her mother, 'wha you sellin?'

'I'm from the council,' the man replies.

We move aside to let him in. He crosses the threshold hesitantly, smiling awkwardly at Yiayia, flinching when he recognizes Tina. Luckily, she fails to identify him and leads him graciously into the living room, makes tea and offers biscuits before asking the man his business.

'We've had a complaint about noise pollution,' he says, 'from someone in the neighbourhood.'

'NOISE! We don make noise, we never at home, we always werkin,' Tina says indignantly.

'Not you, madam, the cockerel.'

'The cockerel he don make noise,' Tina says sternly, her words followed by a piercing

'Ki-ki-ri-kou'. 'Thas no noise, thas nature. Who he can complain bout nature?'

'The next-door neighbours,' I reply.

'I'm not at liberty to disclose the source of the complaint,' the inspector says officiously.

Tina pulls a sour face. 'Thes NATHIN they can do.'

'I'm afraid there is. If after investigation the cockerel is deemed to be a statutory noise nuisance the council could prosecute under the Environmental Protection Act. I'm afraid the noise will have to be abated.'

Tina looks perplexed. 'What is bated mean?'

'We have to stop the noise,' I explain.

'Wharabou tha blady dog cross the roe? Hiss barkin it keep me wake last nigh. Why you no tell them to bate the noise?'

'You can train a dog not to bark, which is the course of action we would take with a dog,' replies the inspector, struggling to maintain his composure. 'Unfortunately the same can't be said for a cockerel.'

Yiayia, anxious to find out why her red-faced daughter is shouting, asks for a translation. On hearing my hurried explanation, Yiayia gets up and disappears into the kitchen, where she can be heard noisily rustling through the cutlery drawer. She returns to the living room with a large bread knife and walks determinedly towards the health inspector.

'*Mama, ti kamnis?*' — Mother, what are you doing? — Tina asks.

'*E tin lisi,*' — here's the solution — Yiayia replies, waggling the long, serrated knife in the air.

Her daughter tells her 'murder is not the answer, though the inspector deserves decapitation' and Yiayia laughs in a slightly deranged fashion while continuing her trajectory across the room, towards an anxious-looking inspector.

'SIT,' Yiayia commands, thwarting his attempt to stand up, 'plees,' and explains to her daughter that the knife is not meant for the health inspector but for the cockerel.

'My matha he say, if you don like the cockerel why you don cat his neck,' Tina explains, running a finger Godfather-like along her throat.

'No, no,' the inspector replies, shaking his head, 'that's not what I had in mind.'

'Wha you have in mind? We letim ran free? Tha berd he make good soup.'

'I need to investigate this matter further. In the meantime, don't do anything rash.'

'I don rash to do nathin,' Tina replies with a self-satisfied grin.

The health inspector backs out of the front

door, without taking his eyes off the knife glinting menacingly in Yiayia's hand.

'Where do I know that man from?' Tina asks.

'He came to inspect the shop, Mama,' I reply.

'The *pesevengi*,' Tina says, calling him a cuckold, 'and those neighbours of ours are unbelievable.'

8

We descend a steep staircase into a dimly lit banqueting hall. Pink helium-filled balloons rise in tight bunches from the centre of circular tables. The resonating hum of voices accompanies our slow descent. Yiayia, leaning heavily on Andy for support, leads the way. Heavy footed and unused to heels, she lumbers awkwardly down each step, impeding our progress. She insisted on walking at the helm, lest she fall and squash the person in front. I stoop at the back, behind my parents, hiding from the gaze of prospective mothers-in-law and general scrutiny, regretting with every painful step the horror I have agreed to wear: a crushed-silk evening dress with a flared skirt and tight bodice, the shiny green fruit of a three-hour shopping trip with Tina. I take solace in the thought that no one who really matters will ever see me in this dress, looking like an oversized fairy dipped in pea green. Then I spot Athena walking across the dance floor and my confidence dissipates. In her long, black, shapeless dress she looks infinitely more striking than the glut of bowed and sequined women vying for the limelight.

Roulla meets us at the foot of the stairs, wearing the artificial smile she saves for public appearances. She has managed to fool an entire community with that smile and regular donations to the church. She is generally thought of as a 'good woman', whose troubles at home are blamed on the actions of an ungrateful son. Support from the 'pious' women of the community has fed Roulla's sickness and strengthened her convictions. I have often heard her say in a melancholy tone, 'I raised a crow to pick out my eyes.' Yiayia says: 'What use is the approval of strangers when you have lost your son?'

En route to our table, Andy elicits furtive glances that spread like a Mexican wave. I walk behind him, proud to be the sister of the most eligible bachelor in the room. Andy's sex appeal oozes like a radiation leak and contaminates a wide radius. His smile ameliorates his handsome face. He flashes it sparingly, revealing a set of straight, white, angular teeth, like a row of miniature halloumia.

We have ringside seats beside the head table, where the happy couple sits, flanked by parents and siblings. Panicos' side is top heavy with two vociferous sisters, their husbands and a gaggle of noisy children. The turkey-mother sits beside her son, proudly accepting congratulations, largely ignoring her husband. Maria looks like a little girl let loose with a dressing-up box and her mother's make-up. She has on pink taffeta, a pink feather boa and a diamanté tiara. She is a dazzling sight, the centre of attention, the pride of her new in-laws. I imagine myself in her shoes, seated amid the suffocating bosom of her new family, and feel a phantom noose tightening around my neck. Maria looks across at me and raises her wine glass in salute, her lingering glance imploring me to be happy for her.

Andy lights a cigarette and settles back in his chair, looking lonely without his friend and partner in crime, without the cousin who should have been here to celebrate the betrothal of his sister. Andy came of age with cousin Peter at his side. The two enjoyed a mischievous boyhood, playing in the yard behind the shop, scrawling graffiti with pea green on every available surface and firing at passers-by with their peashooters. They developed a novel way of killing flies by burning bags of chicken giblets over a gas flame until they were black and sticky like tar, before catapulting them at the bluebottles that settled on the wall behind the bins.

'Enjoin yourself tonight,' Tina says, pouring me a generous glass of Aphrodite, secretly hoping the wine will loosen me up and make me more receptive to an inadvertent introduction.

Kyria Pantelli — Mrs Pantelli — a large, garrulous woman, settles herself down in the vacant seat next to mine.

'My, how you've grown since I last saw you,' she says, viewing me with satisfaction. 'You've turned into a real woman. What size are you now?'

I hail from a culture that deems personal comments perfectly acceptable. I was brought up in a culture that does not. Tina obliges Kyria Pantelli with a fabricated answer, telling her that my dress is a 12 when in fact I had trouble squeezing into a 14.

'It's time we found you a husband,' Kyria Pantelli says, draping an arm across my shoulders.

'Perhaps you can talk sense into my daughter,' Tina comments. 'She won't listen to me. I have talked so much about marriage that my tongue has sprouted hairs.'

'What do you think of Marco?' Kyria Pantelli asks, pointing to a notorious womanizer sitting at a nearby table with a glamorous blonde beside him.

'Isn't that his girlfriend?' I enquire.

'A girlfriend is one thing and a wife is another,' Kyria Pantelli replies, spouting the homespun philosophy that Tina has tried to drum into her own son. 'On second thoughts, perhaps he's too good-looking. You can't trust these handsome types. My husband may be short and bald but he's always been faithful. Have you ever considered Bambo?'

'No,' I reply hastily, feeling highly insulted.

'He may be a little fat but he has a heart of gold and he runs a lucrative grocery business. I have it on good authority that he owns a big house in Haringey and drives a silver Mercedes. He only dresses like a pauper to ward off gold-diggers.'

'If the man was made of gold I wouldn't wish him on my granddaughter,' Yiayia says. 'You're better off a beggar than to marry a man for his money.'

'My sister's daughter married a man for his looks and lost the eggs and the basket,' Kyria Pantelli says, embarking on a cautionary tale about a niece who was presented with two suitors. One was a wealthy, balding accountant, the other was poor but good-looking with a full head of hair. The niece chose the good-looking man and was hastily married. Two years later her husband lost his hair through alopecia, gained considerable kilos and could barely support his family to boot.

'The accountant has a thriving business and his wife has the best of everything,' Kyria Pantelli remarks, 'and my niece . . . she lives in a council house . . . where's the sense in that? Now she says to me, 'Aunty, I wish I had listened to you and married the accountant.''

'If your niece thinks that way, no wonder her poor husband has lost his hair and blown up like a balloon,' Yiayia says scathingly.

'At least the couple is still together, that's what matters. My niece made her choice, wrong though it may have been, and now she has to stick to it, through thick and thin. My niece would never leave her husband. In that sense she is a decent woman, not like certain others I have heard about recently.'

'Who do you mean?' Tina asks, fishing for gossip.

Kyria Pantelli tells us the story of Andricos, a young man who was recently ditched by fiancée number three. His parents, losing faith in the suitability of girls in the UK, went to Cyprus to source a wife. They found a beautiful girl of seventeen in the village of Psevda with 'not a penny to her name' and did the charitable thing. They gave her what every girl dreams of — a husband, a chip shop and a house in Sutton Coldfield. 'Well', this girl was not as 'grateful' as she should have been and life in England 'went to her head'. She refused to work in the shop and spent the day 'filing her nails'. It turned out she couldn't even boil an egg or use a washing machine and 'never ironed a single shirt for her husband'. The family felt duped but were prepared to overlook her faults and try and 'make her into a decent woman'. They never got the chance because she had an affair with the local butcher and was duly sent back to her parents in disgrace. And now Andricos' parents are looking for fiancée number four, confident that bad luck always comes in threes.

'You can blame the girl the first time, you can blame the girl the second time, but the third time you get suspicious,' Kyria Pantelli says, glancing at an adjacent table where Andricos, looking world weary and bland, is sandwiched between his parents. 'I have heard that boy has a problem.'

'What is it?' Tina asks.

'I am not a gossip by nature and would not normally divulge such sensitive information but you have a daughter and have every right to know ... and I'm confident that the Papamichael family can be trusted with a secret.'

'What is it?' Tina asks, unable to contain

her excitement. 'He looks like such a good boy.'

For Tina the term 'good boy' covers anyone Greek, with a sensible haircut and a well-paid job.

'He may well be a good boy,' Kyria Pantelli whispers, her face animated, 'but I have it on good authority that he can't get it up.'

'My God,' Tina says, her eyes bulging like gob stoppers, 'you have saved us from catastrophe, Kyria Pantelli.'

'Why?'

'I had my eye on Andricos for Anna,' Tina replies, letting slip her horrible secret.

'Keep your distance from that boy if you want grandchildren. Anna can do better,' Kyria Pantelli says, standing to leave, 'and please, not a word to anyone about this.'

'I will take this secret to my grave,' Tina replies with requisite melodrama.

I glance across at Andricos' table and his mother looks me straight in the eye, nods her head and smiles. I realize, with utter revulsion, that I have been set up. The proximity of our tables, Tina's insistence on a figure-hugging dress, the chair she graciously pulled out for me to sit on directly opposite Andricos, were all part of a plan to join together this woman and that train spotter. Andricos is window-shopping and I am the possible purchase. I feel his eyes poring over me, sizing me up like a racehorse.

'I'm going home,' I tell Tina, struggling to hold back the tears of anger welling up inside me.

'Are you unwell?' she asks, oblivious to the turmoil and humiliation she has caused me.

'You've ruined my night,' I tell her, 'and left to your own devices you would have ruined my life.'

'But I didn't know.'

'That's not the point.'

'I was only trying to — '

'To fix me up with a desperate man. Is that how little you value you daughter?' I say, standing up to exercise the full force of my lungs.

'Don't shout,' she says, raising her hands in defeat, 'people are looking. Athonis, tell your daughter to keep her voice down.'

'This has nothing to do with me,' he replies, filling his mouth with salted peanuts.

'Sit down, Anna,' Tina pleads. 'You can't leave your cousin's engagement.'

'You've embarrassed me, again, and if you don't stop I'll pack my bags and leave home. I'll join a monastery and turn my back on the world,' I say, voicing Tina's worst fear.

'Bite your tongue,' she says, before offering

a garbled apology and suggesting we swap seats.

★ ★ ★

'Uhg! The *koupepia* are chewy and tasteless,' Tina says, biting into a stuffed vine leaf.

'Not enough meat and too much salt,' Yiayia adds.

'They're inedible,' Tina says, pushing them to the side of her plate. 'Thank God I made the pasticcio, at least we won't go hungry.'

A three-man band plays music from the forties and fifties. Songs made popular by singers like Vouyouklaki and Tony's namesake Papamichael, a glamorous duo, who starred together in tear-jerking dramas and romantic comedies, in the black-and-white films that made my mother's young heart flutter. Tina has a collection of these films on video and watches them on Sunday afternoons, when she needs to rekindle the past and raise her spirits.

Tony turns to his wife and serenades her. '*Asta ta malagia sou, anakatomena, Asta ta n'anemizountai*' — leave your hair tousled, let it blow in the wind — he sings along to the music, his face flushed with happiness, his arms raised above his head. Energized and animated, he is reminiscent of the man in the black-and-white snapshot, with the wavy hair and the sparkle in his eye, a million miles away from the automaton behind the counter. As I watch him sing and twist his shoulders I get a glimpse of the man he really is: an arm-waving, finger-clicking, die-hard patriot with passion in his soul. Like Tina, he fights assimilation and cultural dilution with every stubborn bone in his body but, unlike his wife, he suffers in silence. Tina airs her grievances and feels some sense of relief. He bottles things up because he thinks words are cheap.

★   ★   ★

'Everything seems to be going well,' Roulla says, standing beside her sister's chair, too excited to sit.

'Oh yes, very well,' Tina replies.

'What did you think of the food?'

'Very nice,' Tina replies diplomatically.

Yiayia, for whom diplomacy is a dirty word, tells Roulla that the vine leaves were 'too salty'.

'Mama!' Tina exclaims.

'I'm not one to hide behind my thumb nail,' Yiayia says, munching on an artichoke.

'Doesn't my Maria look beautiful?' Aunt Roulla says. 'And my son-in-law is a very

257

handsome boy, don't you think?'

'Oh yes, sister, and a good boy too. I stake my life on it. That boy is an open book, unlike some in our community. You will never guess what I have just heard from Kyria Pantelli.'

'What?'

Tina recounts the Andricos story, adding her usual embellishments, turning a seedy union into a tragic love story with all the drama and titillation of a South American soap opera.

'Rumour has it that the girl sought comfort in the arms of another man because Andricos has a sexual problem,' Tina says.

'What kind of problem?' Roulla asks.

'You know,' Tina replies, raising her eyebrows, offering no further explanation, throwing Andricos' sexual orientation into question in the mind of her sister.

My aunt makes the sign of the cross. 'Heavens above,' she says, casting a sideways glance at Andricos, 'you would never know by looking at him. He looks so normal. His poor mother must be pulling her hair out.'

I wonder how many more permutations the story will take before reaching its conclusion, what manner and severity of sexual problems will be attributed to the unfortunate Andricos.

'It makes you realize that some people have

problems far worse than our own,' Tina says.

'Some of us stubbornly create our own problems,' Yiayia adds. 'Where's your son tonight, Stavroulla?'

'I don't have a son,' Roulla replies, walking away.

★　★　★

Yiayia gave birth to a long-awaited son after three daughters. An easy labour was followed by forty days in bed, as tradition dictated, nursing her child. Her mother hung out sheets to shield her daughter's house from the evil eye. They called the baby Petros after his maternal grandfather and if family folklore is to be believed, he was a special child. Happy, bright and universally loved. Roulla looked after him when their mother worked, carrying him around on her seven-year-old hip. The two children were inseparable and shared a special bond.

On the day of his third birthday Petros went to sleep with a temperature, on the mattress he shared with Roulla and he never woke up. He died in his sister's arms, from an illness that was never diagnosed. Roulla was convinced she was cursed and blamed herself for her brother's death. At her own request she was subjected to an exorcism, performed in rudimentary fashion by placing her in the mouth of an unlit clay oven and smearing her forehead with an ash cross. Yiayia says her daughter was never quite the same after Petros' death and the trauma of the oven.

Yiayia told me she felt lucky to have lost only one child. Her neighbour gave birth to nine children and lost six of them. 'How did she cope?' I asked Yiayia, chilled by the thought of such gargantuan loss. 'Those were different times,' she replied, 'death was part of our everyday lives. Now we like to pretend it will never happen. The strength of our belief in God helped us through difficult situations.'

Cousin Peter was lost to us in less dramatic fashion. He told his mother over Sunday lunch two years ago that he planned to marry his English girlfriend, who 'by the way' was six months' pregnant. Aunt Roulla, stole the limelight when she fainted and fell head first into a plate of pastichio. Her husband tried to rouse her by throwing what he thought was water in her face but turned out to be zivania. It revived her instantly but stung her eyes and precipitated a fit of screaming. Peter tried to comfort his mother but she shook him off and sent him reeling across the room. She was bigger then and strong enough to fell a man with one blow. Roulla unleashed a stream of curses calling the girl a witch, a slut and a gold-digger. She said if the girl had slept with Peter then she was bound to have slept with others and how could her son know the child was his. Then she gave Peter an ultimatum. 'It's me or her,' she said resolutely. Peter packed a rucksack and walked out. 'I will never forgive him for doing this to me,' was my aunt's egocentric mantra, ignoring Yiayia's wise old adage that 'one can eat a big mouthful but should never say big words.'

Roulla was convinced her son would come home once he'd tasted hardship, that he would return to the fold and fulfil his mother's dreams of marrying a Greek girl and inheriting a fish and chip empire. Peter returned a month later with his girlfriend Melissa to try and heal the rift. His mother broke down, begging him to stay, offering Melissa a generous lump sum for leaving her son. Peter collected up the rest of his belongings and left for good. Roulla had a nervous breakdown. She shrank to half her normal size but became doubly intransigent. Would it were the other way round. She refuses to listen to reason and no one dares push her too far since she threatened to kill herself.

Yiayia saw it all before it happened, in her

daughter's cup. The 'rabbit', a symbol of fertility, below the 'bell' warning of an unplanned pregnancy. She interpreted the symbols and let her daughter draw her own conclusions. Roulla laughed. 'Such a thing is impossible,' she said, 'I've been sterilized.'

Peter rang his mother when the baby was born and told her she was a grandmother — a Yiayia. She said if he wanted to raise another man's child that was his problem not hers. When she heard the baby's name was Sarah she was outraged, saying her son didn't even have the decency to name the child after his mother. She calls her son's girlfriend '*i melissa*' — the bee — and says *i melissa* stung her son and poisoned his mind. So convinced is she that Melissa is some kind of curse she has taken to wearing a blue stone around her neck to ward off the evil eye. It has done her no good so far. Peter continues to favour the curse over his mother.

I wonder sometimes whether my aunt has a psychological disorder that requires clinical attention. She has disowned her son for no good reason and we have stood idly by and watched. Would we do the same if she decided to chop off a limb? Stand in the wings saying: 'It's her arm, she can do with it as she pleases.' I am as culpable as the rest of the family. Perhaps we are all too scared to admit the truth, to put it into words, in case they cart her away and lock her up, in case her disorder is hereditary, requiring us all to take a closer look at ourselves. I intimated as much to Tina, who said: 'Don't worry, your aunt doesn't have a psychological disorder, she's just mad.'

★ ★ ★

Kyria Pantelli's husband Yianni approaches our table, rubbing his pot belly, smoking a cigar.

'Sit down, Yianni,' Tony says, pulling out a chair.

'Friend, I wish I could,' Yianni replies, 'but I have important business.'

'What business do you have on a Sunday, at an engagement?'

'I have a call to make to a business associate. A call that could make me a very rich man.'

'So you're calling the bookies,' Tony says, to the man renowned for losing a small fortune at the betting office.

'Oh friend of little faith. The only gambling I do is in business.'

'Come on, sit down, Yianni, and tell us about your holiday in Cyprus,' Tony says.

'What a holiday that was,' Yianni replies,

sitting down, 'you won't believe what happened.'

'Tell us please,' Tony says, feigning seriousness, knowing he is about to be treated to the finest quality *lafazania* — ridiculous story. Yianni is a well-known *lafazanis* — a teller of absurd and fanciful stories, a cultural phenomenon. He is prone to exaggeration, loves to entertain, he is funny and a pathological liar. His stories are always told with a serious air, leaving you to wonder whether he actually believes what he's saying, and if he does, there are serious grounds for incarceration.

'Well,' begins Yianni, 'you know that I am the greatest fisherman in Cyprus. In my lifetime I have caught lorry loads of fish.'

Tony bites his lip. 'I didn't know that.'

'Oh yes, and I once swam underwater with my harpoon from Larnaca Marina to Paphos Bay nonstop. And I only came out of the water to smoke a cigar. I could have swum all the way to Greece with the energy I had that day.'

Unable to restrain a snigger, Andy starts to cough and Tony pats him hard on the back.

'Anyway, back to my holiday,' Yianni says, scanning the faces of his captive audience. 'I borrowed a fishing boat from a friend and sailed several miles out to sea. I dropped my nets and waited patiently, smoking a cigar and looking up at the stars. A few hours later, I tried pulling up my net but it wouldn't budge. I pulled the net again and it pulled back so hard it dragged the boat backwards. I thought: Holy Virgin I'm going to be killed. I crossed myself and prepared for battle. I grabbed hold of that net and pulled with all my might. I struggled with that net for three days and nights. On the third day I managed to pull it up and you won't believe what I caught.'

'What did you catch, Yianni?' Tina asks, completely taken in.

'Please keep this to yourselves,' he says, lowering his voice.

'Of course we will,' Tina replies.

He scans the vicinity, spots his wife some distance away and deems it safe to whisper: 'A mermaid.'

'My God!' Tina exclaims.

'Don't tell me,' Tony says, his eyes laughing.

'Oh yes,' Yianni continues, 'there she was lying in my net, all shiny and beautiful. I thought, Yianni, you've made it. Your picture will be in all the papers, your name will be published in the *Guinness Book of Records*. I grabbed my harpoon and pointed it at her, ready to fire, but she looked me straight in the eye and said: 'Yianni *mou*, don't shoot me.' And I looked into her sweet face and said to myself: Yianni, be a man for once in your life. And what did I do? I let her go and waved goodbye to a fortune.'

'You did the right thing,' Tony says, placing a reassuring hand on his friend's shoulder.

'I have to go now and make that call. *Adio*,' Yianni says, moving on to the adjacent table and his next preposterous story.

Tony shakes his head and smiles and calls Yianni a *lafazanis*.

'Don't ridicule the man,' Tina says, 'perhaps he speaks the truth.'

'And donkeys might fly,' her mother says.

★   ★   ★

Miriam sits down in the vacant seat beside Tina and listens avidly to a convoluted version of the Andricos story. Malcolm leans over the back of my chair, his breath smelling of whiskey and stale pipe tobacco. Dressed in tailored pin stripe he looks well bred and dashing.

'Anna, you look lovely this evening,' he says, squeezing into the seat next to mine, 'green is definitely your colour. And may I say all the ladies look ravishing this evening, including Mother.'

266

'*Ti lali o Englesos?*' Yiayia asks what the Englishman said.

'*Eben ise bola omorfi.*' 'He said you look beautiful,' I tell her, passing on Malcolm's compliment.

'*Lambron na ton gapsi.*' Yiayia wishes Malcolm were scorched by a burning flare.

Andy offers his chair to Athena, who greets me with unaccustomed exuberance.

Malcolm reaches out and grabs the arm of a passing waitress. 'Double whiskey, no ice, darling,' he says.

'Yes, sir,' replies the young woman, scribbling on a note pad.

Malcolm looks up into her face and tells hcr shc has beautiful eyes.

'Thank you,' the waitress replies, blushing, charmed by Malcolm's flattery.

'Won't you share a glass of wine with us, young lady?' he asks, his tone skirting the fine line between chivalry and lasciviousness.

'No thanks, we're not allowed to drink while we're working.'

'Rules are made to be broken,' says the bastion of silly rules.

The waitress turns to leave and Malcolm gently pats her on the bottom, before turning his attention to Miriam. No one sees the pat, no one sees the waitress glare at Malcolm and hurry away with fiery cheeks. I wonder if this is a case of the drink not the man behaving badly. What little respect I had for Malcolm is decimated in that second.

Miriam takes a cigarette out of her bag and lights up. Yiayia views her with a look of disapproval. Miriam draws the smoke into her mouth and exhales affectedly, the smoke travelling no further than her tonsils.

'She can't smoke properly,' Athena whispers contemptuously in my ear.

'Is no good to smoke,' Tina says to her sister.

'Don't be such a stick-in-the-mud, Constantina,' Malcolm replies. 'There's nothing wrong with Miriam smoking the occasional cigarette.'

Malcolm likes to be thought of as broad-minded, a liberal thinker, light years ahead of his parochial inlaws. Nothing could be further from the truth. In our house, Tina rules the roost; in theirs, Malcolm perpetuates the patriarchal household once run by his father. He expects his dinner at the stroke of six thirty, he eats in the absence of his children, then retires to his study without moving his dinner plate. He lets his daughter have boyfriends, that much is true, but derides and humiliates her if her school work is under par. He denies his children tactile love, to make them strong and independent.

Tonight the twins are at home with a babysitter, while other children their age skid across the dance floor having fun. Malcolm considers such an evening inappropriate for six-year-olds.

Kyria Pantelli hurries across to our table, for the rare opportunity to pry into Miriam's private life and harvest fresh gossip.

'*Ya sou*, Mirianthy, hello, Mr Malco,' she says.

'Kyria Pantelli, you look bountiful tonight,' Malcolm says with exaggerated charm.

'Oh thank you, Mr Malco. You a gendleman,' Kyria Pantelli replies appreciatively, her smile flaring already wide nostrils.

The waitress returns with Malcolm's drink perched on a silver tray. She leans down and tips the glass into his lap.

'I'm sorry, sir,' she says, her voice flat and unrepentant.

'Don't worry,' Malcolm replies magnanimously, 'accidents happen. Anyway, you did me a favour. Surrounded by such a bevy of beauties I needed cooling down.'

'Shall I fetch you another drink?' the waitress asks.

'Yes please. This time no ice, darling.'

★   ★   ★

I blot my face with loose powder, dulling the redness in my cheeks, soaking up a faint film of perspiration. Staring at too glaring a reflection in the toilet mirror, Athena reapplies her pale lipstick while ridiculing Maria's choice of dress, her heavy makeup, her poor choice of partner. Her comments induce a pang of guilt I am far too tipsy to dwell on.

'I'm desperate for a smoke,' she says, pulling me into a cubicle and extracting a cigarette from her handbag. She strikes a match and lights up, drawing the smoke deep into her lungs and exhaling an inch from my face. The sweet smell of burnt sulphur and the taste of wine in my mouth compel me to reach out for Athena's cigarette and put it to my mouth.

'I thought you didn't smoke?' she says.

'I started smoking when I was thirteen,' I reply, the words sounding silly and boastful as soon as they have left my lips, the vision of an ear bud bursting into flames flashing before my eyes.

'I didn't start till last year,' she says, suitably impressed.

★   ★   ★

We kick our feet up to the Sousta, arms linked, legs lagging behind the accelerating

270

pace of the music. I lead Athena and her uncoordinated feet around the dance floor, until the music comes to an abrupt halt and we are both breathless and doubled over with a stitch. Then we dance the Tango to a slow song, cheek to cheek, knocking into smooching couples with our outstretched arms, travelling the length of the dance floor and back again. Tina tries to catch my eye, to implore me to sit down and stop making a fool of myself, realizing that her plan to loosen me up has backfired.

Madame Mimi, queen of the East, shimmies onto the dance floor and we head back to our seats. The evening's exotic highlight looks far from Middle Eastern with her long straggly ginger hair and pale skin but she knows how to kick out her hips and possesses all the requisite folds of skin. She makes her way round the hall, snaking her arms upwards, jangling the bells at her ankles and wobbling her loose belly. She stops at our table and beckons Tony to dance with her. Threatened with decapitation by his wife if he stands up, Tony shakes his head apologetically.

Malcolm obliges, leaping out of his seat, clapping his hands over his head, a cigarette dangling from the corner of his mouth, mimicking Madame Mimi's movements with all the agility of a bamboo stick. He moves closer to the dancer and rubs up against her, to a frenzy of clapping and cheering. Madame Mimi backs away, waggling her finger angrily at Malcolm. Unperturbed he takes a ten-pound note from his pocket and presses it into the dancer's cleavage. Athena turns away. Miriam wears her usual look of amiable blankness, the look she has cultivated for all occasions.

'A bit too much flesh for my liking,' Malcolm says, falling breathlessly into his seat.

Three tables along the belly dancer stops at Kyria Pantelli's table and Yianni goes down on his fleshy knees in front of the dancer. She flicks the tassels of her red and gold costume in his face while he gyrates his shoulders and leans backwards until his bald head is touching the floor. Madame Mimi grabs the end of his patterned tie and pulls him to his feet. He dances like a poodle on a tight leash to a chorus of wolf whistles and dirty laughter. Finally, he slips a twenty-pound note into the dancer's waistband, using his teeth, before collapsing in an untidy heap.

★ ★ ★

Aphrodite, stark and dry, has worked miracles, displacing the crushing weight of my inhibitions with a light and heady feeling of happy intoxication. I have broken through Athena's wall of ice by drinking her under the table, quite literally. Too small and dainty to match me glass for glass she is slumped on a table leg, hidden from view by the hem of a starched white cloth. I stand before the head table and kiss the turkey-mother goodbye on her stubbly cheeks, feeling the sweaty wetness of her face against mine. Panicos squeezes my hand and a jumble of disconcerting thoughts race through my mind. The man who leans across the table to plant a prickly kiss on my cheek could so easily have been mine. The man who says *'gai sta thika sou'* — and to yours — wishing me future wedded bliss, will sleep with my cousin and father her children and grow old at her side.

'Goodnight, Maria, and good luck,' I say, choked by a sudden rush of emotion.

'Thanks,' she says, looking tired and anxious.

'What's wrong?' I ask. 'Are you OK?'

'I'm fine,' she replies, though her troubled eyes tell a different story. They speak of fear and resignation, of a sudden and premature coming of age.

'Ring me,' I say, 'tomorrow if you get a chance.'

A queue of guests forms behind me waiting to congratulate the newly betrothed. Panicos takes his fiancée by the hand and she breaks into a disingenuous smile, a worrying smile, a smile that amplifies the disquiet it tries to conceal. I make my way to the exit, my head full of unanswered questions, tears pricking the corners of my eyes.

'There's a fight outside,' shouts a man from the top of the stairs, setting off a stampede of guests up the staircase and into the foyer where a large crowd is gathered. A woman can be heard screaming abuse, there is muffled laughter and shouts of 'hit him harder'. I squeeze my way through the tight mass of bodies and stand beside Yiayia, to view Kyria Pantelli beating her husband over the head with her stiff, patent-leather handbag.

'You unworthy, ungrateful, filthy, immoral, short arse,' she shouts. 'If an egg fell from your behind it wouldn't break, but still you like to play the big man.'

'Please stop,' Yianni pleads, hunched over, covering his face.

'I won't stop until I've split your head open. How dare you make a fool of me? How dare you dance with any slut that shakes her arse in your direction?'

'*Agapi mou*' — my love — he says, not daring to look up, 'you know how much I love you.'

'Ah, SHAD AP,' she screams, raising her handbag and whacking him once more over the head.

Yiayia shakes her head and says, 'It's no wonder the poor man fantasizes about mermaids.'

9

Irene's Saturday-morning face is a sorry sight. In the cold light of day, without make-up, she looks pale and wizened. Her small, round, wrinkled face is reminiscent of a dehydrated pea, one that needs soaking in water and bicarbonate of soda to plump it up and smooth out its crumpled skin. She orders two bags of chips and rubs the bare arms that dangle like lank rope from her bony shoulders. Around her waist is coiled a beefy pumped-up arm, like an overfed snake in the process of digesting its dinner.

'Ow d'you get that?' Doreen asks, pointing to a faint bruise glinting below Irene's left eye.

'Tripped up,' Irene replies, wincing as she lightly touches her cheek.

'You should be more careful,' Doreen says, throwing Irene's companion a dirty look.

'Yeh, you should watch yourself,' agrees her boyfriend, patting her flat abdomen. 'That's my boy you got in there.'

'What! You're not pregnant again, are ye?' Doreen asks, shaking her head.

'Yeh,' Irene replies with a look of blank resignation.

'How you gonna manage, luv?'

'She's got me now,' the tattooed man says, 'she's not on her own.'

They eat their chips on a frosty forecourt and take turns dragging on a roll-up.

'Peraps this one'll stick around,' Doreen says, 'like a bad smell.'

When Irene starts smooching on the forecourt, a discussion ensues on the perils of promiscuity. Tina insists that an active sex life outside marriage can only lead to ruin and loss of reputation.

'Nowadays people they sex mad,' she says, screwing up her face in disgust.

'What's wrong with that?' Doreen replies, winking at me and grinning mischievously.

'When I was a gel, people they don av sex before marriage,' Tina says, 'and they don av derty minds.'

Tina lives in a fantasy of her own making, erasing details of the past inconsistent with her way of thinking, speaking with unquestionable conviction about issues of morality. With just a few well-chosen words I could annihilate the moral high ground beneath her feet. Our family history is littered with stories of philanderers, gamblers, wife batterers and wayward sisters. Tina's great uncle Stavri had a string of affairs with married women, paying the highest possible price for his

277

indiscretions. He embarked upon an unwise liaison with a buxom woman from a neighbouring village, a village whose menfolk were termed *macherovgaltes* — knife wielders — for whom pride and dignity was paramount, who were reputedly quick to draw a knife on any man looking salaciously at their wives. The husband of the woman in question worked on a cruise ship and spent many months away from home. Great Uncle Stavri paid regular visits to his mistress and made the mistake of boasting of his conquest. When the woman's husband returned home and learnt of the affair he beat his wife to a pulp, before going in search of Great Uncle Stavri and stabbing him fatally in the stomach.

★　★　★

'There's something I need to tell you,' Heather says, pulling me into the private nook beside the salad bar where Tina carries out her unlawful transactions with Dodgy Dave.

'What is it?' I ask, using a pair of prongs to pincer a daddy-long-legs flapping about in the onion rings, before flicking it over the counter.

'It's . . . not easy. I . . . don't know what

you'll think,' Heather says, her laboured sentence coinciding with the noisy electrocution of a fly on the high-voltage bars of the insectocutor.

'I hate that noise,' I say, as another ill-fated fly wings its way toward the blue fluorescent hue and is burnt to a frazzle.

'Anna, I have something to tell you,' she says more urgently, her eyes begging me to listen and understand.

'I know what it is,' I reply, having guessed from the moment she pulled me into the nook that she wanted to confess her feelings for my brother. 'It's about Andy, isn't it?'

'How did you know?'

'I'm not stupid, Heather. It was pretty obvious.'

'I thought you'd be upset,' she says, taking hold of my hand, looking intensely relieved.

'Well I'm not,' I reply, though in truth I don't know how I feel, 'it's the price I have to pay for having a handsome brother. Anyway, I'd better get back to the counter, mum's on her own and those two cretins have come in.'

Kevin and Darren tussle like stags on heat in front of the counter, shoving one another, throwing and deflecting punches, slapping each other across the face. Kevin is quicker and crueller than his friend, planting hard, resonating slaps on Darren's fleshy cheeks, punching him with force below the ribs, laughing at the sight of him doubled over. I shovel chips on to a tray, angry with my father for refusing to ban Kevin from the shop, for subjecting his children to a constant trickle of abuse. I turn my back to the counter and spoon the last of the gravy onto Kevin's chips.

'Eh, wha you doin?' Tina suddenly shouts out. 'Giv me back the knife.'

I turn around to see Kevin slashing the air above his head with the kebab knife.

'He grab it fro my hand,' Tina says angrily. 'Athonis, do samthin.'

'Still want a fight, mate?' Kevin says, jabbing Darren, brandishing the long knife like a foil.

Mrs Collins, sitting on the shop bench waiting for scampi, clutches her handbag close to her chest.

'OK, boys, you've had your fun, now hand back the knife,' Tony calls out from behind the chip pan.

Kevin stares at him defiantly. 'What you gonna do if I don't? Stab me with a chip fork?'

'I'm gonna phone the police.'

'Just fuckin try,' Kevin shouts, pointing the knife at Tony's head.

Mrs Collins runs out of the shop and

across the darkened precinct. Heather rushes into the back and returns with Andy, who doesn't stop to think, who moves too quickly to be caught by the belt strap. He sees the knife poised an inch from Tony's face and leaps across the counter with a yell that seems to emanate from the pit of his stomach. He falls onto Kevin, sending him crashing to the ground, the back of his head scraping the artex wall as he falls.

The knife drops out of his hand and slides across the tiled floor. Darren picks it up and jabs it feebly at Andy, who is so intent on strangling Kevin he fails to notice. Tony grabs the baseball bat, from beneath the range, and throws it like a javelin across the counter, hitting Darren in the chest, causing him to drop the knife and run out of the shop. Kevin splutters and chokes as he tries in vain to loosen Andy's grip on his throat.

'Stop it, you gonna kill im,' Tina screams while Heather covers her face with her hands.

Blood spurts from the gash on Kevin's head, smearing the tiled floor and Andy's white overall. Tony lifts the serving hatch and rushes towards his son, grabbing him by the back of his overall and trying to pull him off.

'LEAVE ME,' Andy bellows, glancing at Tony with wild, bloodshot, accusatory eyes.

Kevin tries to throw a feeble punch but

Andy slams his head down on the tiles and tightly grips his throat, making him gasp and choke. Tony grabs his son by the shoulders and with incredible strength pulls him off and throws him across the shop.

'Go to the back,' he commands, 'and, Anna, phone for an ambulance.'

Kevin is curled up in a foetal position on the floor, clutching his neck, his breathing barely discernible. Tony brusquely sits him up and leans him against the wall just as Mr Frank walks through the door, followed in by a breathless Mrs Collins, who points accusingly at Kevin.

'That's im,' she says, 'the one who threatened Tony with a knife.'

Mr Frank radios for an ambulance before turning to Tony. 'What happened here?' he asks.

'This boy had a fight with his mate,' Tony replies, 'the other one's run off.'

Tony's audacity shocks me, leaves me feeling cold and complicitous, and when Andy walks back into the shop front, still wearing his bloody overall, my legs threaten to give way.

Mr Frank calmly eyes him up. 'Go and clean yourself up, son,' he says. 'Someone might think you've been in a fight.'

Tony tells Andy to go home. Heather

follows him out and halfway across the forecourt they link hands, serving me a double portion of shock. Tina spots the hand holding too and makes the sign of the cross. Heaven help us, she says, if he's holding her hand it must be serious. And only then do I realize what my friend was really trying to tell me. She wasn't admitting to an innocent crush, as I had thought, but confessing to a full-blown affair, to carrying on with my brother behind my back. As I put my hands to my face I discern the faint smell of patchouli oil, passed from Heather's hands to mine, and wonder how I could have ignored the telltale signs and been so blind to the sordid truth.

★ ★ ★

'In the name of the Father, the Son and the Holy Ghost, may the evil leave this man,' Yiayia says, dabbing Andy's forehead with a vinegar-soaked cloth.

'Why don't you take two paracetamol?' Tina tells her son, dismissing her mother's unorthodox cure for a headache. Yiayia shuns conventional medicine whenever possible, taking carob syrup for constipation, camomile tea for stomach pain and a shot of commandaria for insomnia. She rubs zivania on aching limbs rather than medicated rub and clears a blocked nose with eucalyptus oil.

'This seems to be working,' Andy says, stretching out on the sofa.

'Like father, like son,' Tina says, chastising Andy for being hot headed while her husband is out in the garden disposing of the bloodstained overall. On his return to the living room, Tony slips into the terminology of deceit.

'It's his word against ours. We have to stick to our story . . . and, Tina, the fewer words the better . . . your mouth could get us into trouble.'

'I know when to hold my tongue,' Tina replies defensively.

'And someone has to speak to Heather, so that we all get our stories straight.'

'Speaking of that girl,' Tina says, suddenly unwilling to refer to her by name, 'I never expected a son of mine to be messing around with his sister's best friend.'

'I'm not messing around . . . we're getting engaged,' Andy replies, not daring to look at me, his words inducing a painful tightening in my gut.

'What joy,' Yiayia says. 'You see, daughter, St Fanourios has answered your wishes.'

'My wish should have been more specific.'

Tony kisses his son on a vinegary forehead.

'Aren't you going to congratulate me, Mum?' Andy asks.

'Constagulations,' Tina says, briefly lapsing into broken English, before denouncing her fate in florid Greek and castigating herself for giving her son too much freedom. She doesn't faint, there are no signs of a ruptured spleen, she doesn't even raise her voice. She merely rants for a while before asking if anyone wants a cup of tea. I had imagined scenes of high drama not instant resignation. The realization that my mother has teeth but no bite is exhilarating.

'I may have lost one child to this country but I won't lose a second. Don't even think of bringing home a marmalade-eater,' she says to me, with a hopeless flurry of bravado, as if reading my thoughts.

Andy reaches out for my hand. 'You don't mind about Heather, do you?' he asks, as our parents drift away, his eyes filling up.

'Was I the complication?' I ask.

'Yes, we didn't want to hurt you.'

'You haven't,' I lie, turning to leave, to hide my unhappiness at losing a brother and best friend in one fell swoop, at being deceived and lied to by my closest ally.

* * *

Yiayia makes *avgolemoni* with boiled chicken to calm our nerves and settle our stomachs. I battle with my hunger and avoid the soup, eating only toast. I have steered clear of chicken dishes since last Wednesday when our cockerel flew the coop, quite literally, according to Tina. She claims to have seen him fly past her bedroom window on his way to warmer climes. The miracle occurred the day we received a noise-abatement notice from the council warning of possible fines and prosecution.

Lunch is subdued. We sit on tenterhooks, waiting for a visit from the police. A knock at the door sends Andy dashing to his bedroom. Our visitor is Heather, carrying an enormous bunch of flowers for Tina, who has a self-professed preference for 'big things' and is quick to criticize miserly offerings. Heather has heard Tina often enough describing with enthusiasm and exaggerated hand gestures the fruit and vegetables that Tony buys in carton loads from the cattle market. 'The grapes they was as big as oranges' . . . 'the oranges they was as big as melons'.

I had decided during the course of a sleepless night that my friendship with Heather was a sham, that I had been used as a stepping stone to get to my brother. My mind was made up. I would wish my old friend good luck and turn my broad back on her. On to pastures new, I told myself, until I see her standing at the door, with big doleful eyes, looking like a pitiful creature on its way to the slaughter house, and my resolve begins to weaken. I keep my distance for a while, hovering in the wings and avoiding her gaze, until she corners me in the hallway, while Yiayia makes tea and Tina slices up her marble cake.

'What's wrong?' she asks. 'Why won't you speak to me?'

'You've come here for Andy not for me,' I blurt out acrimoniously.

'But . . . I thought . . . '

'I need time,' I say coldly, willing myself to be hard.

'Anna . . . don't shut me out . . . please,' she says, looking distraught, throwing me off my intended course with her tears. I am on the verge of stomping my way upstairs and leaving Heather to stew when a vision of Aunt Roulla and her obstinate face intrude on my consciousness, like an unwelcome alter ego. The thought of the unnecessary pain my stubborn aunt had caused her family makes me feel ashamed. I could bear my friend a grudge, I could ignore her for a while to make my point and then what? I would have to accept the situation and we would all have to get on with the business of loving one another. So I take a leaf out of Tina's book and decide right there and then to forgive, sooner rather than later. I take Heather in my arms, though the hurt is still tender and needs time to heal, and we shed tears for the end of one friendship and the start of another. A friendship between in-laws, with unspoken boundaries and familial etiquette.

We sit together on the sofa while Andy slouches in an armchair, leaving his fiancée-to-be at the mercy of our mother who talks about her son's favourite meals, the godliness of cleanliness and the importance of procreation. Yiayia comes into the room with her incense burner and wafts pungent smoke over Heather's head.

'I am very happy for you, Andreas,' she says, uttering her first full sentence in English.

'*Efharisto*, Yiayia,' — thank you, Yiayia — Heather replies in perfectly pronounced Greek.

'*Mila Eliniga touti?*' — does she speak Greek? — Yiayia enquires.

'*Oi akoma. Theli na mathi*,' — not yet but she wants to learn — Andy replies.

'*Tha tin matho eyo*' — I will teach her — Yiayia announces emphatically.

'*Bos tha katalavi e mia tin ali?*' — and how

will you understand each other? — Tina asks.

'Does your grandmother want to teach me Greek?' Heather asks, smiling at Yiayia.

'How did you understand what she said?' Andy queries. 'I've only taught you a couple of words.'

'I know lots of Greek words. I listen to your mum in the shop. I don't know what most of the words mean but I've heard your mum use them often enough. *Gilia, moutas, pissis* and *pezevengis*,' Heather says, reeling off a list of rude comments: big belly, big nose, miser and cuckold.

'Verigood, verigood,' Tina says, blushing. 'I think is beta you don learn Greek fro me.'

'*Bou emathen I koroutha tounta logia?*' — from whom did the girl learn these words? — Yiayia asks.

'*Bou tin gori sou*' — from your daughter — I reply.

'*Bravo*, Constantina,' Yiayia says, tutting.

'*Eh, to lachisto en kali me yloses*' — at least she's good at languages — Tina replies.

289

Yiayia's *Avgolemoni* Egg and Lemon Soup

Make a stock by boiling a whole chicken in a large saucepan of water flavoured with a chicken cube. Into eight cups of the stock pour one cup of short-grained rice and cook.

Beat three yolks together in a large bowl and add half a cup of lemon juice. When the rice is cooked slowly pour three cups of stock into the egg and lemon mixture, while beating continuously with a whisk. Pour the egg mixture into the saucepan. Add salt and pepper to taste and heat soup through before serving, with an accompaniment of boiled chicken.

10

Tina rushes into the living room, pulling off her flour-dusted apron, straightening the sofa cushions, licking her thumbs to run them along Tony's recalcitrant eyebrows.

'I heard someone knock on the door. I bet it's the police. Athonis, wake up. They've come to take our son away,' she says, voicing the fears that have kept her from sleeping. Tony stretches out on the black leather recliner like a languid cat, exuding garlic-scented breath as he yawns. Infected by Tina's panic, I drop my book and sit up stiffly, throwing off the embroidered blanket warming my legs. I listen as Tina unlocks the front door and ushers someone inside. To my relief I hear an enthusiastic Greek welcome in the hallway.

'Who could it be at this time of night on a Sunday?' Tony says, as Miriam walks into the room, looking like a film star incognito in her Chanel scarf and dark glasses.

'What a lovely surprise,' Tina says, taking Miriam's coat. 'Sit down. I'll make coffee and I will soon be taking *bishies* out of the oven.'

'Hello all,' Miriam says, distractedly scanning the room before asking, 'Where's Mama? I'd like to see her.'

'She normally goes to bed early on a Sunday. Let's go through to her flat and see.'

We find Yiayia sleeping in her armchair, her large feet propped up on the coffee table, an egg-shaped big toe poking through a hole in her dark tights. Tina switches off a blaring television and Yiayia slowly wakes up, looking around confusedly, waiting for the fog that clouds her sleepy eyes to clear.

'Mirianthy,' she says, 'what are you doing here and why are you wearing sunglasses in the dead of night?'

'I've come to see you, Mama,' Miriam replies, unable to muster her usual Avon Lady joviality.

Tina asks me to make three Greek coffees. *Ylyki* (sweet — two sugars) for Yiayia who believes she is too old to diet; *metrio* (medium — one sugar) for Tina who was ordered by her doctor to cut down her sugar intake and *sketo* (unsweetened) for the ever-abstemious Miriam. I load coffees, water and four *karydakia* onto a tray: Miriam's visit provides an excuse to indulge in a crunchy, clove-scented walnut, preserved in syrup. The Papamichael code of hospitality requires all guests be offered something sweet and calorific.

Miriam takes her coffee and turns down the walnut. Tina takes both, negating her efforts to cut down on sugar. I feel a tinge of guilt for doing to her what she does to me, for wafting temptation under her nose and expecting her to turn it down. Tina sips her coffee, saving the walnut for later, to keep from washing the sweet after-taste away.

'How's Athena?' Yiayia asks.

'She's fine,' Miriam replies.

'And the twins?'

'They're good boys. I'm very lucky.'

'And Malcolm?'

'This is good coffee,' Miriam says, looking into her cup.

'We have Bambo to thank for that,' Tina says, applauding the grocer and wishing upon him fine health and a long life.

A fortnight ago Bambo arrived with a vanload of prickly pears. The first of the season. Tina purchased three boxes. She gave half of them away, ate so many she was constipated for three days and left the rest to rot. Our garage is full of fruit at different stages of decay, from sponge-ball soft to green and furry. Tina's realm of fastidiousness ends at the door that leads from the kitchen into the garage, into a manifestation of Tina's alter ego, into a large messy drawer where my mother shoves unwanted items. She blames Tony for the mess, saying the garage is his domain as surely as the kitchen is hers, though it is Tina who fills it with rubbish and perishable foodstuffs. In Tony's real domain, the greenhouse, there is not a curly, crusty leaf or worm-holed vegetable in sight. Our garage has become a no man's land, beyond redemption, full of deceased electrical appliances, large hairy spiders and putrefying fruit.

Miriam upturns her cup in its saucer and slides it along the coffee table towards her mother.

'It's too late for a reading,' Yiayia says, explaining that evil spirits come out after 7 p.m., transmitting negative vibes, turning good news into bad.

'Please, Mama,' Miriam asks.

Yiayia, anxious to discover the cause of Miriam's mysterious visit, has a sudden change of heart. She takes hold of the cup and studies the inside. 'I see an elephant,' she says. 'The elephant symbolizes someone strong and loyal, a close friend or member of the family. Someone who will help you through a difficult situation. The elephant will not help unless you ask. And you must ask, Mirianthy.'

'What else do you see, Mama?'

'I see the aeroplane again. It has risen higher in your cup, until it is almost touching the rim. Your journey is imminent, Mirianthy. You will be travelling with your husband. Can you see him, here beside you boarding the plane, with his thick head of hair?'

Yiayia turns the cup towards us. Beside a sketchy aeroplane there are two grainy lines, resembling Lowry stick figures. One appears strangely feminine with breasts, the other taller, with a mop of straggly hair. Yiayia examines the inside of the cup once more, looking at something intently then seeming to dismiss it. Several minutes pass before she speaks again.

'I am sorry to say this, daughter, but I see the horns of a cuckold in your cup, large and clearly defined. To whom they belong I cannot say. Problems may arise in your marriage. A third party will be involved. You must keep your wits about you, Mirianthy.'

'It's too late for that now, Mama.'

'Why? What has happened, daughter?' Yiayia asks, putting down the cup.

'My husband has left me for another woman,' Miriam replies, taking off her glasses to reveal puffy, sleep-deprived eyes.

Tina throws her arms up in dramatic fashion and looks up at the ceiling.

'How could such a tragedy befall this family?' she says, beseeching God to help Miriam get her husband back. 'A woman is nothing without her husband,' she continues, 'and what will happen to those poor children?' Though she never liked Malcolm, it seems any husband, even a cheating one, is better than no husband at all. Her outburst does little to console Miriam, who starts sobbing.

'This is not a tragedy,' Yiayia says dispassionately. 'Mirianthy, dry your eyes.'

'When a man is faced with temptation, what can he do but take it? Men are weak, Mirianthy,' Tina says sympathetically before resorting to crude interrogation. 'Was it the slut from across the road?'

'No,' Miriam replies, stifling her tears, 'someone worse, much worse. My neighbour's daughter. A girl not much older than my Athena, a girl of only nineteen.'

'Like mother, like daughter,' Tina says, viciously.

Yiayia seethes silently. She knows when not to speak, unlike Tina who talks arbitrarily about the negative influence of television, Irene's unwanted pregnancy and the erosion of family values. She blames fate, the other woman, even God, seeming to absolve Malcolm of any responsibility.

'Don't worry, Mirianthy,' she continues, 'he'll come back.'

'Do you want him back?' her mother asks.

'Yes,' Miriam replies, extracting a crumpled tissue from her sleeve. 'Mama, you have to help me.'

I am shocked by the needy tone of Miriam's voice and her readiness to accept adultery. And I realize then, that in spite of appearances, Miriam is far more traditional than her sister. Tina, who preaches archaic values, would be mercilessly unforgiving if her own husband were to stray.

'Leave things to me and don't worry. Your husband will be back to you within a fortnight,' Yiayia says, making what appears to be an impossible promise to an unreasonable request. Miriam seems reassured. She gets up, thanks her mother and turns to leave, followed out by Tina.

I stay behind to wash up. Yiayia remains seated, muttering curses under her breath, releasing the frustration she was unable to show her daughter. I sit on the floor, close to her feet, and wait for a response to the news. She has a look of distracted intensity about her, like a mathematician mentally unscrambling a problem. Then suddenly, she sits up in her chair as if, eureka, she has hit upon a solution.

'I need a favour,' she says.

'Anything you want, Yiayia.'

'I want you to bring me something of Malcolm's.'

'Like what?' I ask, not daring to question why.

'Something that was once attached to Malcolm's body: a nail, some hair, a tooth, an eyelash, anything like that.'

'But how?' I ask, suddenly regretting my willingness to help.

'You're a clever girl. You will find a way.'

★ ★ ★

Kevin, hospitalized for several days, has mysteriously refused to name his attacker. I have been waiting for the axe to drop, for my brother to be picked up, hand-cuffed and carted away. I have suffered palpitations and sleepless nights, whereas Tony has taken the situation calmly in his stride, as if giving false evidence and perverting the course of justice are second nature. A troublesome life has shaped the man he is today, unflappable and stalwart in a crisis. Tony believes 'every difficulty is for the good' and 'every good brings with it difficulties'.

Tina, who can only keep a secret when it suits her, has disclosed stories about Tony we were never meant to know, cautionary tales meant to steer her son clear of the headstrong path trodden by his father. Her anecdotes only serve to heighten our reverence for a man who tackles problems head on, who has felled a man twice his height with a running jump, who has crushed the fingers of an aggressor in his strong right hand, who would stop short of nothing to protect his family.

Tony bought his first fish and chip shop in the late 1960s, in a rundown part of the city. He took out a hefty loan to start his business and was determined to make it a success. He worked alongside his wife, while Andy and I were left to our own devices in the flat upstairs. I was a lazy baby, content to lie in my cot all day and watch my older brother ransack the flat, emptying cupboards, pulling off wallpaper, shouting intermittently for Tina, who would rush upstairs between customers to console, feed and change her children. Before the evening shift she would rustle up a home-cooked meal and tidy the flat. Only after closing time was she able to prop up her feet to relieve the throb of varicose veins.

Late one Friday night, two men walked into the shop and demanded protection money. Tony refused to hand his hard-earned cash over the counter, claiming the night had been slow. 'Your papa had money in the till,' Tina said, 'I begged him to hand it over but he wouldn't listen.' They left empty handed, warning of violent repercussions. Tony borrowed a handgun from a friend and kept it beneath the counter, loaded and ready for any eventuality. The following Friday the men returned and demanded a double payment. Tony quickly bundled his wife into the storeroom and told her to stay put, before refusing once again to pay up. Tina, who watched proceedings through the keyhole, saw one of the men take out a flick knife and walk towards the door of the flat, threatening to kill the two children sleeping upstairs. She heard her husband threaten to shoot if he took one more step and when he did, Tony fired a bullet into his shoulder. My mother felt a sense of unreality as she watched Tony move quickly towards the second man, put the barrel of the gun in his ear and threaten to blow his brains out if he came back. Then he wiped the gun free of fingerprints and lay it beside the injured man. At this point the accomplice fled, leaving a pool of urine where he had stood. Tony telephoned the police and when they arrived he told them with steely eyes that the injured man had been shot by his friend during an altercation.

The victim pointed the finger of blame at

Tony, who was promptly charged with attempted murder. The local business community clubbed together to pay for Tony's defence, as a thank you for standing up against the protection racketeers. A highflying barrister secured a case dismissed on lack of evidence and the police gave Tony a pat on the back, since the wounded man was wanted for a string of robberies. The shooting did little for business. Customers feared a revenge attack and avoided the shop. Tony took a second job, working in a restaurant, to support his family while Tina was left alone to run the shop and look after two small children. She was petrified at night, when darkness fell and she could barely see beyond the window. Tony acquired the baseball bat he still keeps behind the counter, and taught his wife how to swing for a man's head. 'What else could we do?' Tina says. 'Times were hard and we had no one to turn to.' For several weeks Tony slept downstairs, on the floor behind the range, with a gun at his side, to protect his family and his property.

★ ★ ★

Two pints of red top and a tub of fresh cream sit on the Jameson front step. Tina, anxious to see her sister, walks briskly to the door, cursing the spongy gravel underfoot for impeding the speed of her journey. She picks up the milk and cream, and rings the bell. Miriam answers in saggy jogging bottoms and a shapeless jumper, blinking into daylight. Her hair, left to dry naturally, falls in loose ringlets, softening the angular shape of her face, making her look less formulaic in appearance.

'Come in. Sorry I look such a mess,' she says.

The hallway is littered with toys and discarded children's clothes. Tina steps over the toys and picks up the clothes, draping them over her shoulder, shaking her head disapprovingly.

'What's been going on in here?' she asks. 'And where are the twins?'

'They're visiting friends. I needed some peace today,' Miriam replies. 'Malcolm's moved out.'

Tina turns to her husband. 'Athonis, go and have a lie down in the living room.' Accustomed to a siesta before his evening shift, Tony happily obliges.

'Where's Athena?' I ask.

'In her bedroom as usual,' Miriam replies. 'You can go up if you like.'

I climb the claustrophobic stairwell that leads to Athena's bedroom, hoping I can offer some words of comfort, bolstered by the unaccustomed warmth of our recent encounter. I knock gently on the door and wait.

'Go away,' she says.

'It's me,' I reply, 'Anna.'

After a few seconds, just as I turn my back to leave, she answers with an icy, 'Come in.'

I walk into her room and find she has company. Gordon is sitting beside her on the bed, flicking his floppy fringe from his eyes. Athena views me with her customary dispassion and I know from that look that nothing between us has changed. Only wine, music and necessity will ever connect us.

'How are you?' I ask, for want of something better to say.

'Fine,' she says, throwing me a withering look. 'I wish people would stop asking.'

Her fractious tone leaves me feeling cold, unsympathetic and a little embarrassed in the presence of Gordon. I head for the wicker chair, planning to stay only a few cursory minutes. Gordon lights two cigarettes and hands one to Athena. She gets up and smokes in moody silence beside her open bedroom window. And though I know she must be hurting I am unable to muster the necessary compassion and courage required to help her. She is like a bad-tempered patient, prickly and hostile, for whom the whole world is an enemy.

'My eye, my eye, there's something wrong with my eye,' she screams all of a sudden, causing Gordon to panic and flap his arms around. Athena flicks her cigarette out of the window and blinks frenziedly. I get up and hurriedly pull up her right eyelid. Drowning in the corner of her waterlogged tear duct is a crumpled black insect.

'It's a tiny fly,' I tell her.

'Ugh, get it out, it hurts, I can't see,' she cries petulantly, her high-pitched whine and contorted look of agony making her scarily reminiscent of Roulla. I swipe at the insect with my little finger and flick it away, struck by the sudden realization that Athena, with her predisposition for melodrama and exaggeration, is ironically more Greek than she could ever imagine.

'You poor thing,' Gordon says, his tone faintly patronizing, moving closer to Athena to rock her like a baby in his arms. If he tried to hold me like that I would be tempted to shake him off and trample him underfoot.

I leave the couple to console one another and head for the bathroom to carry out my bidding, quietly descending the stairwell and creeping through the house like a thief. The bathroom is grimy and neglected, greying flannels hang over the side of the bath giving off a musty scent. I open a pine cabinet and rummage through the crusty jars and sticky tubes that cram the shelves. Behind a jar of cold cream, I find a small black comb clogged with Malcolm's thick, brown hair. As I slip the comb into my pocket, someone knocks on the door and tries the handle.

'Just a minute,' I call out, my heart pounding as I flush the toilet and run the water to legitimize my visit to the bathroom, before opening the door.

Gordon is standing outside.

'She's a real drama queen your cousin,' he says, walking past me into the bathroom. His comment, in my ears, sounds traitorous.

★ ★ ★

Tony is snoring gently in the living room. Swamped by Malcolm's expansive leather armchair, he looks like a small boy in an oversized seat. The room whiffs vaguely of fried foods, old spice and garlic. Yesterday Tina made *tsakistes* — crushed green olives with garlic chunks, lemon and coriander seeds. Tony ate the olives with relish, crunched on the garlic and dipped his bread in the oil. Today, we are all paying the price. *'Oofou, vromozoloas'* — poof, you reek

— Tina keeps saying to her husband, screwing up her nose, while he smiles and intermittently regurgitates, polluting his vicinity.

I sit in the living room and wait, the stolen comb pressing into my side. I hear the high-pitched lilt of Tina's voice emanating from the kitchen, monopolizing the verbal exchange. I hear the clatter of dishes, the running of water and suspect that Tina is, without invitation, cleaning the kitchen as she speaks. Half an hour later the two women come into the living room, Miriam visibly rejuvenated. Tina's aptitude for banal chatter has proved a tonic.

'*Oofou*, I will open a window,' Tina says, 'my husband reeks. Last night in bed I could hardly breath. It's a wonder I'm still alive.'

'Leave the poor man alone,' Miriam says.

'Come on, sleeping beauty,' Tina calls out, 'it's time to wake up.'

Tony is easy to rouse. He is used to catnaps.

'What are you making with the fresh cream?' Tina asks her sister.

'Malcolm and I always shared an Irish coffee on Saturday night,' Miriam replies with a faraway look in her eye.

'You should make a raspberry pavlova to cheer yourself up,' Tina says, offering her own brand of food-centred marriage guidance, her super-sweet cure for a broken heart. She offers her sister tips on making the perfect meringue by adding vinegar to the egg white mixture and cooking it in a low oven. Tony's stomach gurgles as she speaks, reminding Tina that we haven't eaten since breakfast.

'We better get home,' she says, 'or we won't have time to eat before we go back to work.'

We linger for a while in the doorway, Miriam physically blocking the exit, seemingly reluctant to be left alone.

'Tomorrow, you must come for lunch,' Tina says.

'No thanks,' Miriam replies. 'I haven't got much of an appetite at the moment.'

'Well the children have to eat. I will send Tony over with a roast. Don't bother cooking.'

Athena runs downstairs wearing a long coat and heavy boots.

'*Athena mou*,' Tina says, opening wide her arms, 'cam hea, darli,' her voice loud and gushing. Athena allows herself to be squeezed, her arms hanging unreceptively at her sides. Gordon follows her down, carrying a khaki rucksack. Tina looks him up and down suspiciously.

'This is Athena's friend, Gordon,' Miriam says, avoiding the word 'boyfriend' in the presence of her sister.

Gordon swipes at his fringe and smiles.

'Mummy,' Athena says, squeezing past her aunt, 'I won't be coming home tonight.'

'Athena, I could do with some company this evening,' Miriam says.

Athena grabs Gordon's hand and walks out, ignoring Miriam's look of desperation and her aunt's open mouth.

★   ★   ★

Tina is uncharacteristically quiet on our journey back to the shop. Under normal circumstances she would be disclosing the minutiae of her conversation with Miriam.

'All right, Anna *mou*?' she says, turning to look at me.

I know as clearly as if a thought bubble were floating above her head that she is wondering how a daughter could abandon a mother in her hour of need. She is speculating on the identity of the marmalade-eater and thinking that maybe her own daughter is not so bad after all. Today she will treat me with care. Tomorrow she will forget how lucky she is and revert to bemoaning her fate and feeling hard done by. She will conclude that Gordon is a paternal relative and blame Athena's actions on the negative influence of a broken home. And nothing will have changed in Tina's intransigent mind.

★　★　★

Mrs Collins listens avidly to Tina's account of Maria's new life. Told in Tina's inimitable style, Maria's engagement has become a tale of love, 'plenty money' and enviable happiness. In reality Maria has moved in with her in-laws and works five nights a week behind a counter. In Tina's romanticized version of reality 'the love-beds they always toogetha' and 'her mather-in-law she treat her like e queen'. Mrs Collins, whose life is pitifully lacking in romance, swallows Tina's rhetoric as if it were a spoonful of thick Greek honey. Tina is an endless source of vicarious pleasure.

'She's a very lucky girl,' Mrs Collins says as she waits at the front of a queue for chips.

'People is make they own lack,' Tina replies, looking across at me.

Irene walks through the shop door and pushes her way to the counter.

'Oi, there's a queue,' shouts a man from the back of the shop.

'I aven't come to eat,' she replies, throwing him a withering look before turning to Tina.

'Where's your son?' she snarls.

'Is no your business where is my san.'

'Tell im I wanna word.'

'You ged oud. The chips is ready and you holdin up my queue.'

A large man standing behind Irene tells her to move aside and let him order his tea.

'I'm not movin till I've seen your son,' Irene says, crossing her arms defiantly.

'What's the problem?' Tony asks, approaching the counter.

'That's the bloody problem,' Irene shouts, spying Andy and trying to catapult herself across the counter. The large man catches her in mid flight and holds her aloft while her arms and legs flail and she hurls abuse. 'You little bastard, you nearly killed my son . . . you should be locked up . . . '

Irene grabs the ill-fated onion jar and flings it across the counter. It smashes on the tiled floor, spraying our legs with glass and vinegar. I examine Tina's varicose legs for signs of injury and see only vinegar-splattered tights.

'Get out or I'll phone the police,' Tony shouts.

'You do that so I can tell em what really appened.'

The large man puts Irene down and tells her to stop shouting.

'I aven't finished yet,' she says, turning with a wild glare to face the queue. 'Did you lot 'ear what I said? That bastard nearly killed my Kevin and I ain't gonna line 'is pockets with my money no more. How d'you think he bought that big car parked outside, eh? With our money. Our money. This lot, think they can come to our country and behave like they own the place . . . '

On and on she goes, spouting venom, unburdening her soul while I fight the urge to grab a handful of her frizzy hair and fling her out of the door like a rag doll. I want to protect my parents from abuse, though I can tell from the disinterested look on their faces that Irene's words make as much impression as a snowflake falling on a whitewashed peak. I feel sick and humiliated, before me a sea of faces searching mine for a reaction. Among the sniggers and shouts of 'shut up, Irene' there are those who listen and nod their heads in agreement. I know their faces. I've been serving them for years, week in week out, with a 'yes please sir' and 'thank you madam'.

'I told you to calm down,' the customer beside her says.

She tells him to 'fuck off' and continues her tirade, until the hungry man, waiting to be fed, picks her up by the waist, carries her quickly outside and drops her on the forecourt. She shouts abuse through the window for a while before adjusting her skirt and walking away.

'Don't take no notice of her, duck,' the man says to Tina, before ordering fish and an extra large portion of chips.

'She's the one who needs lockin up,' Mrs Collins says, quick to offer support.

I feel a sharp pain in my ankle and look down to see blood pouring from the leg of my jeans. I go into the kitchen and remove a small shard of glass lodged above my anklebone, stemming the flow of blood with toilet roll shoved into my sock. I have learnt from example to suffer physical ailments with the minimum of fuss. Yiayia seldom complains about aches and pains and rarely takes to her bed, though she suffers from migraines and dizzy spells.

★　★　★

'No wander that boy he's a trable maker with a mather lie tha,' Tina says, dousing the floor with pine-scented disinfectant.

'I dint know Kevin was er son,' Doreen says. 'I've never seen 'em together.'

'Mr Frank she say that boy he av trable at home,' Tina says.

'What kind of trouble?'

'Domestos violas,' Tina replies, turning a

drama into a bottle of bleach.

'What, luv?'

'Tha boy, they say, he beat ap his matha.'

'So that's why she's got bruises,' Doreen says, 'poor cow.'

★ ★ ★

Somehow, I get through the night without crying, internalizing my anger, compressing it into a small hard ball that sits heavily in my grinding stomach. Tina is unaffected. The shop holds no surprises or disappointments. She has seen and heard it all before. She blames the night's events on a bottle of demonized pickled onions, crossing herself in rapid succession, suggesting Irene's outburst was an act of God designed to rid the shop of a jar possessed. I serve the pub rush on autopilot, avoiding eye contact, fearing any further confrontation. I am a pressure valve ready to blow, straddling belligerence and tears.

At closing time the tattooed man walks into the shop, trailing dirty footprints across the freshly mopped floor. Irene follows him in, her face flushed with drink.

'You ged oud of my shop,' Tina shouts from behind the counter, waving the chip scoop angrily.

'We aven't come to make trouble,' Irene's boyfriend says, 'we've come to talk.'

'We've got nothing to talk about,' Tony replies firmly.

'Peraps you should hear us out. We wanna help your son, don't we, Irene? Lucky for you, Kevin dunt wanna press charges. The boy dunt wanna lose face on the estate. He only told his mum today who beat im up. So your lad's off the hook, so to speak. He could av been locked up, you know. What d'you get for GBH these days . . . five years? His mum ere thinks he should tell the police what really appened, that your lad near on squeezed the life out of him. Personally speakin I dunt think that's such a good idea. Now, if you were to give that poor boy something for his sufferin . . . you know compensation of sorts . . . God knows you can afford it . . . then everyone'd be appy and the police wount need to know a thing.'

'Got any chips left?' Irene asks.

'No,' replies Tina angrily, 'and you both ban from my shop.'

'Steady on, luv,' says the tattooed man, his voice turning nasty. 'If you dunt want trouble then you'd better think seriously bout what I just said. I'll be back in an hour for your reply. And dunt forget I'm only trying to elp your lad.'

When they're halfway across the precinct Tina calls Irene a *'putana'*, vents her fury on the mop and bucket and tells Tony to pay them off.

'I won't be blackmailed,' Tony replies.

'And I won't risk my son going to prison.'

'I have my principles.'

'I saw your principles in action with the pickled onions,' Tina replies, 'and I saw my son's black eye.'

'How much shall we give them?'

'Whatever they want. Money means nothing to me, not where my children are concerned. I would gladly sell my house and live in a barn to protect them.'

★ ★ ★

Irene's boyfriend returns an hour later. Tony lifts the serving hatch, takes him through to the kitchen and hands him the day's takings in a plastic bag, bearing the slogan 'Fish is Fun'. If such a thing were true I would be the happiest soul alive, since ten stone of the slimy stuff passes through my hands every week. The tattooed man takes the money without complaint and winks at me on his way out.

'We had a lucky escape,' Tina says.

'You're right,' Tony replies. 'I was prepared

to give him a lot more.'

'Don't say anything to your brother about this,' Tina says, taking off her overall. 'I don't want any more trouble.'

And with that she quickly changes the subject, reminding Tony that she needs a box of artichokes from the market, to cook with broad beans.

'Come on,' she says, 'let's go home. I need a cup of tea.'

In spite of my festering anger I feel a surge of pride for my mother, for the way she can quickly cast off low spirits like a dog shaking water from its coat. For her absolute refusal to nurture a bad mood and infect her husband and children with negativity.

★   ★   ★

Yiayia listens with a troubled expression to my toned-down version of the night's events. Tomorrow morning she will hear the unabridged version from Tina, complete with bad language and racist overtones. Tina is refreshingly candid when conversing with her mother. She talks without restraint about a whole manner of subjects. Her mild incontinence and infrequent bowel movements are regular topics of conversation. On clearing her bowels after an extended bout of

318

constipation Tina runs to her mother with the good news and Yiayia shares in the joy of her daughter's relief.

'I hear you went to Mirianthy's today. Have you brought me the item I requested?' Yiayia asks.

I remove the comb from my pocket and hand it to her, feeling an inexplicable sense of achievement.

'Lock the door,' she says, rising with surprising agility from her seat to make her way to the kitchen. She opens a cupboard, takes out a flat-bottomed saucepan called a *sagi* and places it on the cooker. Beside it on the Formica counter she sits the comb, a pot of salt, a glass of water, a wooden spoon and a slice of white bread. I take a seat at the kitchen table and watch as she takes a crumpled book from the side pocket of her handbag, opens it and runs her finger along a spiral of coloured text, scrawled on a dog-eared page. Lighting the gas, she begins a rhythmic chant while breaking the bread into small pieces and throwing it into the *sagi*. After adding a pinch of salt, Yiayia dips her fingers into the glass and flicks water into a steaming pan that hisses and spits. Carefully, she pulls individual strands of hair from the teeth of the comb and adds them to the smouldering contents of the *sagi*, filling the

319

room with a pungent, smoky smell. She pours water into the pan and mixes her concoction with the wooden spoon, before turning off the heat to lift up the *sagi* by its handles and carry it on a slow journey around the kitchen table, softly reciting her incantation as she goes. I watch in silence, wondering what strange brew she is cooking up, fearful for my grandmother's sanity. When she has circled the table three times, Yiayia returns the *sagi* to the cooker, makes two cups of tea and settles down in the seat next to mine.

'Yiayia, what were you doing?' I ask.

'I was helping my daughter,' she replies, feeling no need for further explanation.

'How?'

'In a way that my husband would not approve of. But what could I do? Circum-stances have forced me to break a promise.'

'What promise?'

'There are things I haven't told you, Anna, about my life,' she says, embarking on the most extraordinary of stories, about her reputation in the village for curing more than physical ills. Yiayia could rid people of their fears, banish evil spirits and resolve matters of the heart. Her father before her had powers infinitely greater than her own and made a living as a healer and a clairvoyant. Known simply as '*O Magos*' — the Magus — he was

highly respected and immensely feared, us_
his power for both good and bad deec
employing highly unorthodox methods t_
cure a gamut of physical and psychological
ailments. He would rid a child of evil spirits
by running water through a sieve over the
skull of a dog and alleviate jaundice by
concocting a medicine from the root of the
mandragora plant, silk thread and the urine
of the sufferer collected over forty days.

Great grandfather Petros believed Yiayia,
his first born, had inherited his powers and
taught her all he knew. When he died, the
book of incantations, scrawled with curious
symbols and letters, became hers. Many
people sought her help each week for
problems ranging from infertility to tooth-
ache, showing their appreciation with gifts,
mostly of food. When other families lived on
bread and olives Yiayia always had a
well-stocked larder. Until, that is, her
husband forbade her from continuing her
craft, saying it was evil and against the
teachings of the Greek Orthodox Church.
She continued reading coffee cups but ceased
all other practices.

'No one has more faith in God than I. It
was God himself that gave me my gift. These
are not spells,' she says, flicking through the
pages of her book, 'but powerful blessings.

ᵗe one I used today is particularly ᵖowerful.'

'What did you do, Yiayia?'

'Let me explain to you, Anna,' she says. 'When a couple separates, in most cases, both sides must bear some of the blame. Whatever my feelings are for Malcolm, I cannot hold him entirely responsible for the break-up of his marriage. And I must respect my daughter's wish to have her husband back. A man in his forties who leaves his wife to live with a young girl is usually searching for his youth. Malcolm thinks this girl can give him back the years he has lost.'

'And so?'

'And a man of Malcolm's age is likely to sail back to the safety of his port, to the sanctuary of his wife, if problems arise in the new relationship. A rusty ship cannot withstand the rigours of a stormy sea. Sooner or later such a problem will present itself. By then it may be too late. The ship may have sunk. It is essential to strike while the iron is hot, to create a problem while the family can still be salvaged.'

'What kind of problem?'

'A problem that shakes him to the core, that will throw into question his sexual prowess. Tonight's blessing will make Malcolm impotent,' Yiayia says, casually. 'When he returns to port, I shall give him back his manhood.'

I don't know whether to laugh or run for a clove of garlic. I would like to dismiss my grandmother as nothing but a well-meaning crank, but I can't, because part of me believes her far-fetched claim.

'My daughters have never shown an interest in my craft;' Yiayia continues, 'until now I thought my father's legacy would die with me. Anna, I want to teach you all I know and leave this book to you when I die.'

Feeling spooked and slightly exhilarated, I leave the granny flat and make my way to bed.

★   ★   ★

Yiayia is bent over a cardboard box, pulling out old clothes and flinging them over her shoulder, singing a plaintive song about Pentadaktylos, a mountain range under occupation with five indented peaks like the fingers of a hand. A poignant symbol of partition, said to have been shaped by the Byzantine hero Dighenis Akritas. '*Vouno mou Pentadaktyle, me to blati to cheri, pikros vorias bou fisise, kai to kako echi feri . . .* ' A lilting lament, a mournful testimony of loss, an expression of hope.

My five-fingered Mountain
With your wide hand
A bitter north wind blew
And brought misfortune

My five-fingered Mountain
Footprint of Akritas
The star will shine one night
Oh, one night
And with this signal triumph

She sings the simple verses over and over again, in melancholy tones, stopping only when she finds a small glass salt shaker among the jumble. Today is the anniversary of the invasion and Yiayia tells me she is feeling 'heavy-hearted'. Today she will go to church, polish Papou's makeshift altar and sit in a stupor, milling over the events of 20 July 1974. A large part of Yiayia's calendar year is taken up in remembrance of something or other. Saints' days, Independence Day, memorials. Each of these days requires preparation of some sort: the making of *kolifa*, the baking of *antithero*, a celebratory meal, the burning of incense, the execution of antiquated rituals.

On the fifth of January, the day before Epiphany, Yiayia makes syrup-coated dough balls called *lokoumades*. She mixes up a batter with yeast, flour, water and ma: potato, gathers it on a spoon and drops it i. boiling fat. When the dough balls are gold brown she spoons them out and dips them i. syrup. No one is allowed to eat them until she has carried a bowl full outside and attempted to fling them onto the roof where mischievous spirits called *kalikantzari* apparently wait to satiate their appetites and depart. Yiayia doesn't have the strength to throw the dough balls much higher than Tina's bedroom window ledge, so Andy helps her out with a makeshift catapult. He takes great pleasure in littering the roof with *lokoumades*, while Mrs P stands behind her net curtains seething. When she's finished with our roof, Yiayia always throws a good handful over the garden fence in an effort to rid the neighbouring vicinity of demons, an act of good will that only serves to demonize the occupants of number 66, inspiring several pages of poisonous prose. The sweet-toothed Mrs Davis from number 62 always comes round on the fifth of January to collect a plate full of *lokoumades* for the family and soak up the festive atmosphere. 'I've come for my Cypriot doughnuts,' she always says, waving her Tupperware container in the air.

Yiayia adheres religiously to the food-centred rituals leading up to Easter, which t with *Tsiknopempti*, or Smelly Thursday, : name relating to the smell of meat aditionally cooked on that day. Continuing he theme there is *kreatofagou*, or meat-eating Sunday, a day when Yiayia lights the barbecue come rain or shine to char grill lamb, pork, chicken and *loukanika* (spicy sausages). The following week is *Tirini*, or Dairy Sunday, when Yiayia confines her own diet to eggs, cheese and dairy products. The eating fest comes to an abrupt end on *Kathara Deftera*, or Green Monday, fifty days before Easter, a meat-free day when, thanks to Bambo and his well-stocked van, we dine on every conceivable fruit and vegetable. Yiayia fasts stringently for the next fifty days, while the rest of us resume our usual diet until Easter week when we eat vegetarian style with a Tina twist. This should be a period of dietary hardship, a cleansing of one's body and soul, yet Tina fills the house with an infinite number of vegetarian delicacies lest we go hungry or, even worse, lose a few pounds. These include *kolokopittes* — pastry shells filled with pumpkin, cracked wheat and raisins; *tahinopittes* — sweet pastries made with tahini; *eliopittes* — olive bread; taramasalata and tahini.

On Holy Saturday Yiayia makes *paxamadi* (aromatic bread) and *flaounes* (pastries filled

with eggs, halloumi and cheese). When A[...]
was younger she used to pick him up and s[...]
'as I raise this boy, may my pastries rise too[...]
Our fast is broken after midnight mass when[...]
we return home from church in the early
hours of Sunday morning deliriously hungry,
ready to wolf down boiled chicken, *avgolemoni* soup, Yiayia's breads and pastries and
the odd Mars Bar as compensation for a week
of supposed abstinence.

Yiayia rotates the salt shaker in her large
fingers. 'There were so many things I could
have taken, yet I chose this,' she says of the
dated, glass artefact that is more poignant a
reminder than it might appear of the
cataclysmic day her life was turned upside
down.

She talks about the years and months that
led up to the invasion with bitterness and
anger. Of how she listened with a growing
sense of doom to the daily news reports about
the widening rift and escalating violence
between Greek and Turkish Cypriots. Of how
the bitter political struggle between the right
and left wing intensified, setting brother
against brother and father against son. Coffee
houses became dens of political segregation
and heated debate. Archbishop Makarios, the
island's president, was accused by the right
wing of burying the cause of *enosis* — union

h Greece — and a new underground ganization called EOKA B was formed. General George Grivas ('Dighenis'), reportedly disguised as a priest, returned to Cyprus to lead the anti-Makarios forces. There were clashes between the rebels and security forces and several assassination attempts were made against the nation's leader. The Greek military Government financed and encouraged the rebels in their efforts to overthrow the Government.

On the morning of 15 July 1974, my grandparents listened with alarm to a radio broadcast proclaiming the overthrow of Makarios. The presidential palace had been stormed by anti-Government troops and Makarios had allegedly been killed. Anyone who put up resistance was threatened with execution. Those on the far right rejoiced, some celebrated openly in the streets, while Makarios' supporters lay low for fear of reprisals. My grandparents sat beside the radio, waiting for news updates and later that day they were surprised to hear Makarios, speaking from Paphos, saying he was alive and well, urging his people to continue their resistance against the right wing. Papou Andreas said all along that a coup could only lead to disaster and it came, as he predicted, five days later in the form of Turkish bomber planes.

On that day Yiayia rose with the sun as usual, to mop the floors and wash a pile dirty clothes in her deep stone sink. A lunchtime Aunt Roulla took the short walk from her large, whitewashed house to her mother's stone cottage. Peter and Maria played in the backyard with Koko the magpie, while the women prepared lunch. Papou arrived from the coffee house and carried his grandchildren into the house, one under each arm. As the family ate their simple meal of *louvi me ta lachana* (black-eyed beans and chard), they heard a sound like the distant rumblings of an earthquake and then the roar of Turkish bomber planes flying overhead. Papou Andreas grabbed a pistol, a relic from his days with the first EOKA, and ran outside, firing shots indiscriminately into the sky. Yiayia held her breath until the planes had passed by, praying for the safety of the children. Seconds later came the sound of explosions and the sight of flames and smoke clouds rising up in the distance. Aunt Roulla began screaming, fearing that her husband, who worked as a Customs Officer in the neighbouring town, had been killed.

Mothers ran through the streets searching for their children, crying out in panic, while

329

enfolk collected up the guns they kept en in the back of wardrobes. The church ls rang out, summoning villagers to the ain square, setting off a frenzied exodus. Yiayia grabbed her handbag and the salt shaker. She remembers the fleeting thought that flashed incongruously through her mind when she took it and thinks herself ridiculous now. She thought she would be spending the night away from home and took with her the means to make a makeshift meal for her husband more palatable. Even as Yiayia's world crumbled around her, she thought about the dietary needs of a husband who would eat nothing without adding salt. 'If I had known how things would turn out, I would have taken photographs, mementos of our life, things that would have been a comfort to me today.'

The family ran to the village square where women and children were being loaded onto trucks, tractors and rickety buses to be driven to the safety of the British base, some thirty miles away. Yiayia, Roulla and the children were quickly lifted into the back of a crowded double-cabin truck. Papou was told to leave with his family, but he refused to go, saying nothing would drive him from his home, not even bombs. Peter and Maria kissed their grandfather goodbye and asked him to take good care of Koko.

Hundreds arrived in convoy at the British base to escape the bombs and the advancing Turkish troops. On that warm July night they huddled together beneath the trees, believing that by morning they would all return to their homes. Five days passed before my uncle was reunited with his family, finding them by chance as he searched through the camp. A fortnight passed before they were allocated a tent. And while they sat and prayed for their guarantors, Greece and Britain, to liberate them, Turkey landed 70,000 troops on an island with a force of sixteen thousand men, bombed Nicosia and Famagusta and advanced southwards from Kyrenia until it had captured almost half the island. Invading on the pretext of protecting the Turkish Cypriot minority and restoring constitutional order. 'Our guarantors did nothing to protect us,' Yiayia says bitterly. 'They sat and watched us burn.'

Every Sunday at the tail end of lunch, a discussion ensues on the whys and where-fores. Michalis argues that the failed coup gave the Turks the 'green light' to invade and execute their long drawn-up 'Attila plan', to partition the island and form a separate state. Tony blames the Americans and their refusal to antagonize Ankara. 'The Americans knew we had a fair case, but their own self-interests dictated they should support Turkey. They got what they wanted in the end — something Makarios refused to let them have — two bases in the north, from which to spy on the Soviet Union, Eastern Europe and the Middle East.'

What happened to Papou Andreas is only hearsay. We know that Turkish troops captured the village and rounded up all those left behind — mostly men, a few boys and those too old, too infirm or too stubborn to leave their homes. There are unconfirmed reports that they were imprisoned in the local school for several days, that some were shot and the rest were taken to Kyrenia and shipped to Turkish mainland prisons. Papou is one of many men, women and children who went missing, whose fate is classified as 'unknown', for whom there is no corpse and no grave. The relatives of the missing still gather each day at the Ledra Palace checkpoint in Nicosia, with pictures of their loved ones, demanding answers from the Turkish powers that be. To know her husband was dead would be a relief, Yiayia says; it's being in limbo she can't bear. Two years after the invasion, Tony hired a Turkish Cypriot detective to cross the Green Line and discover the fate of his father-in-law. He handed the man several thousand pounds brown paper envelope and never saw h again. Though Tina says her father is dead, know a tiny flicker of hope burns inside he. like the candle on Grandma's window sill. He rose from the dead once, Yiayia says, why not again?

Yiayia is desperate to return to her ancestral home, if only to die. The fate of her mud brick cottage is one she often dwells on. Has it been left to ruin, she asks herself, or become home to Turkish settlers, shipped over from the mainland? Perhaps, like many other properties, it has been sold illegally, as a cheap holiday home. Beneath its stolen eaves there may be foreign holidaymakers, squatting without conscience or decency. 'It makes me sick to the stomach to think about it,' Yiayia says, as she sits waiting for a solution, for the exodus of Turkish forces. She only came to England for a short stay, as did my aunt and uncle, until their homes were handed back.

Peter and Maria arrived first in November 1974, when the nights began getting cold and a canvas tent provided scant protection against the elements. Tony arranged their flights and offered to look after the children until the day of liberation came. Peter and Maria arrived in the UK dishevelled and

ll-shocked. It was several weeks before
ey had the confidence to play or eat with
nthusiasm or talk about the war. Peter and
Andy bonded quickly, sharing the common
love of football and Manchester United in
particular. I shared a room with Maria and
slowly we became friends, though we were a
very different species of girl.

Three months later the rest of the family
arrived, all their worldly possessions contained in a small suitcase. For more than a
year Yiayia refused to hang her clothes in
a wardrobe. 'I'll be going back to my husband
soon,' she used to say. 'What's the use of
unpacking?' She slept on my bedroom floor,
refusing to oust me from my bed and rarely
woke up before midday and then only to
slurp a bowl of soup and go back to sleep.
When she finally accepted her interim fate
and stopped taking Librium she became the
woman I know today. An early riser, a keen
cook, a spiritual mentor.

Nine of us lived in a small three-
bedroomed flat above our fish and chip shop.
I often wished for a solution to the Cyprus
problem, so I could have my bedroom back.
Two years after their arrival, with no solution
in sight, Tony helped his brother-in-law buy
his own shop and the family moved out to
live in the flat above it. Running a chippy was

quite a comedown for a man who was once respected civil servant, unused to getting his hands dirty or his clothes smelly. But Michalis did what he had to do, without complaint, putting the past behind him.

It took a while to adjust to life without my cousins. I had become accustomed to noise and bodies and monumental meal times. Yiayia stayed put, moving from my floor to the sofa bed in the living room and later to her own bedroom in the granny annexe of our new house. With a living space of her own she began storing her belongings in boxes, under the bed, in a corner of the room, on top of the wardrobe. She says she's packed and ready to move if circumstances dictate and is not prepared to lose a single one of her possessions again. 'England is unlikely to be invaded,' I tell her, to which she replies, 'No one knows what lies around the corner.'

★   ★   ★

The sound of urgent knocking on the front door forces Tina reluctantly out of her armchair. She stares for several minutes out of the window, shaking her head before returning, with a disinterested look, to her plump velvet cushion and an episode of *Hart to Hart*.

'Who is it, mum?' I ask, loathe to relinquish the comfort of the leather recliner.

'It's that woman from next door. Let her knock.'

The banging gets louder and wilder, until it can no longer be ignored.

'What's going on?' Yiayia asks, walking into the living room, roused from her after-lunch slumber by the noise.

'It's our neighbour, come to complain. She's got a serious problem, up here,' Tina says, tapping her right temple.

'Something must be very wrong, Mama,' I say. 'If she carries on banging like that, she's going to break down the door.'

'She'd better not,' Tina says, getting up, donning her bolshy face, ready to deflect the slightest criticism.

She opens the door to a feverish-looking Mrs P who cries out in a thick East European accent: 'Help me, my husband he's sick.'

'Come on, Mother,' Tina says in Greek, grabbing Yiayia by the arm, 'the woman needs help.'

We hurriedly follow Mrs P along our driveway, in through her gate and across virgin territory. Her front door opens onto a narrow hall, with a thickly patterned shag pile, leading to a dining room cluttered with pictures, smelling of bleach and stale pre-cooked food. The oppressive room, curtains shut, is furnished with a heavy dining table and an assortment of chun, inelegant chairs. A low wattage bulb shed dingy light on Mr P who sits at the table, gasping for breath, his cheeks red, his waterlogged eyes bulging from their pink sockets.

'The man's choking,' Tina screams. 'Mother, do something.'

Yiayia walks towards the table and whacks Mr P with her heavy hand between the shoulder blades. A piece of gristle, the size of a pineapple chunk, flies out of his mouth and lands at Tina's feet. Mr P greedily gulps in air while his wife smoothes down his hair and comforts him in Polish. And then he notices our presence and freezes like a deer caught in headlights. He looks up at Yiayia, not with gratitude but with fear. And Yiayia puts her hands up, as if to say, we've come in peace, while Mrs P speaks softly in a language that excludes us, quelling his panic.

I take a closer look around the room, at the pictures that jostle for space on lime green anaglypta and a pair of smiling eyes stare back at me from every image, the big dark-eyes of a moon-faced child with bobbed hair and an Alice band. Pictures of the child perched on the saddle of her bike; eating an

...ream by the river; smiling broadly into ...camera; holding the hand of a younger-...oking Mrs P. And though I scan the room, ...aring into every frame, I see no pictures of the same girl in her teens, or wearing a mortar board, or holding a child of her own.

'That's my daughter, Isabelle,' Mrs P says.

'She's very pretty. Where is she?' Tina says, in a tone that sounds inappropriately cheerful for the shrine in which we stand.

'She's gone,' Mrs P replies in a frosty voice that warns us not to pry. A subtlety lost on Tina.

'Where she gone?' Tina asks, expecting to hear nothing more disturbing than a story about a daughter who has flown the nest.

'I lost her. She was taken. Stolen. I sent her out one day to buy a newspaper and she never came back,' Mrs P replies, staring into space.

'*Thee mou,*' — my God — Tina says, reaching for my arm, needing a real daughter to grab hold of. '*Mana exase moro*' — mother, she lost a child — she tells Yiayia, before turning to Mrs P with a grief-stricken look. 'I lost a child too,' she says and for a brief moment a spark of profound empathy seems to travel between the two women.

'It was a long time ago but — ' Mrs P

begins in a softer voice, before she is rudely interrupted by her husband, speaking Pol. in a hoarse, dictatorial voice, telling his wife it seems, that she has said enough. She stiffens and reinstates the familiar look of haughty mistrust we are used to seeing from her upstairs window. The three of us stand in awkward silence, feeling like unwelcome intruders, the animosity instantly restored. The Ps don't ask us to stay for tea, their thanks is muted and spoken through clenched teeth. They accompany us to their front gate, to make sure we are safely off the premises, before scuttling back indoors.

'This is real sorrow,' Yiayia says. 'Every sound of life must remind them of the happiness they have lost.'

Tina nods her head in agreement. 'Well, I won't let their complaints bother me any more. Not after that revelation.'

'And I won't be throwing any more rotten vegetables over the garden fence,' her mother says.

★ ★ ★

When I see her standing on the front step I have a flashback to that dark and rainy Sunday in 1974 when she arrived with Peter, wearing ill-fitting clothes, carrying her ongings in a small canvas bag. She had the ame look of dejection in her eyes back then s she has now. I crane my neck round the door looking for the Mazda and its moustached owner and see Maria's parents climbing out of their Sierra.

Roulla is led into the house by her husband, dragging her feet, wearing a look of unquestionable suffering. She turns her melancholic face towards me but I can't bring myself to ask her what's wrong. This is the look I have come to associate with Peter's departure. It is a look my aunt can muster at the drop of a hat to win a monopoly on sympathy.

Tina walks into the hallway. 'My God,' she says, setting eyes on her sister, 'who has died?'

'No one has died, Constantina, but a tragedy has befallen our house,' Roulla replies, shaking her head.

'Where's Panicos?' Tina asks.

Maria suddenly bolts up the stairs into my room and slams the door.

'Anna, go to your cousin,' my aunt says, 'she's in a terrible state.'

I find Maria sitting on the edge of my bed, her face buried in her hands.

'What's wrong?' I ask.

'I've left Panicos,' she replies, looking up

through troubled eyes, underscored with shadows.

She looks so dishevelled I can't bring myself to ask her why or how. I sit beside her on the bed and patiently wait for her to gather her thoughts. Tears come first. A heartfelt deluge that drenches my shoulder and clears the way for a dispassionate account of the events that led to her separation.

She begins by describing a man who was warm and attentive, who lavished her with gifts and professed his love, who won her heart with his kindness. But there were signs early on that he was a Jekyll and Hyde, prone to angry outbursts and sullen moods. Panicos was polite and charming in front of others but petulant and bullish in his own home. He would shout at his mother over a poorly ironed shirt and sulk for three days after an argument.

'Why did you go ahead with the engagement, if things weren't right?' I ask.

'Because he never got angry with me. I thought his mother was the problem. She was always interfering, sticking her nose in where it wasn't wanted. I was sure things would be different when we got a place of our own.'

'Why didn't you wait then?'

'Because the hall was booked and the dress was made and mum was really happy, e first time in ages.'

ut you had to live with him, Maria, not
r mum,' I say, regretting the accusatory
ne of my voice.

'I thought I loved him, Anna. I thought I
could change him. And there were times
when he was really sweet to me,' she says,
falling silent, fiddling with the finger where
there was once a ring studded with diamonds.

'So what happened?' I ask, itching to know,
unable to contain my curiosity.

'He started going to the casino. Every night
after work. He said he needed a drink to wind
down, to help him sleep. I asked him to take
me too, but he said the casino was no place
for a woman.'

'And . . . ' I say, interrupting another
silence, forcing her along a route she seems
reluctant to travel.

'I waited up one night and confronted him
when he came home. I told him I felt lonely
and neglected. I asked him not to go out so
often. I started shouting, I couldn't help it.
I'd kept things bottled up for so long. At first
he tried to calm me down, until I threatened
to leave and then he went crazy. He pinned
me by the neck against the wall and screamed
abuse at me.'

'Is that when you walked out?' I ask,
struggling to curb the righteous anger

threatening to overwhelm me.

'No,' she replies, 'he started crying and felt sorry for him. I'd never seen a man cry like that before. He cried from the heart, Anna, like he was really sorry. He promised he wouldn't do it again and I believed him. Afterwards, he went to his bedroom and I went to mine and cried myself to sleep.'

'Did you have separate rooms?'

'Yes. What did you think? We had agreed to wait until the wedding;' she replies before spitting out, 'he said he didn't believe in sex before marriage.'

'How could you stay with him after what he did to you?'

'Because things got better . . . he started making a real effort and stopped going to the casino. I got really close to him again and began to believe in our future together. Until the night he ruined everything. The night he went out drinking with a friend, one of the bachelor boys he used to hang around with. I didn't wait up. I went to bed and fell asleep and only realized he was back when I smelt his whiskey breath and felt him pulling up my nightdress. I tried to push him away. I begged him to stop, but he wouldn't listen. He held down my arms and covered my mouth with his hand. *E katastrepse me*' — he ruined me — she says, resorting to Greek for the words at best describe her feelings.

And while I struggle to find words of comfort she talks about the violation with heart-rending lucidity. Of the suffocating weight on top of her, of feeling close to death, of leaving her body and looking down upon herself. Of seeing from a distance something terrible happening to someone else, a woman she wanted to help but couldn't. Afterwards she felt numb and confused and overcome with shame.

'I didn't know where I was or who I was. I just lay there in shock. It took a while for me to realise what had happened. When I saw Panicos lying next to me I knew I had to get away. I was scared he might wake up and do it again. I was scared, Anna, of the very man who was meant to make me feel safe.'

Maria rang the one person she knew who would act without hesitation. She crept downstairs and dialled the number she always kept in her handbag but had never used, for fear of upsetting her mother. She rang the brother she hadn't spoken to in almost two years and talked to him as if they had never been apart. Peter told her to pack her bags and in the early hours of the morning he picked her up and drove her to the safety of their mother's house. On that journey home Maria cried for the loss of her innocence and for winning back her estranged brother.

'I didn't tell Mum and Dad what really happened. I felt too ashamed. I just said I'd been unhappy.'

The next day Panicos telephoned, demanding an explanation, pleading with Maria to return. When she refused to go back, he warned her she would never find another man now that she was 'second-hand goods'. The turkey-mother grabbed the receiver and volubly declared that Maria had never been good enough for her son, which was all that Roulla needed to hear to endorse the separation and back her daughter's decision.

'I kind of hoped it was the drink that made him do it. But I know in my heart that he did it out of spite, to stop me from leaving.'

'Why don't you report him to the police?'

'What would be the point? We were engaged. Who would believe me? Anyway, I'd feel too ashamed to talk about it.'

'What about his next victim?'

'I try not to think about that.'

Maria has since discovered that Panicos is a notorious gambler and that the busiest shop in Birmingham is on the brink of bankruptcy. The turkey-mother has made every effort to blacken Maria's name and Roulla has spread the word about Panicos and his interfering mother. Maria expresses no thirst for retribution, no hostility towards her aggressor. Deep down, she blames herself and her own naïvety. I bite my tongue, hold back the contents of my spleen. Fighting talk won't help her. Only a compassionate ear and time can heal her wounds.

'Please don't tell your mum the truth,' she says. 'I'd never be able to look her in the eye.'

'No, I won't,' I reply; though Tina is in dire need of a wake-up call.

'What will you do now?'

'I'm going to college to study beauty therapy.'

I can't help thinking that in a horribly twisted way, fate has put her on the right track and given me back a sister.

'Can I ask you a question?'

'Yes, anything.'

'Did Panicos like gardening?' I say, asking what seems like an irrelevance in the face of Maria's revelation.

'No. He never went out in the garden,' she says, making a fallacy of Tina's first and lasting impression, inducing a hot flush of anger towards my mother. For seeing what she wants to see. For judging a book by its cover. For having wished such a tyrant upon me.

★ ★ ★

Yiayia spent Saturday morning aboard Bambo's grocery van filling a box with reminiscences of home. *Loukanika*, tahini, halloumi, fresh *anari*, ladies' fingers and artichokes. For lunch she prepared *kolokassi* — Cyprus Taro — with pork. I watched her wash the *kolokassi* and dry it with a towel, before peeling the thick skin of the muddy-brown root vegetable, reminiscent of an oversized sweet potato. She showed me how to cut into the *kolokassi* with a knife and twist the blade to snap off thick, white chunks, to be fried with fatty pork cubes and tomato paste. We ate the *kolokassi* with a salad of rocket, coriander and sweet Cyprus cabbage; thick Greek yoghurt; and bulgar wheat with vermicelli. The atmosphere around the dinner table was lighter than it had been for weeks, the Kevin episode relegated to the backs of our minds, Tina looking forward to an engagement. She is secretly elated by the turn of events that has thrust Heather into the heart of our family.

'We've had our fair share of misfortune of late,' Tina said, soaking up the juices from her plate with homemade bread.

'You're right,' Yiayia replied

'It's been one thing after the other. Mirianthy, Maria and that trouble in the shop. Bad luck comes in threes and we have had our trilogy. I feel something good is afoot, I can smell it in the air,' Tina said with unaccustomed optimism.

'At least your sister is back with her husband,' Yiayia replied.

'I want to talk to you about that,' Tina said, lowering her voice. 'I think it's time to reverse that terrible thing you claim to have done and put the poor man out of his misery.'

'I will. Soon. Today, I don't have the energy to light the *sagi*.'

★   ★   ★

Back at work Tina takes the remote control out of her overall pocket and presses mute. The television above the fruit machine is silenced. Tina strictly controls the volume, according to her televisual preferences. Programmes deemed unworthy of sound include wildlife documentaries, anything vaguely political or satirical, everything on BBC2. The volume is set on loud for soaps and game shows and Royal Variety type entertainment. On this occasion Tina silences the television to win the undivided attention of Mrs Collins and cleanse her soul of its recent trauma.

'That boy he was no good, Mrs Collie. No good,' she says, with an air of melancholia.

'She picked a bad un, poor girl,' Mrs Collins replies.

'His matha she was worse,' Tina says, accepting none of the blame for helping to orchestrate her niece's failed engagement.

'Mother-in-laws can make or break a marriage,' Mrs Collins says.

'When my chudren they get married I don interfere. They can do wha they like, I don be in their way. If they wanna cam and see me they can cam, if they don wanna see me, I don say nathin.'

'Wharabout when the grand kids come along, Teen, you still gonna take a back seat?'

'Aah, thas diffren. NO ONE he's gonna stop ME seein MY grankids, wheneva I wan.'

'I see mine twice a week,' Mrs Collins says, 'my daughter-in-law brings em round. She's good like that.'

'My Heatha she's gonna be the same. HEATHA, you hear Mrs Collie, what she say?' Tina calls out to Heather, sitting on the window ledge.

'Yes, Mrs Papamichael,' Heather replies.

'And you don call me Mrs Papamichael no more. You call me Matha.'

'Yes, Mother.'

Heather has chosen the route of diplomacy over confrontation, instinctively knowing how to handle Tina. She agrees with her demands and keeps quiet when she expresses her unrealistic hopes for the future. 'My son and my daughta-in-law they gonna tek over the shop and werk side-by-side.' Heather has no intention of working behind the counter. She is headed for a career in dentistry and, what's more, she has cajoled Andy into following his boyhood dream of becoming a racing driver. Unbeknown to Tina, he has started taking driving lessons at Silverstone.

Doreen comes into the shop, wearing her Sunday best, carrying a tray of cream cakes.

'You late,' Tina calls out, 'and why you dress lie that for wek?'

'Cause there's great cause for celebration, Tina duck. Eight score draws.'

'Was tha mean?'

'It means my villa in Spain, luv. It means £250,000,' Doreen screams excitedly.

'Blady Nora,' Tina says, 'you win £250,000 and you only buy cream cakes. Whes the champagne?'

'There's plenty of time for champagne. Right now there's work to be done,' Doreen says, taking off her coat. 'You dint think I'd leave you short staffed, did you? I'll be stayin on until you find a replacement.'

Doreen lifts the serving hatch and comes behind the counter, her face aglow. Yiayia's shoal of fish has swum its way to Doreen and no one is more deserving. We gather rou[nd] her, offering congratulations and eati[ng] chocolate éclairs while Doreen shows us [a] list, hurriedly scribbled, of all the things she plans to do with her money.

'I'm gonna put half of it aside for the boys,' she says, 'to giv em a good start in life. I'm gonna buy a small villa in Spain for the holidays and a house in a nice part of town. Me and Alan, we're gonna open up our own business. We're not gonna fritter our money away on rubbish.'

'Good on you, luv,' Mrs Collins says.

'And I'm not gonna forget my friends neither. I'm gonna buy Albert an electric wheelchair so he can get out more and you, Teen, I'll buy you anything you want, within reason. I know you've got expensive tastes!'

'I don wan nathin, bat why you don buy this shop? Is a good business.'

'That's not such a bad idea. I could run this place with mi eyes closed. I know the clientele. And better the devil you know, eh? Let me speak to Alan.'

I allow myself to dream, for a few happy moments, of a normal life without The Shop, of weekends free to lounge, of clothes no longer infused with oily smells, before glancing at my mother in her chequered overall and feeling a pang of guilt for wishing ay the fabric of her life.

'And what are we gonna do, if we sell the shop?' Tony asks.

'I'm gonna open up a café. I'm gonna serve sandwiches and my own cakes. At five thirty I'm gonna close up, go home and put my feet up, like everyone else,' Tina says without real conviction and I know in my heart that she has no intention of selling the shop, of jeopardizing her livelihood, of handing over a business she has built from scratch.

'Av you 'eard the latest about Irene?' Mrs Collins asks.

'No,' Doreen replies, biting into her second éclair.

'She's must av ad a small windfall of her own. She and that boyfriend of ers av been living it up, spending a fair amount on drink, dressin up in posh clothes. That boy of ers, Kevin, e's done a runner. They say e's gone to London to find work, cause he can't stand living with Irene and her new fella.'

'Good riddance,' Doreen says, 'that's one less difficult customer.'

Euphoria carries us through the night. We talk of new beginnings and welcome ends. The sound of laughter reverberates. We drink cinnamon-scented Typhoo and eat chip butties, leaving the men to run the shop.

Yiayia's *Chirino Me Kolokassi* Pork with Cyprus Taro

Wash, dry, peel and chop a kilo of *kolokassi* — Cyprus Taro. In a heavy saucepan heat two tablespoons of corn oil and fry half a kilo of pork, cut into small pieces. When the meat has browned; transfer it to a dish and add *kolokassi* to the pan. Cook on a medium heat for fifteen minutes. Return fried pork to the pan, add half a cup of tomato purée dissolved in hot water, a cup of sliced celery and salt and pepper to taste. Bring to the boil, cover pan and simmer for an hour, or until sauce has thickened. When *kolokassi* is cooked add half a cup of lemon juice.

11

I sit on the granny-flat sofa, munching fig biscuits, listening to Yiayia's contented snore. She went straight to bed after a rich lunch of rice pilaff and *stifadho* — beef cooked with onions, peppercorns, cinnamon and vinegar. My eyelids grow heavy and sleep carries me gently, on a magic carpet, to a distant land and a tranquil dream, one that has me sitting in the branches of a carob tree, looking out onto a fertile landscape, dotted with orange and lemon trees. A profusion of daisies carpet the ground, raising their yellow florets skyward. Corpulent bees disappear inside the bright-blue petals of hyacinths and white butterflies flutter erratically above patches of long grass. The gentle hum of cicadas is accompanied by the twitter of birdsong.

In the distance I see a couple approaching, walking slowly through the trees. A tall, slender man holds the arm of a stout, heavyfooted woman. She plucks a leaf from an orange tree, rubs it between thumb and forefinger to release the scent and puts it to her nose, blurred by the white glare of the sun. The statuesque man moves robustly, while the woman walks with a stoop and the characteristic gait of arthritic hips. As they approach my carob tree I recognize the couple as my grandparents and feel a sense of elation. Papou Andreas twirls the ends of his long, grey moustache, his grey-green eyes glinting, while his wife wears an expression, hitherto unseen, of womanly contentment. Hidden behind a screen of dense foliage, I feel like a voyeur, spying on the most intimate of moments.

I wake up feeling cold and irritable. I cover my legs with the sofa blanket and try in vain to return to the tree. Though I can't sleep I keep my eyes shut and try to recapture the scene in my waking mind. All of a sudden I hear a guttural sound emanating from Yiayia's room. I get up to investigate and find her lying open-mouthed, a rasping exhalation of breath exuding from her throat. The sound is unearthly, as if her soul is being expelled by force up through her oesophagus. I know instinctively that I am hearing her last breath.

★   ★   ★

Time quits its normal passage while we wait for the paramedics. Tina sits on the bed, stroking her mother's soft forehead, refusing to believe the truth, claiming she can feel a pulse. Tony comforts her with 'perhaps' and 'let's wait and see'. I stand in a corner, my stomach in knots, hoping for a miracle. The paramedics arrive and eject us from the bedroom. Their diagnosis takes only minutes. Tina cradles her head in her hands and begins to wail.

'*Mana mou, manoulla mou*,' she cries out, 'why have you left me?'

Tony holds her in his arms, trying to absorb the shock that rails through her system. She cries like an orphaned child, as if a husband and daughter are no consolation for the death of her mother, as if suddenly the weight of the world has been thrust onto her shoulders and she must carry it alone.

I am a spectator in the midst of confusion. Possessed by a feeling of unreality. Tony sends me upstairs, to spare me the sight of death and the sound of Tina's unrelenting sobs. I stand at my bedroom window and watch the duty doctor arrive to certify death. Then Yiayia's body is loaded onto the ambulance and driven away. Mrs Davis stands at the foot of the driveway, looking distressed, unable to venture inside. I watch with dry eyes the arrival of Andy and hear my brother's cry of anguish in the hallway downstairs. Tina's sisters arrive one by one. First Roulla, then Miriam. Each arrival riggers a caterwaul that washes over me.

Someone walks into my bedroom and sits down on the bed. I don't have the energy to turn from the window and talk.

'How are you?' The unwelcome voice is Athena's.

'Fine,' I reply, using the word that covers all evils, forcing myself to turn around and look at her.

'Why don't you sit down?' she says, patting the bed.

'I'd rather stand,' I say, feeling wretched but forcing a smile, loath to show my feelings and project my gloom.

'Well,' Athena says, casually, stretching out her legs, 'I don't think we should be too upset. The old woman had a good innings.'

Athena's words of cold comfort only serve to annoy. In them I hear the influence of Malcolm's dispassionate nature. Now is the time for tears and heart-felt commiseration not lazy analogies.

'I never thought of Yiayia as old,' I reply. To me she was an ageless being and I had come to think of her as immortal.

'Is it true,' Athena asks whimsically, 'that she kept all sorts of rubbish under her bed? Daddy says she's probably got a small fortune stashed under there as well.'

I feel a sudden rush of anger and the

irrepressible urge to lash out at my cousin, to grab her by the skinny arms and throw her roughly out of my room. For showing no respect. For failing to understand the magnitude of my loss. I have lost my friend, a Guardian Angel, my lucky rabbit's foot. When Athena speaks again, I hear the intonation of her apathetic voice but her words have no meaning. My fury is so intense it begins to scare me. I try to calm myself down, to repress the tidal wave of emotion welling up inside me.

Slowly the fury subsides but disorientation and a feeling of weightlessness takes its place. It's not a pleasant weightlessness, not the buoyant feeling of flight I have in my dreams, but a frightening, uncontrollable loss of self. I want to run out of the room, to escape from Athena and the horrible sensations that have me in their grip. I hear the sound of my heartbeat resonating in my ears, banging like a drum, louder and faster, as if my heart is on the brink of exploding. And then I start gasping for breath and all I can think about is not wanting to die. And this strangulating breathlessness is the last thing I remember.

★ ★ ★

Birdsong wakes me and early-morning sunlight pleasantly warms my head. For a moment I think the day is just like any other. That I have woken up, safe and sound, from a horribly vivid nightmare. Then I catch sight of Tina, colourless and red-eyed, viewing me anxiously from the foot of the bed. On the chair beside me is Dr Smeeton, our GP, scribbling out a prescription.

'You gave your cousin quite a scare last night,' he says.

'Did I have a heart attack?'

Tina frantically crosses herself.

'You wouldn't be tucked up in your own bed if you had.'

'But my heart. It was beating so fast and I couldn't breathe.'

'You had a panic attack, which isn't surprising in the circumstances.' The doctor explains that I was breathing so quickly I was expelling oxygen which caused me to faint.

'If you feel these symptoms again,' he says, 'take deep breaths and try to slow your breathing.'

I am chilled by the thought of reliving the terror of last night.

'Now you need to rest and come to terms with your loss.'

★ ★ ★

The house is eerily quiet. I get out of bed an[d] head downstairs, uncertain as to how [I] should be feeling, knowing where I need to go. I open the door of the granny flat without hesitation or fear and head for Yiayia's bedroom. The bed is unmade; the room is as it was, in a state of ordered chaos. The smell of jasmine tonic and mothballs is as overpowering as ever. I pull a Frytick box onto the bed and empty its contents. A child's crocheted cardigan is among the jumble, unworn, smelling of new wool. There are letters, Papou's green beret and the small white seashell that meant so much to her. I put it in my pocket. I will treasure it, where others will throw it out without a second thought.

The saggy black handbag she has carried with her since 1974 sits on her bedside table. I open the side pocket and extract the book of incantations, flicking reverently through the flimsy pages, stopping at the impotence page and tracing my finger along the spidery coloured print. Along the pis, deltas, omegas, along mysterious symbols and letters. Smooth to the touch, the old paper is reminiscent of Yiayia's skin. I close my eyes and imagine I am stroking her hand, soft and translucent, frail and bone-crushingly strong. The tears, I thought had passed me by, come gushing. I ıake no effort to hold them back. I cry for Yiayia's death, for the unpredictability of life, for feeling lonely and needing strong arms to comfort me. I cry until my soul is partially purged of its emotional log-jam. Then I lie back on the bed, exhausted and stingy eyed. I wrap myself in Yiayia's fleecy bedspread and close my eyes. And in that floaty state between wake and sleep I feel her spirit hovering near by.

★ ★ ★

We travelled many miles over land and sea, just as she foretold, to take her back to the island of her birth. Her daughters had wanted to bury her in the family grave, alongside her ancestors, but partition prevents access to Yiayia's village. So they made arrangements instead, through their cousin Elengou, for Yiayia to be buried beneath the shade of an olive tree, as she had requested, in a cemetery on the fringes of a refugee estate.

On the day of the funeral we gathered at Elengou's house, a rundown pre-fab with a rusty, corrugated-iron roof. We walked the short distance from the house to the church, through the rambling estate of matchbox houses, built after the war to house the glut of refugees, many from Yiayia's own village. The houses were only meant as a temporary measure before the refugees returned to their homes. No one expected these shacks to be occupied more than a decade after their construction.

Hundreds came to pay their respects. Friends, neighbours and extended family. They crowded round the coffin, below an intricately carved iconostasis, for their last glimpse of a woman who left the island after the war and refused to return until her home was handed back. It was comforting to know she had not been forgotten. Everyone she loved was present. Everyone except Athena, who refused to travel two thousand miles for a funeral, welcoming the prospect of having the house to herself for a week, turning Yiayia's death to her own advantage. This act of inclemency severed the frayed cord between us. As it snapped I felt free at last from the damaging influence of her negative spirit.

Yiayia's daughters filed passed the casket, one by one, accompanied by their husbands, staring through the small glass panel. Roulla lingered longer than the others, talking to Yiayia, her face betraying a mixture of despair and regret. A mass of bodies closed in tight around me, pushing me along, towards the coffin. The church, hot and humid, cooled only by an ancient ceiling fan, began to feel suffocating. Plump sweat beads ran down my torso, soaking in my trouser waist band. I felt a panic coming on and remembering the doctor's advice, I took slow deep breaths as I inched my way closer to the glass panel. I had decided not to look. I thought I would faint at the sight of her. I tried to turn my head and look away, but the temptation to glance at Yiayia's face was overwhelming. I thought I'd see something ghoulish and frightening, but I didn't. I saw a wax effigy with rosy cheeks and lacquered hair. A defunct shell with the spirit long gone. And I felt a sense of relief, knowing she was elsewhere, hoping she was back in her village, walking through a fertile orchard, arm-in-arm with her husband.

★ ★ ★

A glossy-black hearse, resembling a milk float, led the slow procession that travelled on foot to the cemetery. It was a long and bumpy walk, difficult in heels, which led out of the shabby estate to open countryside, strewn with evergreens. As we walked through the tall wooden gates of the cemetery, small brown pods crunched underfoot and the smell of eucalyptus disinfected the sterile air with its medicated scent.

We gathered round the open grave, beneath a slender olive tree, to watch Yiayia's clumsy descent into the parched earth. The coffin lunged and snagged its way into the ground, balanced on two ropes, held either side by relatives. 'Let her down on that side' . . . 'pull her up, pull her up' . . . 'I can't hold her much longer' . . . they called out, over the melodious voice of the priest, as if launching a ship. The sisters each threw a handful of earth on to the coffin and held hands.

I stood beside Roulla, handing her tissues on request. She was remarkably composed for a neurotic, suddenly assuming the role of older sister, offering her younger siblings emotional support. As we stood at the graveside, a pretty little girl in a thin crocheted top started pulling on Roulla's skirt. She looked down and smiled.

'What a beautiful child,' she said.

The green-eyed girl looked up through a mass of golden curls.

'Yiayia, Yiayia, pick up, pick up,' she said.

'Where's your Yiayia, darling?' Roulla asked, looking around her.

'Yiayia, Yiayia, pick up,' repeated the child.

Roulla picked her up.

'Where's your mummy and daddy?' she asked.

The child pointed to a couple standing a

nort distance behind us, to Peter and Melissa, viewing us with awkward smiles. Roulla looked at her grandchild and her eyes filled with tears. She clutched Sarah to her breast and nuzzled the little girl's neck. Then she reached out for my shoulder and I felt her legs give way. I grabbed Sarah from her arms as she slumped heavily to her knees and buried her head in her hands, crying out like a wounded animal: 'Forgive me, son, please forgive me.'

I felt like an extra in a Greek melodrama. The crackly black-and-white kind that Tina watches on video. The kind that feature young men who fall in love with unsuitable, penniless women or visa versa, whose parents rant and rave and refuse to give their blessings. After much crying, soul searching and financial deprivation the young couple usually steals away to a bell tower to commit suicide or one of them catches pneumonia and is close to death, at which point their parents repent and ask for forgiveness. Cut to the final scene. A violinist playing at a wedding celebration and a happy family reunion. And I can't help thinking at the end of these films — once I've stopped crying — that such heartache is a waste of time when the ending is a foregone conclusion. When love always wins the day.

Peter ran over to his mother and gently lifted her back onto her feet.

'It's all right, Mum, don't cry,' he said. He held her in his arms while she sobbed, and the funeral gathering looked on sympathetically, thinking she was crying for her mother and not because of her own stupidity.

'I have been a fool, son,' she said, looking up. 'It took my mother's death to make me a woman. Her heart burned with the desire to see her great grandchild and I denied her that wish. And now it's too late. She's in her grave and will never see the angel that God has placed before me.' And with that line, my aunt's lifelong theatrical ambition is realized. She has assigned herself the starring role in a drama of her own making. Cue violins. Roll credits.

'Don't worry, Mum,' Peter said, 'Yiayia saw the baby lots of times. Andy used to bring her to our place every Sunday. She made the top that Sarah's wearing.'

Roulla looked shocked. Then relieved.

'Sarah really loved her,' Melissa said.

My aunt started howling again.

'Yiayia crying, Yiayia crying, wa wa,' Sarah said, mimicking her grandmother.

Roulla laughed through her tears. Uncle Michalis walked towards us, his face glowing with inappropriate joy.

'Papou, Papou,' Sarah screamed, lurching forward into his outstretched arms.

'You've seen her too?' Roulla said. 'It seems I am the only fool in this family.'

'Nothing and no one could have stopped me seeing my grandchild,' he said, 'not even your nagging.'

'Give me my granddaughter,' Roulla said, grabbing Sarah from her husband's arms and walking away, towards a clump of eucalyptus trees.

'I think we've lost our daughter,' Peter said turning to Melissa, 'with Mum it's all or nothing.'

★   ★   ★

After the burial we gathered at Elengou's house and sat on plastic chairs in the small front yard, amid a hotchpotch of fruit trees and flowering plants. Neighbouring yards were similarly planted with figs, lemon trees, jasmine and honeysuckle, each tiny patch of land an oasis of stunted greenery, masking façades of cracked and crumbling plaster. A steady stream of people came in through the wooden gate to offer condolences. There were emotional reunions and many tears shed. They exchanged stories about the woman who read their coffee cups below a burgeoning lemon tree, who made the finest halloumi, who was daughter of 'the Magus'.

Malcolm sat beside his wife, hands slumped in his lap, uncharacteristically subdued, while the twins chased up and down the quiet dirt track outside the house or swung from a makeshift swing, made from a baby's potty, suspended from the thick branch of an olive tree. I couldn't help wondering if Malcolm's return to his wife had anything to do with Yiayia's spell. If so, who would now undo the damage done? I felt a tinge of guilt for conspiring with my grandmother and at the same time ridiculous for giving credence to such irrational notions. I chased these thoughts from my mind, telling myself there was no such thing as magic.

Elengou ate her way through a mountain of pastries: *Tiropittes, eliopittes, kolokopittes.* She patted her rounded belly as she munched, blaming grief for her gluttony. Elengou lost her husband in similar fashion to Yiayia. She was only thirty when her husband went missing but she never remarried. Elengou, with her cat-like eyes and anomalous crown of blonde hair, oozed sensuality. She seemed such a waste of generously clad woman, her thwarted bodily energies channelled into a hedonistic love of food.

Maria spent the afternoon in the company of Minos, a curly haired man who insisted on speaking broken English. Maria tried to engage him in Greek but he was keen to impress. I liked his generous smile and his self-deprecating humour.

'What d'you think of him?' Maria said eagerly, taking me to one side.

'He seems nice,' I replied.

'We're gonna keep in touch. We've exchanged addresses. Who knows, when I've finished my course I may come back. This place is my home. I never would have left if it wasn't for the war.'

'And his name begins with M,' I said, reminding Maria of Yiayia's prophetic insight.

'One step at a time. I'm not rushing into anything. Not this time.'

With the sun glinting on her olive skin, she looked radiant and serene, at one with her surroundings. I knew in my heart that one day soon, I would lose her again, not to a man, but to the soil from which she was plucked.

★ ★ ★

I sat with the sisters and Elengou beneath a stunted orange tree. Roulla could speak of nothing but her granddaughter.

'You should hear her talk,' she said, 'she's a clever little thing. And look at those eyes. They are exactly like mine. They should have called her Stavroulla.'

'I don't want to hear any more nonsense,' Miriam said.

'You won't,' Roulla replied, 'I have learnt my lesson. Doesn't she look like an angel though? God took away my mother and he gave me a granddaughter.'

'Don't you have any grandchildren yet?' Elengou asked Tina.

'No. But my son is getting engaged soon,' Tina replied.

'What about Anna? Isn't it time you started looking for a husband?'

'Oh no, my daughter's going to university. Marriage can wait,' Tina said, her head raised haughtily, speaking the words I have waited so long to hear, making me wonder whether Yiayia was working miracles from the grave. 'I don't want her following in my footsteps. Soon we may have a doctor or a lawyer in the family,' she continued, adding her own spin, since I have expressed no interest in either profession. I let her talk, embroider the facts and take pride in her daughter's aspirations.

When she finished her coffee Tina instinctively upturned her cup in its saucer. Looking at it, she began to cry and her sisters followed suit. I picked up the cup, peered inside and saw infinitely more than coffee grains smearing white ceramic. I saw a panoramic landscape of roads, rivers and mountains. A journey by plane, a rabbit, a bell and a cockerel as big as my thumbnail. I sat with the sisters, unravelling their destinies, with a newfound eloquence and a captivating aura.

THE END

We do hope that you have enjoyed reading this large print book.

Did you know that all of our titles are available for purchase?

We publish a wide range of high quality large print books including:
Romances, Mysteries, Classics
General Fiction
Non Fiction and Westerns

Special interest titles available in large print are:
The Little Oxford Dictionary
Music Book
Song Book
Hymn Book
Service Book

Also available from us courtesy of Oxford University Press:
Young Readers' Dictionary
(large print edition)
Young Readers' Thesaurus
(large print edition)

For further information or a free brochure, please contact us at:
Ulverscroft Large Print Books Ltd.,
The Green, Bradgate Road, Anstey,
Leicester, LE7 7FU, England.
Tel: (00 44) 0116 236 4325
Fax: (00 44) 0116 234 0205

EVERYTHING HAPPENS FOR A REASON

Kavita Daswani

Priya has married a handsome young Indian man living in America. Though she has moved from Delhi to Los Angeles — land of Hollywood excess and celebrity craziness — she still lives the life of an obedient Hindu wife: cooking, cleaning and obeying her in-laws in all things. So when her mother-in-law suggests that she goes out to work, Priya is a little surprised. But not half as surprised as her husband and his family would be if they knew the reality of her new job. Because Priya has just become the hottest, most in demand and most envied showbiz reporter in Hollywood. And they would NOT approve . . .